"I'm
gain the

"You
knew . .

"Yes,
less. Cou
ows don't frighten easily.

"Well, this is London."

"Yes, and I plan on winning a horse, a very fine horse, the best stud in all England."

Her eyes flashed with challenge. "Not if I have my way." She took a step back toward the ballroom, then stopped. "You know, you had your chance to steal Tanner away from me."

"Steal? You said I could *have* him."

"Yes, but you didn't take advantage when you could have. Why?"

She appeared so regal, so beautiful, standing in the moonlight, and Tye realized that the old ghosts had finally been banished between them—at least for him. The past was forgiven.

Perhaps he had come to London for this moment . . .

Other Books by
Cathy Maxwell

CATHY MAXWELL

The
WEDDING WAGER

AVON BOOKS
An Imprint of HarperCollinsPublishers

This is a work of fiction. Names, characters, places, and incidents are products of the author's imagination or are used fictitiously and are not to be construed as real. Any resemblance to actual events, locales, organizations, or persons, living or dead, is entirely coincidental.

AVON BOOKS
An Imprint of HarperCollins*Publishers*
10 East 53rd Street
New York, New York 10022-5299

First Avon Books paperback printing: November 2001

Avon Trademark Reg. U.S. Pat. Off. and in Other Countries, Marca Registrada, Hecho en U.S.A.
HarperCollins ® is a trademark of HarperCollins Publishers Inc.

Printed in the U.S.A.

10 9 8 7 6 5 4 3 2 1

For Wanda and Paul Escobar,
and Julie Lawrence

I am wealthy in my friends.

Love is repaid by love alone.

St. John of the Cross

Chapter 1

Every English village had to have at least one eccentric—and Mary Gates, the old squire's daughter, was Lyford Meadows's. She dressed in men's clothing, was capable of outswearing a stable hand, and claimed to be as good as any man alive, if not better . . . especially when the subject was horses.

Tye Barlow stifled the urge to swear aloud himself as he spied her winding her way through the crowded yard. He'd not wanted her here. Had hoped she'd stay away. Why didn't Mary know her place like other women?

Instead, she moved among the completely male crowd of buyers assembled at Lord Spender's stables for the horse auction with an easy, loose-limbed grace, seemingly oblivious to the surprised but appreciative silence trailing in her wake. Conversations stopped. Eyebrows raised. Speculation appeared in men's eyes.

Tye understood their response. Mary was a beauty, the loveliest woman in the shire, a fragrant red rose among the smell of muck and horses. Aristocratic breeding might mark her high cheekbones and straight, elegant, patrician nose, but in the depths of her sea-green eyes was a hint of fire, a trait passed to her from some Viking ancestor who had raided these parts . . . and she had a sensual, full lower lip that begged to be kissed.

Nor did her unconventional dress disguise womanly curves. Her buff breeches were baggy in the seat, her brown wool jacket overlong, and yet from the scuffed toes of her worn boots to the rakish tilt of her beaverskin hat, her mannish dress enhanced feminine attributes in a way that excited masculine imagination. Her sole concession to her sex was the trim of lace edging her snowy white neckcloth, a cool, silent thumbing of her nose at the world.

Mary did what she liked and didn't give a damn what anyone thought.

She stopped to greet Lord Spender and removed her hat. Sunlight caught and held on the gold-silver splendor of her pale blonde hair. Pulled back in a simple queue, it reached her waist and swung with the movement of her body like a bright and dazzling lure.

Men gaped in stunned admiration. Several of them, the outsiders, moved closer, their predatory instincts aroused. Tye frowned. If she were smart, she'd move her tail nearer to where he stood—alongside her brother-in-law.

Of course, Mary always bragged she knew how to handle unwelcome attention. And as much as she vowed she didn't need or want a man in her life, he suspected she knew exactly how attractive she was. In fact, right now, she appeared to flaunt it—and there didn't seem to be a man in the area who could resist her.

Save himself.

Because he knew her. Too well.

Behind her vibrant beauty was the stubbornness of a high-strung broodmare in foal. And when Mary kicked out in anger, she always hit her target.

Her estate bordered his. Her grandfather had given his grandfather a precious stake of land in gratitude for years of devoted service, and her family had rued the day since. In retaliation, her father had feuded with Tye's, a feud Mary gleefully carried forward and he resignedly upheld in self-defense.

Over the years, she had misdirected his water to her use (convincing the magistrate *she* was completely within her rights), attempted to move the property line no less than seven times (Tye had won *those* skirmishes), and beat him out of two sales of his foals by swaying the buyers to purchase hers instead—for a better price!

Ah, yes, Mary Gates was a major pain in his arse.

As if she sensed she was being watched, she slowly turned and looked through the milling crowd directly at him. She placed her hat on her head at a jaunty angle and gave him a small salute. Instantly, Tye was on guard. She was up to something. His frown deepened and she laughed.

He turned to David Atkinson, the local horse doctor and her brother-in-law. "What is Mary doing here?"

Atkinson pulled his pipe from his mouth. "You couldn't have expected her to stay away from the biggest horse event of the season? Not Mary."

Tye had expected it. In fact, he'd gone to great pains to keep the news of Spender's sale from her. It had not been easy. He'd personally waylaid any handbills that could have gone in her direction and sworn his friends to secrecy.

"You didn't tell her?" Tye accused.

"No, but I would have." David shrugged. "She's my sister-in-law."

"I pity you."

David grinned. "There are times," he admitted.

Brewster, the local pub owner, confessed, "I told her."

Tye confronted him. "You knew I didn't want her here. You promised."

"Come, man, Mary's one of us. She has to be here. It's the sale of the Stud," Brewster said in his defense.

"I told her, too," Blacky said. He was a barrel-chested man who ran the village smithy. "She has admired the Stud as much as any of us. He's been a part of our lives and now he will be gone. I remember when he won his first race. I made a handsome profit and have always backed him since. I can't believe Spender is selling him. 'Tis a pity this day, I tell you. The sky should be black."

"Aye," Brewster said. "What will Lyford Meadows be without the Stud?"

Tye understood their sentiments. He'd watched Tanners Darby Boy grow since the horse was a green colt, had even had a hand in his training. To date, Tanner was the winningest horse in all Britain. Spender was a fool to sell him just because the horse had gone lame. The foals thrown from Tanner would be worth a fortune—a fortune Tye intended to make.

He'd come to this auction not as an observer but as a bidder. He had eight hundred carefully saved pounds to his name and he'd spend it all if need be.

As if reading his mind, Brewster asked David, "Who do you think will buy him? Appears all of England is here."

"And some from foreign parts, too," Blacky said with a dark glance at a group of Europeans.

"Next to them Spaniards is Frenchies. Can you believe it? The smoke from our cannons has barely cleared and here they are trying to buy our horses."

"He'll go to whomever can afford him," David said flatly. "Spender told me he doesn't care who buys him as long as the price is high."

"How much do you imagine he'll bring?" Brewster asked.

Blacky shook his head. "A winning horse like Tanner with years of breeding ahead of him? Five hundred, maybe as high as six or seven."

"He'll bring in seven times that as a stud," Blacky said with disgust. "Why sell now?"

They all looked to David for the answer. As horse doctor, he had the most reliable gossip. He didn't disappoint. "To give to his nephew. That's him down front." He nodded to a ruddy-faced young man who appeared barely old enough to shave and whose lime-green waistcoat and red jacket made him stand out like a rooster among sparrows. Worse, the gent wore blue velvet boots. Tye couldn't understand why any man would put anything but good leather on his feet.

"He's Spender's heir," David continued. "The old man dotes on him, and a more selfish, priggish lad you'd have to travel far to meet."

"But to sell the Stud . . . ?" Brewster said.

"The lad wants to go to London and live in style," David said. "Spender wants him to be happy. Besides, he can't let a horse of Tanner's caliber fall into the nevvy's hands. The lad's not a horseman. Has no appreciation for the beast. This way, Spender raises the blunt and ensures Tanner goes to a man who will see the horse's line continues to rule the racecourses."

"And what of Lyford Meadows?" Brewster asked. "The Stud was like one of us. We were all so proud of his every victory."

"I don't think either Spender or his nephew cares what the horse means to the village," David answered.

But Tye did. If all went well, he'd be a hero this day, although he kept his own counsel.

Vicar Nesmith wandered up. "I say, Barlow, knew I'd see you here. I'm to ask if you can come to the vicarage for dinner Sunday. Grace made me promise." Grace was the oldest of the vicar's five daughters, each of them lovely and sweet . . . and anxious to marry.

"Oh," Blacky said, as if remembering something he'd almost forgotten. "Clara is hoping you will join us for dinner tonight." He lowered his voice. "I was supposed to ask yesterday but I forgot, and you'd better say yes or she won't give me a minute's rest. Having an unmarried sister is becoming a burden beyond compare. You and me will have our meal then sneak out to Brewster's for a pint to console ourselves over the loss of the Stud."

A tingling along the back of Tye's neck warned him Mary had approached even before her mocking voice said, "Ah, yes, the Buck of the Parish is in demand."

Tye frowned. "Mary," he said, a curt acknowledgment.

"Barlow," she countered.

The others were friendlier. There were times Tye suspected they all actually liked her. As the late squire's daughter, she was accorded respect, even if the man had been a bastard beyond compare.

The vicar said with an apologetic shrug, "Barlow is the most eligible bachelor in the parish. Just because you don't want him, Miss Gates, doesn't mean the other lasses aren't going to chase him."

Brewster snorted. "Now that would be a sight, Miss Gates and Barlow courting."

The others laughed, sharing a good joke . . . but Tye and Mary didn't. For the briefest second, his gaze met hers, and he wondered if she was remembering a time when she hadn't been so adverse to him. A time when he'd avidly given chase—?

As if reading his thoughts, she gave him her back. "Yes, that would be a sight, wouldn't it?" she arrogantly agreed with the others and lifted a tankard of punch from the tray of a passing servant. "What is your motto, Barlow? 'Love them all; settle on none'? Fortunately, I have higher standards than dallying with former servants." She referred to his grandfather having served as her family's head groom.

Several jaws dropped at her insult. Mary pushed the limits. He'd be justified in leveling her and she'd have naught to say in her defense.

Nor was she in any position to attack him. Not after the scandal she'd created. How long had it been now, nine years ago, when she had been sixteen and he turning twenty? Yes, here was the opportunity to set her in her place, right there in front of them all—but then, something about the defiant lift of her chin coupled with the hint of troubled shadows in her eyes brought him to his senses.

She hadn't had an easy time of it. Her father had been a gambling fool who had practically destroyed Edmundson, the family's horse farm, with his excesses and grand ambitions. She'd kept the estate together with hard work and shrewd management. And then there were the rumors of an affair between herself and Lord Jergen's son. 'Twas whispered her father had practically thrown her at the man who had taken advantage of her and subsequently jilted her.

Tye didn't know the truth. He did know that at one time Jergen's son had been enamored but had returned to London alone. Shortly after, Mary had donned her breeches and forsworn men.

If her life had been different, she could have been a biddable lass, happily married with children clinging to her side. Instead, she ran Edmundson for her fourteen-year-old brother, Niles, who was away at school. She did a good job in spite of the fact everyone knew the family lived from hand to mouth.

Yes, Mary Gates had learned the hard way how to squeeze a shilling. Any dreams she'd harbored of a wealthy husband and secure position in society were lost. Tye could let her have her pride.

Fortunately, Lord Spender decided the time had arrived to start the auction. He was a self-important man who clung to the era of wigs, snuff, and satin jackets for special occasions, and his horse sale was a major event. His belly overflowed his breeches and strained at the silver buttons of his vest. The slightly askew angle of his wig gave testimony to the strength of the punch he was serving.

"His dandified nephew must cringe every time he spends company with the man," David said from the side of his mouth and Tye agreed. However, today the pompous nevvy seemed at peace. Anything for money.

Lord Spender relished the moment by welcoming them with a few modest jokes. Tye crossed his arms impatiently, anxious for the sale to begin.

At last, Spender called up the auctioneer, a Welshman he had imported for this event. The villagers muttered to themselves that this was one more slight his lordship had handed them. Brewster could have run the auction better.

Tye didn't join in the black comments. Tense with the waiting, he stood a little to one side of his friends. He noticed Mary did the same.

The auction started with the presentation sale of several inconsequential broodmares. Fine horses all, but not the caliber of Tanners Darby Boy. Tye had always believed Spender should have invested in better mares. The prices these animals fetched were low. He chomped at the bit for the sale to move on.

Then, at last, the moment arrived. With the proper flourish, the Welshman announced Tanner. The crowd of buyers perked up with interest. Several moved forward toward the front. A groom led the strutting bay stallion out—and Tye had never wanted anything in the world as much as he wanted this horse.

Tanner had been England's premier winner until an accident on the field eighteen months ago had cut short his racing career. His breeding was impeccable as was his conformation: long back, short head, powerful legs. He was the embodiment of the very best in a racehorse.

"Turn him around, turn him around. Let them see all of him," Lord Spender urged his groom, and then beamed with pride as the lad complied, retracing the horse's path before the half circle of buyers. The horsemen craned their necks, evaluating the Stud with seasoned eyes. These were men who appreciated good horseflesh and knew it came at a price.

Abruptly, the horse stopped. His ears pricked up and he scanned the crowd, intelligence in his dark brown eyes. His gaze honed in on Tye.

For a heartbeat, Tye couldn't breathe. Couldn't move. The horse was *choosing* him. He felt it all the way to his bones.

The consequences of this moment vibrated through his body. He and his father, God bless his soul, had dreamed of owning a stud like Tanner. With him, Tye would make Saddlebrook the finest breeding stable in England. Maybe the world.

Standing close by, Mary appeared to be having the same reaction. "He's magnificent," she said under her breath.

Tye nodded agreement. His gaze shifted and he evaluated his competition. Every man in the yard wanted Tanner, but up at the front stood Alex Harlan, the duke of Marlborough's stable manager. Tye knew him well. Harlan could outbid him. Tye prayed that he wouldn't.

The bandy-legged Welshman stood on a stool and called out for their attention. "Here he is, gents. The horse you've come to see, and a fine and dandy master he is!"

While the auctioneer extolled Tanner's virtues, Tye tried to relax. A bead of sweat rolled down his spine, his every muscle tense.

He and his friends stood toward the back, separate and apart from the outsiders who had come to bid. But while Blacky, Brewster, David, and the others talked among themselves, he concentrated on the Stud. Mary stood close at hand, as quiet and sober as himself.

At last the Welshman clapped his hands together with a resounding noise that gave Tanner a start, but didn't spook him. The horsemen nodded approval as Tanner was known for steady nerves. The auctioneer called for an opening bid that made most men blanche. Tye was unsurprised by the price, but still he crossed his arms and waited.

He noticed Mary crossed her arms, too, and he couldn't help an inward smirk. She might claim she couldn't stomach him and, yet, here she was at his side. He shook his head.

The auctioneer wheedled, and the first price called out came from Alex Harlan. After that, the bids flowed heavily.

Those who initially jumped in the fray for the devil of it quickly dropped out. Serious buyers came down to three men—a Spaniard, Harlan, and a Sussex breeder. The price hit five hundred pounds and the breeder bowed out.

At last, Tye dared to let himself believe he might win the horse—and, maybe, even have a bit of blunt left over.

The crowd commiserated with the defeated Sussex man and handed him a tankard of punch. The last bid had been the Spaniard's. The auctioneer looked to Harlan, who took his time thinking. A good sign to Tye.

"I don't want that horse to go to a Don," Brewster muttered, referring to the Spaniard.

Blacky agreed grimly. Vicar Nesmith and Mary didn't comment. They were both spectators to the event before them.

But Tye was a player. He could remain silent no longer. If Harlan was indecisive, then a new bidder might push him out. "Five fifty," he shouted.

There was a rustle in the silence as all turned to see who the newcomer was.

Tye felt a flush of pride, especially as Brewster, the vicar, and Blacky looked at him with new respect.

"Good man," Lord Spender said with a clap of his hands. "Glad to see you in the fray, Barlow."

"Right you are, Tye," Brewster encouraged. "Right you are. Keep that horse for us."

The Spaniard bid. "Five seventy-five."

A murmur went through the other buyers. Harlan's eyes narrowed as he considered the bid. He looked to Tye, who met his gaze unflinchingly.

For a second, Harlan appeared ready to bid—but then, he took a step back. He was done.

Tye could have collapsed with relief.

"I have a bid of five seventy-five from the gentleman from Spain," the Welshman said. He looked directly at Tye. "Do I have a counter?"

"Six hundred," Tye said, his voice stronger, more certain.

"Six twenty-five," the Spaniard responded.

"Six fifty," Tye shot back. Their gazes met across the crowd of men. Beside him, Blacky clenched his fist in excitement. The vicar and Brewster were almost dancing on their toes in anticipation.

"You're going to do it, you're going to do it," Vicar Nesmith repeated over and over.

The Spaniard considered the horse and then conferred with one of his companions. Tanners Darby Boy lifted his head, alert to his role in this drama.

"Six sixty," the Spaniard said, but this time, his bid was more tentative and Tye knew he had won.

"Six seventy-five," he said firmly.

A slight smile lifted the corner of the Spaniard's mouth.

"Sir?" the auctioneer prodded, hoping for a bid.

One glance back in Tye's direction and then the Spaniard shook his head. He was out.

Tanners Darby Boy was Tye's.

Brewster grabbed Tye by both shoulders from behind, squeezing them with joyful bonhomie. The crowd was on his side and it was a triumphant moment, one Tye would never forget in his life.

The auctioneer repeated his bid. "I have a final bid. Six hundred and seventy-five pounds. All in . . . all done . . ." He raised his hand to slap against the table—

"Seven hundred pounds," Mary's clear voice rang out.

For a stunned moment, Tye thought he was hearing things. The others whirled toward her, as surprised as he.

She didn't look at any of them. Tye wanted to believe his mind was playing tricks, but then the auctioneer announced, "We have a bid from the gentle—ah, I mean, young lady for seven hundred pounds. Will you counter, sir?" he asked Tye.

Tye couldn't take his gaze off of Mary. "What are you doing?" he furiously whispered to her.

She flicked a disdainful glance in his direction. "Buying a horse."

"No, I*m* buying the horse."

"Not if I outbid you."

"You don't have the money."

The set of her mouth hardened. "Obviously I do or I wouldn't be bidding."

Tye glared over her head at David, expecting

an explanation. His friend shrugged. He was as taken aback as any of them.

"Sir? Do you counter?" the auctioneer called to Tye.

Tye struggled to pull together his scrambled brains. He was going to make Mary pay for costing him more money. He didn't know how but he'd sit up nights thinking of a way. "Counter? Yes, yes, I do." He looked at Mary as he said grimly, "Seven twenty-five."

"Seven fifty," Mary replied without batting an eyelash.

Tye's temper bubbled to the surface. She was fueling the bid. He knew it. This was one more of her attempts to tweak his nose, to let him know the Gateses didn't consider him worthy of such a horse.

Well, he'd show her. A Barlow had as much pride as a Gates. "Eight hundred pounds."

His bid was met with hushed surprise and then excited murmuring from the buyers. Eight hundred pounds—all he had in the world. And it would be worth every shilling to put stubborn Mary Gates in her place.

Tye crossed his arms, satisfied.

"Eight hundred fifty," Mary responded.

Tye's jaw dropped. He closed his mouth. "You can't—" He looked to David, to the vicar and Brewster and Blacky. They shook their heads.

They didn't know Mary Gates had this kind of money either.

For a stone-cold second, Tye almost dropped out. He should let her win the bid. Then she would have to publicly admit she didn't have money. She'd be humiliated. She'd never be able to show her face in the village again.

He looked to the horse stamping restlessly, his mind working. He could sell one of his mares. He could practice more economies. "Nine hundred," he heard himself say crisply.

The spectators roared with approval. Many had traveled a good distance for this sale. This was the kind of action that would keep the horse world buzzing for months—years, even. And they had ringside seats.

"Nine fifty," Mary said, cool as you please.

Tye's mind reeled at the sum.

"Well, the good news is the horse isn't going to leave the village," Tye overheard Brewster whisper to Blacky.

But didn't they understand? If he let Mary Gates have Tanners Darby Boy, the horse would be lost to him. A Gates would never allow a Barlow breeding rights.

Tye took his future in his hand. He gambled. "Nine seventy-five."

Mary shifted, her jaw tightening and Tye felt a surge of relief. She was going to cry quarter. She had to. 'Twas madness they were engaged in.

He held his breath, waiting, and was just about to release it when he heard her say faintly, "One thousand pounds."

"I beg pardon, miss?" the auctioneer said, cupping his hand to his ear. "I could barely hear you."

"One thousand pounds." This time her voice was strong and clear. Each syllable was like an arrow piercing Tye's body.

One thousand pounds! The amount echoed in his brain even as the number was repeated by the crowd. 'Twas an astronomical amount for a horse, even one as great as Tanner.

Tye tried to think of how he could raise more cash and couldn't. It was impossible.

He looked at Mary. She stood straight and tall. How could she have so much money? He was not only her neighbor but her rival. He'd been raised to be aware of the Gateses and everything they did. Their families were intertwined. She couldn't have that much blunt without him knowing.

But he didn't have the money either.

If he outbid her, he could lose everything.

"Sir? Do you bid?" the auctioneer asked.

Tye felt all eyes on him. Marlborough's man, the Spaniard, and all the others, including a beaming, anxious Lord Spender.

He knew what they were thinking. They were wondering if he was going to let a woman get the best of him. They wanted to know if he was man enough to set her in her place.

And the answer was . . . no.

Saddlebrook had been his father's life. It was his life. He'd not lose it for one horse, even if owning that horse would give him his dream.

There would be other horses, but he knew he'd never forget this moment when Mary Gates made him say, "I pass."

"Then, all in, all done—*all sold*," the auctioneer announced, "to the lady for one thousand pounds."

At last, for the first time since the bidding had begun, Mary turned and looked at him. She smiled.

Tye could have cheerfully murdered her.

Chapter 2

Mary had known Tye Barlow all her life and she'd never seen him as angry as he was now.

She'd bested him.

Her father would have been proud. Better yet, *she* felt proud.

She returned his glittering anger with a cool stare—but inside, she was doing a jolly jig.

Their gazes held. She refused to blink first. They'd done this before for what seemed like hours at a time. However, today, Tye was apparently not in the mood for games. His jaw hardened. His eyes seemed to sharpen into pinpoints and then, abruptly, he turned and stomped off, leaving her behind to draw her first full, relaxed breath since the auctioneer had accepted her bid.

Vicar Nesmith grabbed her hand. "Bless you, Miss Gates," he said, pumping her arm. "You've saved the day. Tanners Darby Boy will stay in Lyford Meadows."

Brewster half-hugged, half-clapped her on the back while Blacky seconded the vicar's praise. "Aye. You're a right one, Miss Gates. And I tell you, that horse is worth his weight in gold. *Gold*," he repeated as if she didn't understand the importance of the word.

Her empty tankard of punch was taken from her and a full one pushed into her hand. Other villagers surrounded her now, thanking and congratulating her.

It was a heady moment for a woman who all too often felt the outsider.

"You don't think Barlow is upset?" she asked Blacky, knowing the answer but curious to hear his response.

"Pissed mad," the blacksmith said, lifting his cup to his lips, but he froze when Vicar Nesmith pointedly cleared his throat. Sheepishly, Blacky corrected his statement, "Beg pardon, Miss Gates. But Tye's not a man accustomed to being bested."

"Especially by a woman," Brewster added with a snort, and others agreed with him.

From the corner of her eye, she caught David's frown and knew her brother-in-law was not happy with her. Well, he could be pissed mad, too. She'd won the horse fairly.

Always the peacemaker, Vicar Nesmith leaned forward. "What the fellows mean is Tye is upset, but he'll get over it. He's a good, honest man—a bit headstrong at times—but he'll soon agree having a stud like Tanners Darby Boy right next to his own farm will be a fine thing. Why, he'll have access to the horse for his mares any time he wishes."

"Not a likely chance," David responded, "and Tye knows it." He drained his tankard and handed it to one of Lord Spender's servants. "The old squire would turn in his grave at the very thought of his daughter helping a Barlow."

"He's already turning in his grave over your marriage to Jane," Mary replied smoothly. "If you remember, I supported the decision."

David's smile turned less cynical. He touched the tip of Mary's nose, a brotherly gesture. "Aye, and I thank you for it. But be honest, Mary, will you let Tye breed his mares with Tanner?"

The expression on her face told all. Barlow's mares were the envy of all who saw them. The foals thrown off Tanner would be champions. A Gates would never give a Barlow such an opportunity.

Fortunately, she was saved from answering by Lord Spender's approach, his step a bit wobbly from punch. Happiness beamed from every pore in his body. "Congratulations, Miss Gates," he said, straightening his wig. "A fine horse you have. I weep to part with him but can't tell you how pleased I am Tanner will be staying in Lyford Meadows. I hated making the decision to sell him."

"Then why did you?" Brewster demanded rudely. Other villagers nodded agreement.

Sensing the atmosphere was not congenial, Lord Spender hooked Mary by the elbow and led her away. "Come, you need a good look at your horse." He lowered his voice and confided. "I feared there were those who were still angry with my decision to sell Tanner."

"No, they are upset over the way you chose to sell him," Mary corrected. "If you had accepted the offer I made last week, you would have saved us all the worry over Tanner's fate."

"Now, Miss Gates, I had to be fair. Tye Barlow cooled his heels every day in my study making the same request. An auction was the only equable solution. I do like and admire both of you. Excellent horsemen, I mean, er, horseman and -woman."

"And you wanted to drive up the price," Mary replied without mercy.

"That too. You were forced to double your offer."

"Yes," she replied dryly, not liking the thought, then pushed doubts away. She changed the subject. "Barlow visited you every day?"

"Like yourself. Both of you are amazingly persistent."

"Except only one of us owns the horse," she responded smugly.

"Yes, and now my nephew Henry will receive his chance at London. He is very accomplished, you know. Don't have children of my own. His presence has been a blessing in my life. Here we are, Miss Gates. Your horse."

Unlike most stallions, Tanners Darby Boy was known for his gentle nature—another reason Mary had wanted him. At close to seventeen hands tall, a belligerent stud would have been too much for her to handle. Instead, Tanner stood at ease amongst the conversation following his sale, watching her with soulful brown eyes.

"You remember me, don't you, boy?" she whispered, raising her hand to rub the velvety texture of his nose. Tanner nuzzled her palm.

Reverently, she walked around him, the stable lad holding the lead rope stepping out of her way. She smoothed the sleek, chestnut-colored coat. Copper highlights glinted in the sun. Tanner turned his head in her direction, responding to her touch. He was perfect. Completely perfect.

Mary had coveted the Stud from the first day she'd laid eyes on him as a colt. He'd only been a day old but she'd known he was going to be a winner. Now, he was hers. With him, she would reclaim her family's heritage and, yes, establish a reputation for herself that would free her of the mistakes of her past.

She ran her hand down his right front leg, feeling the muscle. "Is this the one he injured? I can find nothing wrong."

Sentimental tears pooled in Lord Spender's eyes. "Aye, he's healed, but he'll never run the same. Broke my heart when the accident happened." He blinked the tears away. "I hate to seem indelicate, Miss Gates, but there is, um, the matter of settlement."

"The money," Mary said flatly. She hadn't quite worked out the details of the money, but she deemed it best not to mention this little concern to his lordship. Later, when they could have a private moment, she could work out the financial arrangement. Certainly the brilliant nephew didn't need money immediately, or would accept payments. She took the lead rope from the lad, ready to take her horse home. "May I bring it to you on the morrow?"

Lord Spender smiled indulgently and took the rope from her, handing it back to the stable lad. "Of course, Miss Gates. Your word is good with me. But the Stud will stay here until our business is concluded."

"Of course," she murmured, pushing away a twinge of doubt. Again, she stroked the horse's gleaming coat, admiring the line of his back. The muscles rippled beneath the skin. Everything would work out. Tomorrow, she would plead her case in private and Lord Spender would agree to some sort of consideration. There were ways. God would help her think of something. After all, she'd been praying every single night—

Barlow's hand came down on top of hers, pressing it flat against the horse's skin. He held it in place. In spite of Tanner's impressive height, Barlow glowered down at her from the other side.

When he was angry like this, Mary had to concede he was rather good-looking. He boasted sharp, cobalt blue eyes, straight black hair, broad shoulders, and a muscular physique that made other men appear puny.

However, Mary knew what sent female hearts fluttering was not his perfections, but his imperfections. His grin was slightly uneven, like that of a fox who had raided the henhouse. A scar over his right eye added to his devil-may-care expression, and there was a bump in his nose from the day years ago when he, Blacky, David, and Brewster had brawled with a neighboring village.

They'd won.

Of course, she wasn't one of his silly admirers. She knew better than to trust a man who could make a woman's brain go a little daffy.

"Barlow," Lord Spender said in friendly greeting. "Too bad about your bid on Tanner here. I know you wanted him. But I'm certain as Miss

Gates's neighbor, she'll give you breeding rights, what eh?"

At the mention of breeding rights, Barlow's grip tightened on her hand like a vise. Mary refused to wince, and Lord Spender, being as short as he was and full of his own punch, didn't notice anything amiss. The stable lad did and wisely backed away.

She understood why the servant would want to run. Barlow's presence could be overwhelming. Too masculine. Too forceful.

The heat of his anger flowed from him through their hands to her. The force of it could have toasted her toes. Mary refused to be cowed.

"What do you want, Barlow?" she asked.

A tense muscle worked in his jaw. His angry eyes never left hers as he said, "My lord, your nephew wishes a word with you. He has with him a gentleman from London he'd like you to meet."

"He has?" Lord Spender scanned the crowd for his nephew and then smiled and nodded when he spotted him. "Must go meet this gentleman, then. You'll excuse me, Miss Gates? Barlow is here. I imagine the two of you have much to talk about."

"Yes, I'm certain we do," Mary replied pleasantly through clenched teeth. She attempted to ball her captured hand into a fist. Barlow didn't remove his. The stallion swerved his massive head in their direction as if asking what they were doing.

The moment Lord Spender tottered off, Mary forcibly yanked her hand free. "What do you want?" she demanded, using the horse as a barrier between them.

Barlow leaned forward, his deep voice low. "You *stole* this horse from me."

Mary could not believe her ears. "What?"

"You deliberately drove up the price because you didn't want me to have this horse."

"*I* drove up the price?" She shook her head. "Sorry, Barlow, but *you* were the one who made me pay *twice* the amount I'd intended."

"*Me?*" He took a step forward, stopped by the presence of the stallion. With an irritated frown, he said to the stable lad, "Put this horse up."

"Keep him right here," Mary countermanded.

"He doesn't need to stand in the sun all day," Barlow said.

"He's not just standing here," she snapped. "His new *owner* is inspecting him."

The stable lad looked from one to the other, uncertain whom he should listen to. But when Barlow turned and gave the lad the full force of his heated gaze, the servant caved immediately. Touching his forelock to Mary, he mumbled something about needing to give Tanner a turnout and escaped with the horse.

Now, there was no obstruction between Mary

and Barlow's anger. She refused to show fear.
"Bravo, Barlow. How admirable of you to bully a
stable hand. But you can't intimidate me. I outbid
you. The horse is mine. Good day."

She would have turned and marched off, but
he grabbed her by the crook of the arm and
whirled her back around.

The suddenness of his movement caught her
by surprise. She lost her balance and fell against
his body. 'Twas like hitting a rock wall. He
steadied her by gripping both her arms, but he
didn't let go. Instead, he stared down, his gaze
intense.

"Mary, I know you don't have the money for
this. What are you doing? 'Tis madness. You can't
afford that horse."

She felt a flash of panic. How did he know the
state of her fortune? She'd always been careful to
keep up appearances. She was certain no one outside of her family suspected—and she'd only told
Jane and Niles what she absolutely had to.

Their faces were inches from each other. She
could make out the line of his whiskers and smell
a hint of the bay rum shaving soap he used. For a
guilty second, she was tempted to blurt out the
truth . . . then pride took over.

How dare he manhandle her. And the state of
her affairs was her business, not his.

She gave his black scowl right back at him. "I

can afford the horse, Barlow, and I've bought him. He's mine. And you are a sore loser."

Her words hit their mark. His hold on her arms loosened as if she'd struck a physical blow. She jerked away. Two steps and she could breathe easily again.

"Your stubborn arrogance will ruin you, Mary."

His accusation stung. She wasn't arrogant. Proud, yes; arrogant, no. Calmly, forcibly, she said, " 'Twas a business decision, Barlow. Nothing personal."

The daggers in his eyes told her he didn't believe her. "And how do you think you are going to find the funds to pay the horse's price?" His low voice was meant for their ears alone.

"I have plenty of money," she replied stiffly.

"God, Mary, stop this pretense. You're done up. It's not your fault. Your father—"

"Don't *you* dare mention my father. Not after what your family did to him—"

"I did nothing and if you think so, then you're a fool."

His blunt verdict robbed her of speech. They were back in each other's space again, almost toe to toe.

"If I were a man," she said, "I'd call you out and run you through."

"But you're not a man, Mary. Yes, you are good with horses, but damn it all, you are still a woman. The only thing I haven't seen you do yet is spit, and I'm expecting you to do that any day now. Return to being yourself, to what God made you, and sell Tanner to me—"

"I knew you were coming to this point," she said with satisfaction. "Well, your methods of negotiation are not to be admired, Barlow. Insults have never won over a buyer. And I'd *never* sell Tanner to you. Ever!"

Gently, Vicar Nesmith interrupted. "Ah, see you are congratulating Miss Gates again, Tye. Good lad. But you can't hog the lovely lady to yourself."

His presence suddenly reminded both of them they weren't alone, something Mary had forgotten in the heat of the moment. She turned and discovered the other villagers had gathered round. She caught Blacky staring into the bottom of his empty tankard as if wondering how it had gotten that way. Even Brewster appeared a bit moony-eyed from drink and David had already left. Embarrassment at what could have been overheard shot through her.

However, she noted that the good vicar's eye was clear and bright, but he'd never repeat what he'd heard. His discretion was one of the many things Mary appreciated about the cleric.

Barlow's manner turned formal. He touched the brim of his hat. "You must excuse me. I should be returning to my stables." He didn't wait for her to leave but strode off, his long legs eating the distance to where the guests' horses were tethered.

Mary watched him go. She should feel relieved. She didn't.

How did he know her financial affairs?

Someone pushed a tankard of punch in her hands and someone else asked her what plans she had for the Stud, an effective diversion. 'Twas easier to shove disturbing thoughts from her mind and give in to her dreams.

Tomorrow she would worry about Barlow and money. Today, she wanted to savor the heady thrill of victory. The Stud was now hers and she'd do anything to keep him.

Absolutely anything . . . and for no other reason than to tweak Barlow's egotistical nose.

Chapter 3

The next morning, Mary woke with a head heavy from strong punch and a fear Lord Spender might not accept her terms. She'd thought of an arrangement to meet the purchase price. Of course, last night, flush with drink and the euphoria following the sale, her idea had sounded completely rational.

Today, she had to face Lord Spender. Optimism met reality. It wasn't a pleasant meeting. Even if she succeeded in convincing Lord Spender, the price would still place a strain on Edmundson's already tight financial state, that is, until Tanner started paying for himself . . . which could take a year or even two.

Worse, she'd overslept. Depending on his mood, Peter, her stable "lad" who was actually well past sixty years of age, might or might not have fed the horses and started the chores. With a groan, she forced herself to sit up, regretting every sip she'd taken of Lord Spender's punch.

A painful ten minutes later, she'd braided her hair, pulled on her clothes, and splashed water on her face. She started down the stairs, wincing at each creak of the stair treads.

Edmundson was a stately old country house, comfortable but a touch rundown. There was no extra money for repairs. But there would be, she promised herself, when Tanner's foals started winning. The first item she'd buy with her new fortune would be a thick runner for the stairs. Then she'd never have to hear another creak again or freeze her toes on the bare wood.

As she passed the room the family always referred to as the morning porch on her way to the front door, she came to a complete halt. Her sister, Jane, sat at the breakfast table sipping a cup of tea. The trio of dogs who usually slept in the front hall begged at her feet. At the sight of Mary, they wagged their tails and lumbered over in greeting. Mary leaned against the doorjamb.

At first appearance, the only trait the two sisters appeared to share were the same slashing eyebrows. Jane was four years younger with curly, golden hair and a petite, very buxom figure. She was pretty, but everyone agreed Mary was the beauty.

However, as sisters, they were close and were both known for their tenacious natures.

"David told me you paid an astronomical price for Tanners Darby Boy," Jane said instead of a simple "good morning."

"I paid the price I had to." Mary pushed away from the door frame. "If you wish to tell me what a fool I am, you'll have to tag along. I've work to do."

"You also suffer a bit from yesterday's brandy punch?" Jane hazarded. She held up her teacup. "It's my mint tea. David swears by it after an evening of drink."

Mary crossed to her sister in two strides, took the cup, and gulped down the contents. The brew was lukewarm and sweet and her needy body soaked it up. "It's not bad," she admitted, then turned on her heel and started out the door. Jane hurried to catch up.

"If you are here to lecture me, you can return home," Mary threw over her shoulder.

"Would you listen to me if I did?"

Mary grabbed her floppy brimmed barn hat from a side table. "No." She threw open the door.

The day was overcast and threatened rain. The two sisters didn't say anything as they walked to the stables. The dogs dutifully trailed behind. The mint tea did seem to alleviate the headache until Jane asked casually, "So, do you have the thousand pounds for the Stud?"

Mary skidded to a stop and looked her sister straight in the eye. "What do you think?"

Jane frowned. "I was afraid of as much."

Mary had a tough question of her own to ask. "And Barlow knows I don't have the money. Have you been talking to David about my financial affairs?"

An impatient sound was Jane's reply. "It's not a secret, Mary. *Everyone* knew Papa gambled too much and they've watched as you've let one servant after the other go."

"I've *pensioned* them off," Mary corrected proudly. "It was what Grandfather would have done. After all, they've all worked for the family for years."

"Yes, I know, and *you* are the one who has had to sacrifice to accomplish it. Papa would have worked everyone until they dropped where they stood. Has it really been six years since he died? Everyone thought Edmundson would fall to pieces, but you saved us." Jane hooked her arm in her sister's and moved toward the estate's brick stables. "You've given Niles and me so much, but at what cost? And what have we done for you in return?"

Jane had never talked this way before. Of course, for the last two years all she could do was think of David. But this talk . . . it made Mary uncomfortable. "I don't want anything. Everything I've done has been for Edmundson."

She pulled her arm from Jane's and swung open the stable's huge, white painted main doors. Several mewing cats let her know she was late and they were hungry. The horses moved restlessly in their stalls and a few nickered a greeting.

Mary inhaled the smell of hay, fresh air, and horses. She preferred their scent over any perfume save the bouquet of honeysuckle. The flower always reminded her of her mother and had been her chosen fragrance back when she'd been the belle of the parish.

Whiskers, a black and white tomcat, leaped forward and deposited a dead mouse at Mary's feet. Jane squeaked in disgust but Mary cooed, "Good, Whiskey. Such a good cat you are. Off with you and the others. I have the horses to feed. Then, I'll come to the house and reward you properly."

The cats took off running. The dogs joined in the morning ritual, chasing them. Mary picked up the mouse by the tail and tossed the wee thing out the barn door. Jane shivered and pulled a face.

"You are so missish," Mary complained, yanking open the grain bin.

"And I've never understood why you wish to live here alone."

"I'm not alone. I have the horses, the cats, the dogs."

"I'm talking about human companionship."

"There's old Peter."

"Really? He never seems to be around," Jane said doubtfully. "Shouldn't he have fed the horses by now?"

"He naps. Often," Mary explained. In truth, he was past ready to be pensioned off too, but he refused to even discuss the issue with her, and stayed on out of loyalty.

Mary started to measure feed, not wishing to pursue the subject, but Jane caught her arm.

Her expression searching, Jane said, "You can't tell me you haven't wished for more."

"Like what?" Mary asked. "I have my horses, Edmundson—"

"Like a husband, children."

For a second, Mary couldn't speak, overcome by yearnings she didn't want to admit to herself. She'd had too many of these alien feelings since Jane's marriage . . . feelings that were never to be, not for her.

She quickly hardened her resolve. "I don't." She pulled out the measured scoop and headed for the first stall. Portia, her favorite broodmare, greeted her by stamping impatiently for food.

Mary might economize on other facets of the estate, but not on anything concerning the horses. Edmundson boasted eight horses—mostly mares, the others geldings—down from the twenty back in their grandfather's day, but that would soon change now she had the Spender Stud. "I'm going to put Tanner in the end stall. It's the largest and I can separate the other horses from him."

"David always says stallions should have their own shed," Jane replied, although she'd never had much interest in the managing and training of horses. The irony, of course, was her marriage to the local horse doctor. Mary surmised David must prefer a wife who had conversation in the evening that differed from what he'd been hearing all day.

In truth, she liked her brother-in-law and had been happy to sanction the marriage. Jane had married for love—which was the way Mary felt it should be, even if she didn't trust that traitorous emotion herself. When it was returned, love could be full of the happiness Jane had found with David. If unreturned, love stole your self-respect . . . honor . . . everything worth valuing or holding sacred—

The still almost overwhelming sense of betrayal threatened to engulf her. She pushed her anger away. Instead, she focused on Tanner. With him, everything would be set back to rights. Edmundson would thrive and all would respect her family name again.

Mary swung open another stall door. "No, I want Tanner here with the others." She poured the grain into the feed bucket. Honey, a cart pony, pushed her velvety soft nose in the way, anxious to eat. "Don't be so greedy," she cooed. She went on to the next horse.

Jane had picked up another scoop and helped with the feeding. For a few minutes, they worked in companionable silence. When they'd finished, Jane handed her the scoop and said, "I think you are wrong."

"About what? Putting the Stud in here?"

"About sacrificing yourself the way you are for Edmundson." Jane looked around the barn as if gauging the width of its stone walls and the height of its rafters. "Edmundson is a place, sister, not a family. And I don't believe you when you say you don't long for a husband and children. I know you too well."

Mary slapped the grain bin door shut. "I realize you are happy with the married state, but understand I am quite pleased with my lot in life."

She swooped down to pick up the water bucket, ready to take it to the pump to be filled, but Jane blocked her way.

Raising a placating hand, Jane said, "Very well, I accept the fact you are happy. Now, let us talk about a matter which *will* interest you. You are in over your head with Lord Spender's horse."

"Not you, too." With a shake of her head, Mary moved past Jane toward the barn door, but then stopped. She turned. "I hadn't intended to pay so much, and I wasn't going to bid until I realized Barlow would win the horse."

"You should have let him have it."

"I couldn't. You know that."

Jane shook her head. "No, I don't. Tye is a good horseman and he's a fair man. You could have let him have the stallion. Then your only expense would be breeding fees."

"Aye, and his farm will prosper with trade Edmundson could have had. I can't believe you would even suggest such a thing. The Gateses give no quarter to the Barlows." She marched outside and started priming the pump.

Jane followed. "You sound exactly like Father."

"And why not? Everything he said was going to happen has. Barlow grows wealthier while we suffer. He is trying to take everything from us. Can't you see, Jane? Well, he can't have the Stud."

"Tye hasn't done one thing—"

Mary dropped the bucket and whirled on her sister. "Why do you keep defending him? Father would be in an uproar to hear you speak in such a way."

"Father was *always* in an uproar," Jane countered. "Mary, Father wasn't the be-all and the end-all. You and I have very different memories of him. He was an ill-tempered tyrant—especially as he grew more bitter."

Mary opened her mouth to tell her she was wrong, but then had second thoughts. Only she knew how right their father had been with his distrust and recriminations. *She'd* let him down. She'd let them all down. If not for her foolishness, she would have married well, and Edmundson's coffers and stables would be full.

Guilt almost suffocated her.

Jane gentled her tone. "I've been thinking, Mary. Ever since David told me the price you are paying for the horse, I've been racking my brain for a way to raise the funds . . . and I believe I have a capital idea."

Now she had Mary's interest. "What is it?"

Jane smiled, but a small worry line marred her forehead. "You could marry."

"What?" The word exploded from Mary. "Marry?"

"Yes, to a *rich* man."

For a stunned second, Mary was silent and then she burst out laughing. She laughed long and hard. When she could gather her breath, she said, "That is a ridiculous idea. Besides, I don't want to marry."

"But you should. It's time."

"Not for me. My home is here."

"Mary, be sensible," Jane said with a hint of frustration. "When Niles turns eighteen, Edmundson will be his and then what will you do?"

"There will always be a place for me at Edmundson." Mary really hadn't thought that far ahead.

"A place? Niles will marry someday and have children. You won't be the mistress anymore. Niles's decisions will carry weight in the stables and his wife's in the house. What will you be, dotty old Aunt Mary left to watch after the children? Is that what you want?" Jane asked sadly. "I mean, David and I will always have room for you . . . but you deserve more."

More. There was that cursed word again. Mary took another step away. "I don't want to marry. Ever."

"Before you reject my idea, hear me out. David's Aunt Alice and I correspond. She knows I have a sister of marriageable age and she's offered to introduce you among her eligible gentlemen friends—several times, in fact. She's a mettlesome sort but apparently very well connected, and she has managed to find several women husbands. For a small fee, of course. Very small. It's more of a hobby of hers."

"You want me to go to *London* to find a husband?" Mary asked incredulously. "At the ripe old age of twenty-six?"

"You are not that old," Jane replied. "And you'll never find a husband here. They—" She broke off from what she was about to say, bringing her hand up to her lips as if to stave off the words.

"They all know me," Mary finished for her.

"And respect you," Jane said loyally, but with a

telltale flush to her cheeks. She made an impatient sound. "Oh, come, Mary, there isn't a man in Lyford Meadows, save Lord Spender—or Tye—who has the money to buy the Stud. Only in London will you find a man rich enough."

At that moment, old Peter called her name. The women looked up and saw him hurrying toward the barn as fast as his stout legs could carry him. He took a moment to catch his breath before announcing. "Mr. Barlow is here to see Miss Gates. Rigged out like a dandy he is and waiting for you in the front hall."

Mary closed the pump handle. "His Sunday best? Well, well, well."

"Well what?" Jane demanded. "Why is he here?"

Hooking her arm in her sister's, Mary purred, "He wants the horse and he's decided to grovel. Come along, Jane. This should be fun."

Chapter 4

Mary and Jane came through the rear entrance of the house through a room she used for muddy boots and her rain kit. Spying Barlow impatiently pacing the perimeter of her front hall, Mary stepped back before he had the opportunity to see her. She signaled for Jane to take a peek.

"Look at him," she whispered. "He is not a man who enjoys cooling his heels. No doubt he is more accustomed to women waiting for him." She added with satisfaction, "But not this woman."

Jane bumped her arm. "You are enjoying this too much."

"Yes, I am." Mary stepped out into the hall and approached her enemy with a swagger in her step, feeling very much like Sir Francis Drake when he'd boarded a captured Spanish galleon. Ah, yes, power was a heady emotion.

"You clean up well, Barlow," she said. And he did. She'd never seen him turned out so fashionably. He wore his bottle-green Sunday church coat and had polished his riding boots. He'd even shaved—at ten o'clock in the morning, no less.

She also understood why all the other girls fawned over him. His back was straight and strong, his shoulders broad, his eyes intelligent. White breeches hugged powerful thighs. Trained to recognize good bloodstock, she had to admit Tye Barlow was a well-made man . . . and he was on his knees before her.

She was going to enjoy this interview.

"What do you want, Barlow?" she demanded.

Jane made a sound of annoyance at her rudeness that Mary ignored. This wasn't a social call. Mary knew what she was doing.

The lines of Barlow's mouth tightened, his blue eyes grew serious, stoic. He held his hat in his hand. "I've come to talk to you about Tanners Darby Boy."

Mary savored this moment. "You want to buy him from me," she said softly.

"God, yes!" The words exploded out of him. Humbleness evaporated and he tossed his hat on the side table and took a step forward, taking charge. "Mary, we must talk. There has to be a solution for the both of us."

"I'm not interested in talk, Barlow," she replied breezily. "But I wouldn't mind listening to you *beg*." She strutted into the parlor, flopped down on the settee, and placed her boot heels on a wooden footstool. "I'm waiting."

Barlow hesitated, peering into the room as if imagining her father lurking in the corners. Then she realized he'd never been this far inside Edmundson. Her father would never have let a Barlow past the front step, let alone in the door.

She looked around the room, and for the first time noticed how bare the furnishings had become. The vases of fresh cut flowers, colorful rugs, and figurines that had filled the room when her mother had been alive were long gone. Most of those fripperies had been sold to help pay her father's gambling debts. What items were left Mary had given to Jane upon her marriage.

Worse was the layer of dust covering everything. Mary wasn't a housekeeper, and without servants it was impossible to keep it up. There was no time. What time she did have she spent in the stables, where the leather and the fittings gleamed from polish, cobwebs were banished on a daily basis, and floors swept clean.

All that remained of her privileged former life was the portrait of her mother and father hanging over the fireplace mantel. In spite of the painting being worth a pretty penny, Mary hadn't had the heart to part with it. 'Twas all she had left of her parents.

Now she felt her father's disapproving presence hover over this interview. She looked to her sister, who stood politely waiting for their guest to make a move to enter the room. "Come and sit down, Jane. We must listen to what Barlow has to say."

"Mary, behave," her kind-hearted sister warned, but Mary wasn't interested in "behaving." She'd longed to tweak Barlow's nose for ages and now she could.

"I'm waiii-ting," Mary reminded him in a singsong voice. "I don't have all day. I'm to meet Lord Spender this afternoon."

Her quip spurred him to action. He marched into the room, his shoulders square, his expression defiant. Immediately, the air in the room seemed to change, swirling with the vitality of his presence. He started to sit in the chair opposite the settee but she stopped him with a wave of her hand.

"Ah, ah, Barlow. A gentleman never sits when a lady is standing." She glanced pointedly in her sister's direction.

Bright color rose up his neck as he straightened. "Sorry," he said to Jane.

"Oh, Tye, don't worry." Jane cast a ruthless glance at Mary. "I'm just ashamed my sister doesn't have better manners." She sat down on the other end of the settee, giving Mary's legs a rough push off the footstool as she did so.

Mary didn't take offense. Instead, she puzzled over Barlow's obvious embarrassment at her "gentleman" gibe. She'd thought nothing could discomfit him. Perhaps he wasn't as cocksure of himself as she'd surmised.

In truth, she was jealous of him, as had been her father. Tye Barlow had the most fortunate luck backed by talent. His father had been a good horseman, but Barlow was better. Too many times, Mary had heard her father curse him—and then wish he'd had a son like him in the next breath.

Niles had been too young to feel the sting of those words but Mary had felt them.

Uncomfortable with the memories, she armed herself with sarcasm. "Groveling doesn't come natural to you, does it?"

"No more than it does to you," he muttered as he sat. He leaned forward, his expression earnest, and came right to business. "Edmundson can't afford Tanners Darby Boy. Not at the price you bid."

Mary replied silkily, "Are you accusing me of purchasing a horse I can't afford?"

To his credit, he didn't back down. "The selling price is outrageous for *anyone*. Meeting it will place a strain over everything you own."

True. "What makes you so certain?"

He glanced at Jane, who lowered her eyes. He barged forward, "It's common knowledge you are holding this place together with straw and spit, Mary. And no one thinks the worse of you," he hastened to add. "There are many who respect you. But what good is spending what cash you have on a horse if you have nothing left over to properly develop him?"

"I won't sell the horse to you."

"I knew that before I came here," he said ruefully. "But I have an offer that may interest you."

"You'd best make it quick, Barlow. I'm growing impatient. And if this is your idea of groveling, you aren't very good at it."

He didn't rise to the bait but pressed on, "What I'm proposing is that you and I split the cost of Tanners Darby Boy. Half of the horse will belong to you, half to me."

Jane stirred with interest but Mary sat tight. Split a horse? No. Still . . . she couldn't stop the quickening of her pulses at the thought of only paying half the purchase price. "Go on."

"Our agreement would be very straightforward," Barlow said. "We'd have breeding rights for our own mares. Before accepting stud fees from others, we'd have to both agree upon the commission. Profits would be split equally. Our estates border each other's so there is no *physical* impediment to us working together."

It sounded funny to hear him refer to his farm as an estate. Her father had always scoffed at the name they'd chosen, Saddlebrook. More important, Tye's proposition sounded reasonable. *Too* reasonable.

"Of course, we'd keep the Stud at Edmundson," Mary said.

He sat back with a shake of his head. "Don't be silly. The animal will be stabled at Saddlebrook."

There it was. She'd known she couldn't trust him.

"Why is that, pray tell?" she asked, her voice carefully neutral. Jane gave her a nervous glance.

"Because my stables are better, for one reason," Barlow said, apparently oblivious to the insult he was delivering. "They're newer and larger. He's a big horse. He needs the space."

"There is no horse in the world that needs more space than what Edmundson offers," Mary said firmly.

Barlow locked his gaze with hers. "Another reason is the breeding itself. It can have difficult, even dangerous, moments—*as you know*. A man of my size can handle a stallion like Tanner. He's not for the weak."

Mary sat straight up. "Weak?"

Jane placed a placating hand on Mary's arm. "I'm certain Tye wasn't calling *you* weak," she said with a pointed look in Barlow's direction.

He picked up his cue like an actor trained for the stage. "Of course not. You are very strong . . . for a woman."

Mary rose, suddenly tired of the game, especially if it meant Jane favoring Barlow's petition against her. "I'm every bit as capable at managing a stallion as you are, Tye Barlow. You want Tanner for yourself and you believe you can bamboozle me with this talk of a partnership."

He came to his feet. Anxious, Jane rose, too, as if thinking she might be called upon to tear the two of them off of each other.

"I am not trying to deceive you in any way," he said. "But I've thought hard about this, Mary. You are a fine horsewoman, probably the best in England. You know what you're doing. But my stables are more modern and that is something other horsemen like to see."

Mary snorted her opinion. "Why? The mechanics of breeding haven't changed since, oh, let's see . . . the beginning of time?"

Barlow frowned at her sarcasm. He shot a glance toward Jane, then said bluntly, "The truth is people from outside Lyford Meadows don't know how to take you."

Jane made a soft sound of distress. Barlow attempted to soften his statement. "I mean, we all in Lyford Meadows know and accept you. But outsiders are different. They won't know how to deal with a woman walking around in breeches and running her own breeding farm."

Mary felt her blood begin to boil. "What are you saying, Barlow? Do you fear I will be taken advantage of?"

Jane moved between Barlow and Mary. "Please don't lose your temper," she begged her sister. "But Tye is right. You know David and I worry how people might misconstrue your connection with a breeding farm and living alone here."

"I have Peter," Mary returned.

"Yes, dear, I know, and everything is all very respectable. But if something *should* happen, I fear Peter would not be any protection."

"I've been on my own for years," Mary said, not liking the direction of this conversation. "I'd thought I'd won this argument between us long ago. I've made my own way."

"Yes, among us in the village," Jane quickly agreed. "We all love you. But what Tye is saying is that the fame of Tanners Darby Boy will bring men to Edmundson who might not understand your position here. Men who perhaps aren't gentlemen. Horsemen can be very rough."

"Then I will teach them to understand," Mary vowed, "with my whip." She walked over to the mantel where she could face the two. They stood together and she felt betrayed. "I make my own rules," she said, her voice ringing. "I do what I want. I don't need a man to stand in front of me."

Barlow stepped forward. "I respect your independence. We both do. But we are concerned—"

"Concerned?" Mary laughed. "You want the horse in your stables."

"No, it's not—" He paused, and then as if frustrated by his own argument, replied honestly, "You're right. But, Mary, see the sense of it. You've never left this village. You know nothing of the outside world. Didn't you notice the way the men ogled you at yesterday's horse sale? If Brewster, Blacky, myself, and the others hadn't been there, you would have been dragged into the bushes for all your pride."

Jane gasped at the crude picture his words drew. Tye half-turned, dull color again creeping up his neck. "I'm sorry, Jane. I was perhaps too blunt. I forgot myself."

His apologizing to Jane touched a raw nerve Mary hadn't known existed. He had not begged *her* pardon, and she was the one he'd maligned! Boldly, she declared, "You needn't worry about me, Barlow. Lyford Meadows is no different from the world beyond. I've already fought that battle—and I didn't need you for protection."

"Mary . . . ?" Jane said with a touch of distress.

Mary ignored her sister. This was between herself and Barlow, who had taken on the expression of a guard dog whose territory had been invaded. "No harm came to me," she informed him. "And your domineering protectiveness is further proof of your overbearing nature. You believe everything and everyone in Lyford Meadows should dance to your tune. Well, I won't. I also question if you are more worldly than myself. Where have you traveled in your life? Newmarket? Ah, yes, I remember, you once went to Oxford. Decadent, worldly city it is."

"But I'm a man," he responded, a glint in his eye. "There is a difference in how the world perceives us. You don't understand, because we've all coddled you."

"Coddled me?" His accusation was preposterous. "I've made my way on *my* own." She stabbed the air between them with her finger. "Tanners Darby Boy is *mine*, Barlow, and I'll not be needing such 'help' as you are offering. Now, take your manhood and get off of my property before I fetch my horse whip."

He didn't budge. "If you were to try such a thing on me, I'd pull the whip from your hands, snap it in two, and—and—"

"And what?" she dared, taking a step forward.

He sliced the air in an angry swipe of his hand. "Damn you, Mary. You are stubborn, pigheaded, foolish—"

"I am *not* foolish." His accusation raised old ghosts. Mary doubled her fists, ready to bop him if necessary. "I may be the other things, but I am not foolish!"

"Well, you are playing the fool now," he answered. "If Tanner escaped his pen and got at the mares, there'd be no way you and old Peter could stop him. He's too much horse. Someone, some way, has to get reason through your thick head."

"*My* thick head? You insufferable, arrogant—" She searched for the right word. "*Toad*. A woman stands up to you and you can't take it, can you? Well, here is a bit of news, Barlow: Not every woman is willing to simper and jump to your command just because you think you are the parish buck! For once, you've met your match."

Jane stepped between them. "Please, both of you—"

"Stay out of it," Mary said ruthlessly. "This is between Barlow and myself. It's time someone took him down a notch. He's too full of himself."

"And how would you know?" he countered. "Your nose is so up in the air, it's a wonder you can see past it."

That comment took her back a bit. "That's not true. I get along with everyone in Lyford Meadows. *Except you*."

He opened his mouth, his expression telling her he was about to set her straight, but then he shook his head. "Why am I arguing with you? It's a senseless exercise."

"You just can't accept an opinion from a

woman, Barlow. Your response is to threaten to manhandle her."

"Manhandle—?" He leaned forward until his nose almost touched hers. "I've never forced myself on a woman. Ever. But don't you worry. You are the *last* woman I would touch. You are difficult, obstinate, irritating, rude—"

"Heavens, such a vocabulary," she sniped.

"Bull-headed," he concluded. "I don't know why I even thought it a good idea to partner with you." He marched to the door, but then stopped. "And let me tell you something else. You'll *never* own Tanners Darby Boy, Mary. I feel it in my gut. And my gut is always right."

Mary jumped up on her footstool, needing to bring herself up to his plane. She wasn't about to let him cow her. She braced her legs to keep her balance and said, "You're a sore loser, Barlow. A *bloody* sore loser."

He scowled, his expression ferocious and then confessed, "You're right. For once, you're right. Good day." He stomped out of the room, grabbed his hat up off the side table and slammed the front door with such force the front of the house shook.

Mary crowed with triumph. "I told him. And it felt good." She punched the air with one fist and jumped off the stool.

Jane appeared stunned and slightly frazzled, as if she could collapse at any moment.

With an impatient sound, Mary said, "Don't be such a puss, Jane. Barlow can handle it."

"But you both . . ." Jane raised her hand to her head. " 'Twas like watching the clash of the Titans."

Mary laughed, pleased with the comparison. She always enjoyed a confrontation with Barlow—especially when she came out on top. Of course, now that he was gone, 'twas like all the energy had been sucked from the room.

It was often like that between them. When he was around, she felt invigorated, challenged. But once he'd left . . . well, she could always sense his absence. 'Twas like a hole that could not be filled.

What was it about Barlow that made everyone, herself included, so keenly aware of his presence?

"He is too full of himself by half," she muttered, attempting to answer her own question. "Telling me that I know nothing about the ways of the world. I know a good deal more than he imagines." Her last words sounded more bitter than she'd intended. She didn't like what they might or might not reveal in front of Jane, who was usually attuned to the nuances.

But instead, her sister asked bleakly, "So, how are you going to pay for the horse?"

The flush of victory evaporated. "Do you doubt me, too?"

"I asked a simple question. Don't take after me like you did Tye."

"I am level-headed," she assured Jane. "After all, after Papa died, I picked up the reins of managing Edmundson and have done fairly well."

"You've done very well, but I worry. A thousand pounds is a fortune."

Mary placed her hands on Jane's shoulders. "Tanner is worth a fortune. Here, come with me." She led her sister to the next room, the study. Ledgers lay open on the desk, one on top of the other. Mary reached for a wood chest on the book shelf and blew off the dust. She carried the heavy coffer to the desk. Clearing aside her bookkeeping, she set it on her desk and raised the lid. Inside were coins.

Jane's eyes widened to the size of saucers. She reached out to touch the money.

"I've saved it," Mary said proudly. "Six hundred and thirty-two pounds. Of course, most of it is my dowry. Mine was larger than yours, remember? Father had expected me to snare a rich husband and had financed me accordingly."

Jane dropped the coin in her hand as if it had turned into a glowing ember. "But your dowry is for when you marry."

Mary snorted. "Be sensible, Jane. I'm twenty-six. Marriage is not part of my future. This money has been going to waste. I'm going to use it to purchase Edmundson's future. I'm going to buy Tanner."

Jane shook her head. " 'Twas meant for *you*. Not Edmundson."

"Edmundson *is* all I care about," Mary stressed.

"But what if you meet someone who makes you want to have children? Someone whom you can love and who will cherish you? What will you have to offer?"

Mary looked into her sister's eyes. "There is no *someone* as you describe for me." No, her foolishness of falling in love with a faithless man years ago had ruined her. But she couldn't tell Jane that. There were still some secrets, even between sisters as close as they were. Instead, she said, "I have no need for any man. Edmundson is all that is important."

"Is it enough?" her sister asked sadly.

"Yes . . . if I own the Stud."

"But, Mary—"

"Enough! This horse is all I want, all I've dared to let myself want. I've won him. He's mine. If I lose him now, I'll never gain respect."

Jane's gaze dropped to the dull coins in the chest. For the space of several heartbeats, she was quiet. Then, "You still don't have enough." She paused. "Perhaps you should reconsider Tye's offer."

Mary's pride came up like a shield. "No. He wants control while giving me only a token voice in the decisions. Well, I'm not that green."

"But you are still almost four hundred pounds short. David and I have some savings to offer but it won't give you everything you need."

"Oh, Jane, thank you, thank you, thank you for understanding. But I don't think I will need your money." She pulled a legal parchment from the desk. "I'm going to offer Lord Spender the Dower House for the balance."

"Can you?" Jane asked. "I thought it was part of the estate."

"It is, but it wasn't included in the entail since Grandfather gifted it solely to Mother. Certainly it is worth four hundred pounds."

Her sister appeared doubtful. "There isn't much land attached to it. Just the house and immediate grounds. Not really enough property to make a difference. And what of Niles? Isn't it legally his? What if he wants to keep the property?"

"Jane, he's a boy. What does he know? Besides, Tanner will make Edmundson famous and Niles will be happy."

"Have you discussed this with Uncle Richard?" Jane asked, referring to the distant relative who served as Niles's guardian.

"We haven't heard from him for years! I've been the one making decisions concerning Niles and having to arrange money for his schooling. I'm not going to start consulting Uncle Richard now."

The lines of Jane's mouth flattened. She wasn't particularly pleased with the turn of events. "I wish there was another way . . ."

"There isn't."

A heartbeat of silence and then Jane said with more loyalty than conviction, "Well, perhaps it will work."

Mary closed the lid. "It *must* work."

Chapter 5

Lord Spender must have been peeking out the windows eagerly waiting for Mary because when she arrived, he charged out of the house, almost barreling over his butler.

"Timely as always, Miss Gates," he chortled. "Is that the money?" He tapped one finger on the chest she carried on the saddle in front of her. "Come into the house and let us have a bowl of punch to celebrate our mutual good fortune!"

Mary didn't want to have another thing to do with Lord Spender's punch. "A simple cup of tea will be fine for me, my lord," she demurred as she dismounted. A groom in burgundy and black livery took Portia's reins.

"May I carry the chest for you?" Lord Spender asked, holding out his hands.

"No—no, not until we've concluded our business." Secretly, she feared he would wonder why the chest wasn't heavier.

To her relief, he played the gallant and didn't argue. Instead, he said to the groom, "Tell Hadley to prepare Tanners Darby Boy. I'm certain Miss Gates wishes to take him home with her today."

Mary felt a twinge of guilt as she nodded agreement. *Everything will work out,* she promised herself. After all, events happened for a reason. One way or the other, she was meant to own Tanner. She knew it in her heart.

Taking off her hat as she stepped into the house, she almost tripped over a stack of bandboxes. Backing up, she nearly tumbled on top of a trunk. "What is this?" she asked Lord Spender. "Are you traveling?"

He dismissed the stacks and stacks of luggage with a wave of his hand. "These are my nevvy's. He's on his way to London, you know."

"Already?" Mary responded, a sinking feeling about their upcoming interview churning her stomach. She shifted the weight of the chest from one arm to another.

"Oh, yes," he said. "He's a young man, anxious and full of his own sense of purpose. Does my heart good to know I can grant him his wish to take on London. Here, hand your hat to William." He said to the butler, "Bring a cup of tea for Miss

Gates and a big tankard of punch for myself to the library."

"Yes, my lord," William responded and, taking Mary's hat, left the foyer.

"Come now, to my library," Lord Spender directed.

Following him down the hall, Mary ventured, "London is a dangerous city. Perhaps it would be better if your nephew stayed in the country a bit longer."

"Nonsense!" Lord Spender opened the library door and then paused. He leaned close to Mary, his eyes growing misty, the red tip of his nose a sign he'd already imbibed. "I want to tell you how happy I am that you won the Stud. Your father and I were good friends . . . or at least, I imagine I was the closest thing he had to a friend."

"You are right, my lord," Mary murmured truthfully.

"Well, he could be a harsh man—but he knew good horseflesh. He is the one who discovered Tanner, you know, back when the horse was a yearling. He couldn't afford him at the time, but since he owed me money, he paid off the debt by tipping me off. Best return I've ever had for my money."

If only her father had gambled less and purchased the horse himself, she thought bitterly, then Edmundson wouldn't be ready to fall down around their ears.

But then, she, too, had been responsible for the family's reversal of fortune. Her father had gambled everything he had on her marrying a wealthy man and she'd failed, becoming another one of his bad risks.

She prayed her luck had changed, for she was about to stake all.

His wood-paneled library was a true man's domain. The walls were lined with books she doubted anyone had ever read and the furniture was oversized and comfortable. Lord Spender offered her a chair.

"I'd prefer to stand right now," she said, too nervous to relax. She drew a fortifying breath for courage—and then frowned. A recognizable scent hung in the air, but she couldn't quite place it. Strange. She placed the chest on his desk.

Lord Spender made a low, happy sound in the back of his throat. He walked around the desk, eyeing the chest with undisguised pleasure.

Mary hated spoiling his joy, but she knew she couldn't keep her guilty secret a moment longer. In one breath she spoke, "I-don't-have-all-the-money."

Her confession came out in such a rush, Lord Spender paused as if uncertain that he'd heard her correctly.

Slowly, he sank into his chair behind the desk. "You don't have the money?" He pointed to the chest. "What is this here?"

Mary's mind scrambled for words. "I have *most* of the money. It's in the chest in front of you."

At that moment, their privacy was interrupted by the arrival of a liveried manservant carrying their drinks, which he set on a side table. Lord Spender rose, crossed to the tray, took his mug of punch, and drained it. "Shut the door on your way out," he ordered the servant.

The moment the door closed, he returned to the desk, flipped open the chest, and ran his fingers through the coins. They hit against each other with a soft metallic ching. He sounded remarkably sober as he barked out, "How much?"

Awkwardly Mary said, "Six hundred and thirty-two pounds. The bulk of it. Enough to send a young man to London in style for years."

The corners of Lord Spender's mouth turned down. "Not if he has Henry's tastes. Henry can't cut the dash he wishes without the full thousand pounds." He sat in his chair and stared out the library's sole window, his expression distracted. "What am I going to say to him? There will be a terrible row."

She pulled the deed to the Dower House from inside her jacket and offered it to him. "Here. I offer something better than money."

"There is nothing better than money, Miss Gates," he assured her. "Your father should have taught you that lesson."

"Oh, yes, there is," she countered. "These are the papers to the Dower House. It's a fine property and worth well over four hundred pounds. Why, with it, you'll be the largest landowner in the parish."

He made no move to take the papers. "I already am the largest landowner in the parish. Besides, what do I want with a house that's little more than a cottage? One in need of repair at that?"

"You can give it to your nephew. He can sell it." She placed the deed on his desk.

Lord Spender shot out of his chair, pushing his wig back as he lifted a distressed hand to his forehead. "My nevvy doesn't want land. He wishes to go to London. He has great prospects there."

Mary couldn't imagine anyone turning down property . . . unless it was for a horse.

Lord Spender kicked his desk in frustration. "You're like your father," he said half to himself. "Yes, that's it." He raised his voice. " 'Tis as if I've made a pact with the old devil himself. This is exactly the sort of trick he would have pulled—promising me payment and then gulling me into accepting a pittance of what he owed."

Her face turned hot. "I am not my father. And how dare you slander him! Over the years, you've made three times the money he's ever owed you from Tanner. You said so yourself."

Lord Spender pointed a plump, beringed finger at her. "Ah ha, see, there you are—trying to talk around me the way your father would have. Always thinking of every angle, that's the way he was. A sly boots if ever there was one." He backed away as if she had turned into some evil thing. "I should have sold the horse to Barlow while I had the chance. He was just here, warning me he didn't believe you had the money!"

"Tye Barlow was here?" Cold anger spread through her limbs. And then, she recognized the scent she'd noticed when she'd first come into the room. Barlow's shaving soap.

"He left not more than ten minutes before you arrived."

She clenched her fists. "That scoundrel. That back-handed sneak—"

"I told him I wouldn't do it," Lord Spender said. "I trusted you. But now I must pen him a note this very second and tell him the horse *is* for sale." He headed toward his desk.

Not to Barlow!

Mary blocked his path. "No, wait, please. He doesn't have the money either. Not a thousand pounds."

Lord Spender considered a moment. "Yes, but he'll have more than you have." He stepped around her. "I can't disappoint Henry." He opened the top desk drawer to pull out a sheet of foolscap, picked up his pen, dipped it in ink—

Mary snatched the paper out from under the pen. "I'm getting married." The words flew out of her mouth seemingly of their own volition.

Her declaration was met with a long pause. Lord Spender shook his head as if clearing his ears. "Married?" He drew back slightly. Then, "You?"

Mary swallowed, her throat suddenly dry, her pulse rising. She thought fast. "It's a secret, a family secret. I didn't want anyone to know, but my intended is rich. *Very rich.* He wants me to have the horse."

"Then why doesn't *he* give me the money?"

"Why doesn't he—" she repeated half to herself and then plunged into the worst series of lies she'd ever told in her life. "Because he doesn't know I purchased Tanner. But he'd asked me what I wanted for a wedding present, and I haven't had a chance to tell him yet," she confided. "But he'll give me anything, including Tanner, once he knows. He dotes on me. Worships me."

"You're getting married?" Lord Spender repeated the words as if the idea was still beyond his comprehension. His rheumy gaze took in her loose braid, her breeches-clad body, and her scuffed boots.

She wished she'd dressed better.

"I'd not heard a word of this," he said at last.

"The banns haven't been read, have they? Why, we'd all notice if the banns were announced linking *your* name with some gentleman."

"No, they haven't been announced," she said honestly, "because he's not from Lyford Meadows."

"Where's he from?"

"London." It was the first word to leap to her mind. "The banns will be read in London."

Lord Spender sat in his chair with a frown. "I'm one of the deacons of the church, Miss Gates, and I must inform you the banns should be read here, too, in the bride's parish. 'Tis the law."

"Yes . . . but . . . he's wealthy enough to afford a special license."

"Oh. Well, why read the banns at all then?" His gaze narrowed thoughtfully. "Something isn't right here." He rubbed the side of his nose. "I can sense it."

Mary threw caution to the wind. She came around to his side of the desk and knelt before him. As she took his hands in hers, she prayed he didn't notice she was shaking. "Trust me, my lord. My intended is very well connected. He could help your nephew when he goes to London."

"He could?" Lord Spender pursed his lips as if nibbling the bait she'd thrown out.

Mary set her hook. "I'll tell you everything, but you must promise to keep my story a secret."

"A secret?" he whispered back. For a second, he wavered and then curiosity got the best of him. "You may count upon my discretion."

"I've been betrothed for years," she confessed.

His eyes widened. "Years?"

She forced what she hoped was a carefree laugh. "Father arranged the betrothal before I reached my majority. 'Tis why I've remained single. I've been waiting for him." Lying didn't come easily to her lips—but she was getting better.

"What's his name?"

She wasn't ready to make up a name. She covered her mouth with a finger. "Please. I can't. You would be shocked if you knew."

"I must say, no one in the parish has even suspected such a thing. I mean, after the disaster with Jergen's son . . ." His voice trailed off. With a glance at the door as if to check to see if anyone eavesdropped, he asked, "Tell me, Miss Gates, *is* it Jergen's son?"

"What?" she exclaimed, surprised by his conclusion.

He leaned forward. "I mean, now that the old Lord Jergen has passed on, his son has inherited the title. They say he is a force to be reckoned with in London." Speculation appeared in his eyes. "As I remember, Jergen was furious over his son's infatuation with you. 'Twas said, the son was besotted, but the father refused to countenance a match between you."

"My intended is not him," Mary said stiffly.

Lord Spender sat back, his expression disappointed. "Ah, well, I was only guessing. Why was Jergen's son in the area back then? Oh, yes, he was visiting his aunt and uncle. Everyone in the parish thought he was going to come up to scratch. We were all certain of it. He was so attentive. Must have been a heady thing to have a young man due to inherit such wealth courting you. The other lasses were livid with jealousy. But then he left." He cocked his head, his gaze narrowing slyly. "Many believe—well, *you know*. After all, you spent a great deal of time *alone* in his company. But then, people will talk about anything whether it is true or not. Especially jealous young ladies."

Heat crept up Mary's cheeks. Not for the first time did she regret her reckless behavior back then. She had no excuse save youth and naïveté. Both she and her father had demonstrated a lapse of judgment. Of course, she'd trusted John and had believed he loved her. Instead, he had crashed into her life with his promises, stolen her heart, her trust, and her innocence, and left without a backward glance.

She also knew the gossips still whispered. Some of the villagers might have guessed; some might even know. She steadfastly refused to comment.

In truth, she'd blocked much of the aftermath

of their affair from her mind. She'd been stupid, foolish. She had wanted to marry for love. Not money.

Well, now she knew love did not exist. At least, not for her. Jane may have found it with David, but Mary knew love was too rare to be found by everyone. And a lover's rejection was too painful to be lived through again. It left one heartbroken, exposed, shamed.

Her father had been the one to warn her to never breathe a word of what she'd done to anyone— not even to Jane. And so, Mary had donned her breeches, pulled back her hair, and dedicated her life to Edmundson. This was her absolution, her price to pay for disgracing herself and her family—and for losing her head over love.

She ran her thumb across the back of Lord Spender's hand. His skin was thin with age, the blue veins prominent. "Nothing," she heard herself lie tightly. "Nothing happened between myself and Jergen's son."

He frowned. "Nothing?"

"Nothing. Lord Jergen's son had more pressing engagements in London than flirting with an inconsequential squire's daughter, and so he went his own way."

"Ah, but you were a beauty in your youth. You still are. You could have landed him. All the young men drooled over you. Jergen's son could not have done better."

"Yes, well . . ." Mary cleared her throat. "Thank you, my lord, for your compliment. However, the man I am going to marry *is* better than him."

Lord Spender hummed with interest. "More powerful?"

"And richer," she replied boldly.

"Does he know you march around the neighborhood in breeches?" he asked bluntly. "Does he mind how *independent* you are?"

"He loves me for who I am," she said, wishing such a man did exist.

"Why haven't you married before now?"

Mary attempted a helpless sigh. "After Father died, I needed a little time—"

"He died years ago!"

"Yes, but you know how he left our affairs. Niles needed me." In her meekest voice, she added, "And I needed time. My betrothed cared enough to give it to me. Now I'm ready." Mary rose to her feet. "He's been waiting patiently all these years. He's so kind and thoughtful. Everyone respects him. He's understanding, too. He knows I had to put Edmundson first and he's the only one who hasn't criticized me. He supports my decisions." She added softly, "He loves *me*, just the way I am . . ."

She was brought back to reality by Lord Spender's gruff, "To my way of thinking, the man should tie you to the hearth until you learn your place. Buying horses you can't pay for—" He snorted. "And don't think I don't know you bought before you could pay. I should have never let you in to my sale," he said, jabbing the air with one finger.

She shook her head. "No, my lord, never say that. Please. I want Tanners Darby Boy more than I've ever wanted anything in the world. You don't know what I'm willing to sacrifice to gain him."

His expression softened. "But I can't wait forever. My nephew—"

"*Tomorrow.* Jane and I are leaving for London tomorrow. When I come back to Lyford Meadows, I will be a married woman. You must give me a chance."

"Miss Gates—"

"*Please.*" She put everything she had in that single word, including a melting gaze that had, at one time, made men her slaves.

For a heartrending second, she feared he would refuse—and then he said, "How long will you be?"

Mary caught her breath and did quick calculations. How long did it take to find a husband? "Three, four months."

"Four months! I can't wait that long. Henry will be furious as it is." He pulled a hand free and reached for his pen.

"Two, I meant two months. 'Tis not such a terribly long time, is it? I'll be back sooner if I can."

Lord Spender silently debated the issue. Mary

held her breath, knowing the horse's fate was about to be decided. She feared the worst . . . and then he said, "My nephew will be disappointed."

"My husband will make the wait worth his while. He'll introduce him to all the best circles and make certain he is invited to the most important affairs."

"I will expect him to do so." His gaze fell on the money chest. "And I can offer him this."

Mary panicked. She was going to need money to finance her husband hunt. She grabbed the chest before he could touch it.

"Actually, this is my dowry. I was offering it to you as a sign of good faith but you can understand I should give this to my husband first." The words, "my husband," felt strange on her lips.

"But you brought it here," he protested. "You already said the money was mine."

"That was when I thought you would let me have the horse. Now, you must wait for my husband. Besides, you can't have me traveling to London dressed like this. You said as much yourself." And she would need the Dower House as husband bait. Her face might win her notice, but London gentlemen yearned for property. She snatched the deed up from the desk and tucked it in her coat.

His gray, bushy brows came together. "My nevvy will kick up a fuss."

"I do not ask him to wait long. Besides, you know Tanner belongs at Edmundson. In your heart, you know it."

The pleading finally won him over. He stood. "You are a good lass, Miss Gates. Over the years, your misfortunes have troubled me deeply. I wish your father had been a different man, but he wasn't." He drew a deep breath and released it slowly. "I will give you two months to wheedle the full amount from your intended. 'Twill be my wedding gift to you. And although every bride needs her dowry, I will take four hundred pounds to keep my nephew happy."

Mary didn't balk. She counted the money out quickly. Two hundred pounds should be enough to introduce her to a husband. Why, there were people who lived for years on that sum. "Thank you, thank you, thank you. You will not be disappointed." She punctuated her feelings with an impulsive buss on the cheek.

Her kiss flustered him. "I want to see you happy. Two months and no more, Miss Gates. My nephew will not wait longer."

"Two months," she promised, and headed for the door before he could change his mind.

Forty minutes later, she rode up to the cottage Jane shared with David on the outskirts of Lyford Meadows. Still holding her precious chest of money, she banged on the door.

Jane answered. Before she could speak, Mary said, "Did you mean what you said about David's aunt finding a husband for me?"

"Yes, of course. As I said, matchmaking is her passion, provided we finance the venture."

"Good." Mary shoved the chest in her sister's arms. "We leave tomorrow."

Chapter 6

SEVEN DAYS LATER

"**W**here is Mary?" Tye demanded without preamble the moment he spotted David in Farmer Sower's barnyard applying a poultice to a draft horse. He dismounted and dropped the reins, a signal to Dundee to stay.

David looked up from the draft horse's hind haunch. "Well, hello, how are you?"

Tye frowned. "I've been looking for you for the good part of three hours and I'm in no mood to shilly-shally around. Where's Mary?"

"Who says she is anywhere?" David countered with a touch of irritation as he finished tying off a bandage around the poultice. Reaching for the mortar and pestle he'd used to mash the herbs, he rose, stretching his back at the same time. With a nod to Farmer Sower's son, who held the horse steady, he said, "Keep him quiet now. We'll see if that poultice draws out the abscess. I'll be by on the morrow to have another look at him. Tell your father."

"Yes, Mr. Atkinson," the tow-haired boy said, and led the horse away to the stall.

Tye planted himself right in front of David. "You know she is missing."

"Who is missing?"

"Mary," Tye said with annoyance. "I've concluded she's been missing a week. I've not seen her anywhere—including church. I've just come from your home and it appears Jane is gone, too." He was a touch proud of his sleuthing.

David frowned. "How did you reach that conclusion?"

"The place is a mess. You were never a tidy bachelor. She's been gone as long as Mary."

Sheepishly, David confessed, "I don't like lying. I was never good at it, especially with you, so don't ask me any questions." He started for his wagon.

Tye dogged his steps. "They have both gone somewhere together, haven't they?"

"Visiting," David said, grabbing the word as if a life line. "They've gone visiting. Relatives."

Tye shook his head. "There is something afoot. Lord Spender still has the Stud, his nephew left Lyford Meadows in a huff after a tiff with his uncle the servants said could have waked the dead, and Mary has hired a village lad to help old Peter with her horses."

"You have been busy, haven't you?" David threw over his shoulder. "Spying is not an honorable activity."

"I have a horse at stake," Tye replied tightly.

David opened the box where he stored his supplies and equipment on his wagon, his expression grim. He put the mortar and pestle away.

Tye reached over and closed the lid. "Where is she?" he asked quietly.

For a second, his friend wasn't going to tell him. He could read David's resistance in his expression. "I'm not surprised you don't want to tell me," Tye said. "This is what happens when a man marries. He feels more loyalty to his wife than his friends. Even friends whom he has known since they were in nappies. Even the *friend* he'd asked to stand up with him when he married."

David muttered something about troublesome sisters-in-law and wanting his wife back. Then, louder, "What difference does it make?" He looked his oldest friend in the eye. "Jane and Mary have gone to London to visit my Aunt Alice."

"The aunt who attended your wedding?" Tye remembered her. She'd made a fool of herself flirting with him, angling for a place in his bed—

which she had not landed. He'd not been impressed with her London airs. Nor did he admire brazen women. If there was chasing to be done, he wanted to be the chaser, not the chased. "Why would they want to visit her?"

David motioned with his head for Tye to step closer. Farmer Sower's son was busy filling water buckets and didn't appear to be paying much attention to them, but Tye did as he asked.

In a low voice, David said, "Jane took Mary to London to find a husband. My aunt is going to sponsor her on the Marriage Mart."

"A husband?" If the earth had opened up beneath him and God had announced it was Doomsday, Tye could not have been more surprised. "For *Mary*?" Recovering his initial shock, he tilted back his head and laughed loud and long. The idea was unbelievable.

"Well, why not?" David answered. "She has to marry sometime or else she could end up living under my roof and *that* is not going to happen. Mary and I rub well together as long as we are free to go our separate ways." He started to climb in the wagon.

Tye pulled him back down by the tail of his coat. "Why does she want a husband? She's never acted like she's wanted one before." Except for Lord Jergen's son, he reminded himself. Oh, yes, Mary had wanted him.

David looked down at the fistful of jacket in

Tye's hand. He released his hold. "Because it is past time she marries," David explained.

Tye rejected the explanation. "She's on the shelf, and has been for years. Why, she must be twenty-five, twenty-six?" And he was approaching thirty. He *was* thirty. He frowned. They were both growing a bit long of tooth.

"That was my thought," David agreed, "but Jane made me see Mary might have excellent prospects in London. After all, beneath the muck, she has her looks . . . the men in London don't know how difficult she can be."

An unfamiliar emotion flitted through Tye at David's rational explanation—jealousy.

He couldn't be jealous.

Not over Mary.

However, the idea of "Mary the wife" didn't sit well with him. "Why now?" he demanded. "She's never needed a husband before. To the contrary, she's bragged about not wanting one."

"She needs money. You know that. Jane told me about your confrontation with Mary at Edmundson over Spender's Stud. She told me the two of you were so angry with each other, the walls shook. Mary refuses to partner with you and Jane has convinced her she can marry for the money she needs."

Tye slapped the side of the wagon. "I *knew* she didn't have the money. That minx. Bidding the price up when she couldn't pay—" He stopped abruptly and turned to his friend. "Mary wouldn't sell her freedom for a horse." He stated a certainty.

"For the Stud she will," David replied.

Tye stared out over Farmer Sower's fields, attempting to grasp this new turn of events. Mary was not acting like herself. For years, he'd relied upon her behaving in a certain manner. Now, she'd up and gone to London and he didn't know what to think. Mary didn't do things like this . . .

"She's going to marry a man wealthy enough to buy the Stud," he said slowly, the reality finally taking shape in his mind.

"She won't," David said confidently. He hooked an arm over the side of his wagon and confided, "Aunt Alice knows eligible men because she makes sort of a career out of matchmaking. It's how she makes ends meet. She charges lasses like Mary a small retainer to introduce them to the proper sort like law clerks and maybe a banker—but she doesn't know any male with the blunt to throw a thousand pounds away on a horse. Wait two months and Tanner will be yours."

"Does Mary know this?"

"No, and I wasn't going to tell her. I'm not certain even Jane is aware." He sighed. "Nor would she care. My wife won't be happy until her sister has a husband. Any husband."

"Why should she worry? Mary seems happy enough."

"Tye, every woman should be married. And man, too." At Tye's snorted opinion, David said, "I know you won't believe this but I've never been happier since I wed Jane. She is my light, my reason for being, my helpmate."

"You appeared to me to be doing very well before you met her," Tye said flatly.

"On the surface, perhaps, but underneath, in my soul, I needed Jane."

Tye inched back. This conversation was too strange—and too personal—for his taste.

David noticed his withdrawal. "You won't know what I mean until you fall in love yourself."

"I've fallen in love a hundred times," Tye assured him. "I could never settle on just one when there are so many lovelies in the world."

Besides, he knew from experience love, *real* love, was not everything they claimed it to be. When it wasn't returned, love could be shattering. Even now, years and years later, he remembered the pain as if it had happened yesterday. And the worst part was that Mary never gave any indication that she remembered what she'd done to him. No, she'd cut him loose as callously as a hussar and had never looked back.

His friends didn't even know there had been anything between them. Tye kept this part of his past secret. As far as he knew, Mary hadn't ever spoken of that time to anyone either . . . but, of course, it was always there between them, coloring the way they reacted to each other whether she would admit it or not.

And he'd learned over the years how to protect his heart.

David continued his lecture. "No, you've only fallen in lust. I'm talking about *love*. There's nothing like it."

Tye pushed away from the wagon. "I don't know if this conversation is the sort of thing men discuss. Next thing, you'll be spouting poetry."

Anger flared in David's eyes. "Does Blacky appear a poet? Or Brewster? We all feel the same way. There isn't a one of us who regrets we married. Mayhap the time has come for you to try it."

Tye gave an exaggerated yawn.

His friend's mouth closed with a snap, anger in his eyes. "You are hopeless." He climbed up onto the wagon seat and picked up the reins. "You'll probably waste your life flirting with every passing girl, bedding widows, and die an old bachelor like Lord Spender who has nothing but his pompous nephew for family."

His verdict stung. "I'll marry. Someday. When I'm ready." To David's continued skepticism, he added, "I just haven't found a woman who inspires in me what Jane does in you."

It certainly hadn't been Mary. And he realized

in a rare flash of insight, in many ways, because of Mary he'd been avoiding the commitment of marriage.

The realization was decidedly uncomfortable, and not something he wanted to explore too closely. Although he couldn't stop himself from saying, "I still don't understand why Jane finds it so important for her sister to marry, beyond the horse, that is."

David studied the reins in his hand a moment, then said quietly, "Jane and I want children. Lots of them. Brewster already has one. Blacky and his wife have one and another bun in the oven, so to speak. But Jane and I . . ." His voice trailed off with unspoken concerns.

"You'll have children. It's the natural order of things," Tye said. "Provided you keep doing what you should be doing to get there."

"We are," David retorted. He shook his head. "But she hasn't taken. I think her worries about her sister are to blame. I believe, once Mary is wed, Jane will be pregnant in a fortnight." He shifted his weight, his tone taking on a more positive note. "Tye, give Jane two months. She'll have her sister wed and the Spender Stud will be yours."

"Provided Mary doesn't find a rich husband."

"She won't."

"But what if she *does*?" Something about Mary's husband hunt made him restless. Nor was

he willing to trust Fate. Not when Mary wanted
Tanners Darby Boy as much as he did. He knew
her. She'd get what she wanted. Especially if it
meant his not getting it.

He turned on his heel and headed for his horse.

"Hey," David called after him. "Where are you
marching off to in such a hurry?"

Tye didn't even bother to pause. "London."

Coming to London was not a good idea.

In her youth, when her father had been groom-
ing her to make her Season debut, Mary had
imagined London as a city of dreams. Clean, urbane, sophisticated.

Instead, it was sooty, dreadfully crowded, and
the smelliest place she'd ever been.

She missed her horses, her home, her village,
and *fresh* air. She'd also taken a dislike to David's
aunt, Alice Peebles.

The feeling was mutual.

They had met at David and Jane's wedding.
However, it was one thing to meet a person for a
happy family occasion and an entirely another
issue to live under her roof.

Mrs. Peebles turned out to be dictatorial and
condescending—two traits Mary never could
abide, especially from another woman. She wore
her butternut-colored hair high on her head like
some living image of the Roman goddess Hera,

painted her lips, and ran around in gauzy royal purple dresses and matching sandals.

Her first words to Mary had been the judgment, "We must change everything." And she'd set about to do exactly that—at Mary's expense.

Everything cost money, and Mary's precious dowry had dwindled considerably. Mrs. Peebles arranged for diction lessons, dance lessons, hairstylists, and dressmakers. Special creams were purchased at exorbitant prices and rubbed into Mary's complexion. Her hair was pulled and twisted every which way, her every privacy invaded, and each endeavor, both large and small, cost, cost, cost!

However, instead of embracing Mrs. Peebles's strictures and working with the dance instructor, the seamstress, and the hairdresser, Mary sabotaged their efforts in little ways. She fidgeted so dresses had to be fitted and refitted, deliberately stepped on the dance master's toes so he limped for days, and ducked whenever a pair of scissors or hot tongs was brought anywhere close to her hair. Her gravest offense was to ignore all of Mrs. Peebles's rules of etiquette.

She didn't understand herself why she was behaving in such a contrary manner. She wanted to blame her damnable pride. It had gotten her into more than a few scrapes over the years. But in truth, this trip had raised memories that kept her awake late into the night. This was London, _John's_ home. In Lyford Meadows, Mary could pretend he didn't exist. Here, there was the possibility their paths could cross.

The finery, the frills, even the dresses Jane and Mrs. Peebles wanted her to wear, served to remind Mary of the vulnerable girl she had once been back when she'd believed in love. Then, she'd anxiously given all in a desperate attempt to please John and her father—only to have her lover leave abruptly without word or assurance and her father turn his back on her.

Over the years, she'd coped by hiding that vulnerable girl behind breeches, bravado, and fierce independence—and she wasn't certain it would be wise to resurrect her. Yet, she desperately wanted Tanners Darby Boy. If Barlow won the horse, the Gateses would be doubly disgraced by her hand and she couldn't let that happen.

Grappling with conflicting emotions, and oh yes, her pride, Mary proceeded to balk at every request with the restraint of a stubborn mare refusing a jump. Meanwhile, a surprisingly determined Jane put the best face on her antics and urged Mrs. Peebles to plan on.

It was decided Mary would have her debut at a soirée hosted in the home of Mrs. Willoughby, a good friend of Mrs. Peebles—and paid for with Mary's coin. Mrs. Peebles assured her that important, eligible, and definitely handsome men of discerning taste would be presented to her. Jane was delighted; Mary was reticent.

Matters came to a head the day before the Willoughby soirée as Mary was being given a final fitting for the cream-colored gown she was to wear. She stood on a low stool in the middle of Mrs. Peebles's bedroom while Madame Faquier, the dressmaker, poked pins every which way into the dress. Often she would miss and prick Mary's skin, then complain if Mary flinched or uttered a protest. They'd been at it for an hour and Mary's temper was growing shorter.

Jane was elsewhere in the house doing needlework. Mrs. Peebles sat in a side chair, sipping tea laced with brandy and supervising the fitting. Her nasal voice grated on Mary's strung-out nerves. The pressure of tomorrow night's debut loomed amongst them.

Then, Mary's foot went to sleep. She wanted to tap it, to wiggle. She wanted to scream.

"Miss Gates, stop moving around," Mrs. Peebles snapped. "Madame, the bodice on the dress doesn't fit well. Something is wrong with the cut of it."

Madame bridled at the complaint. "The dress is not at fault," she said in accented English. "If Miss Gates insists on wearing a heavy petticoat beneath my design, what am I to do?"

"The heavy one? I thought we'd purchased new ones?—" Mrs. Peebles's voice broke off as a new thought struck her. She gave a long, suffering sigh. "Oh bother. Take it off, take it off. Let us see what you are wearing, Miss Gates."

Before Mary could protest, Madame peeled the dress up over her head, scratching her with the pins as she did so. She found herself standing in front of them wearing nothing but her stockings, garters, chemise, and pantaloons. Mary's face heated with embarrassment.

"Where are your stays?" Mrs. Peebles demanded, rising from her chair. "And why are you in these linen underthings? I thought we ordered cotton?"

"I had them delivered," Madame replied quickly.

"I don't like them," Mary said. "They are too—" She waved her hand over herself, not knowing how to express her sense of modesty without sounding silly. But in truth, the light, finely woven cotton made her feel naked—and too feminine in ways she'd not felt in years. "These are *my* clothes—from Lyford Meadows."

Mrs. Peebles walked around her, inspecting Mary's person. "The problem," she said to Madame, "is not the dress or the underclothes. She has no bosom."

"I do too," Mary protested.

Mrs. Peebles harrumphed her opinion, then boldly reached out and squeezed Mary's breasts together. "*Now* she has something. That's a nice bit of cleavage. Do you have an undergarment that can poof her up here?"

Mary pulled back and crossed her arms over her chest. "I don't want to be poofed."

Madame rolled her eyes. "So provincial."

"Yes," Mary agreed hotly. "In Lyford Meadows, we do not squash other women's bosoms."

Mrs. Peebles raised her eyebrows. "You want to make a favorable impression for your introduction into Society tomorrow night, don't you?"

"Not if you have to touch my bosom."

"Here," Madame said, digging in her box of sewing supplies. She pulled out two handfuls of sheep's wool. "We stuff her bosom with this, like so." She started to tuck the wool in Mary's bodice.

Mary slapped her hands away and jumped down off the stool. "Leave me alone."

Madame threw her hands holding the wool in the air. "*C'est impossible!* She does not understand fashion."

"I don't need wool stuffing to give me—" Mary broke off, too embarrassed to say the words. She waved her hands at her chest. "—Poof."

Mrs. Peebles had no such sense of delicacy. "Breasts. They are called breasts, Miss Gates. Every woman has a set and many stuff them."

Mary dug in her heels. "Not I."

"You don't have to stuff much," Madame said,

pressing the wool puffs together with her fingers. "*Un peu.*"

"No," Mary answered.

Mrs. Peebles's gaze narrowed. "I've had it with you, missy. Every young woman who has come to me has found a husband. You will not upset my record. I won't let you. Your sister is a good, biddable girl, but you are too headstrong by half."

"People who really know me call me bull-headed," Mary announced proudly, remembering Barlow's words.

"Well, in this house, *my word* is law," Mrs. Peebles said. She pushed the gauzy sleeves of her dress up her arm and took a menacing step forward. "And for over a week, you have attempted to thwart me at every turn. Well, I have had enough of your defiance. Now, you will let Madame sew the stuffing into the bodice of your chemise if I must wrestle you to the floor and hold you down while she does so!"

"I'd like to see you try," Mary dared.

"Madame, have your needle and thread ready," Mrs. Peebles ordered.

"*Oui*, Madame Peebles," the Frenchwoman said. She came to stand behind her benefactor.

Mary picked up the stool, using it to hold them at bay. Mrs. Peebles blinked in surprise. Obviously, she hadn't actually expected resistance.

Well, she had chosen the wrong woman to threaten.

A knock sounded on the door. Howard, her butler, said from the other side, "Mistress Peebles, may I interrupt you?"

Mrs. Peebles smiled, the expression putting a shiver down Mary's back. "Reinforcements, Miss Gates." She raised her voice. "Howard, come here."

Her butler opened the door. "Madame, you have a—?"

"Grab her," Mrs. Peebles ordered, pointing at Mary.

The butler's eyes widened. "I beg your pardon?"

"Grab Miss Gates!" Mrs. Peebles barked. At the same time, both she and Madame Faquier lunged for Mary.

But she was ready for them. She threw the stool. It missed Mrs. Peebles but sent Madame Farquier tumbling backward. Before the surprised butler could react, she slipped out the door.

"Chase her!" Mrs. Peebles commanded.

Mary started for the bedroom she shared with Jane, then stopped. They'd catch her there for sure. So, instead of running down the hall, she took off down the stairs for the ground floor, shouting for Jane at the top of her lungs.

Howard, Mrs. Peebles, and Madame gave chase, the two women adding their own opinions to the ruckus.

Mary's stocking feet slid on the wooden steps but she didn't mind. As soon as she found Jane, they were leaving this house. No one was stuffing her bosom!

In the front hall, she hesitated, trying to decide which way would be best, and then chose the back parlor. Jane loved to sew there in the afternoon because the light was better. Howard leaped at her from the bottom step, but she dodged in time and went running.

The door to the back parlor was open and Mary barged right in. Jane had heard the commotion and was halfway to the door. They almost ran into each other.

Mary steadied both of them. The maroon and yellow furnishings were dominated by two high-backed sofas and a comfortable cushioned chair in front of the hearth.

"Mary, what is the matter?" Jane asked.

"They're after me," Mary said. "They want to stuff my bosom and I won't let them!"

"They what?" Jane said.

Mary didn't bother to explain because Howard and the dressmaker careened into the room. Mrs. Peebles brought up the rear. Quick as a cat, Mary hopped up on a sofa ready to dive over it. Her feet sunk into the feather cushions and she almost lost her balance. Once again, Howard came close to getting his arms around her. She avoided him, knocking over a prized vase on the sofa table. Mrs. Peebles screamed with rage and dove to save the vase.

Mary decided the time had come to move. She leaped across the tea table between the two sofas—and then gave a start in midair.

From the feather recesses of the opposite sofa where he'd been sitting, enjoying the escapade, Tye Barlow stood up.

Mary would have crashed into him, save he reached out and caught her in a firm grasp. Her body against his, he set her feet on the floor.

In the cobalt depths of his eyes, she could see her reflection and the light of a thousand dancing devils. "Mary," he drawled, "I see you are taking London by storm."

Chapter 7

Mary was so shocked to see Barlow in the flesh standing in front of her, she couldn't speak. Her mouth moved, but no words came out.

He chuckled, enjoying her discomfort. "I'm happy to see you again, too." Then his gaze dropped and brushed the line of her chemise along her breasts. A new heat, hot, instantaneous, appeared between them. Obviously, he didn't mind that she didn't have "poof."

Her breasts tightened, growing fuller. Her nipples pressed against the well-worn linen.

Barlow noticed and released her as if she'd turned into a firebrand. Hot color flooded her face.

But while Mrs. Peebles, Jane, and the others gaped, as surprised by the situation as herself,

Barlow had the wits to remove his jacket and put it around Mary's shoulders. He edged away and nodded to those in the room he didn't know as if to pretend he hadn't seen Mary in her small clothes.

With as much dignity as she could muster, Mary gathered the wool coat around her. It was so large, she could have swam in it, and it smelled like him—shaving soap mingled with clean air, fragrant earth, and the slightest hint of horses.

The wave of homesickness was staggering.

She found her voice. "What are *you* doing here?"

Jane quickly collected her wits. "Tye had business in town and decided to pay a call."

"I didn't know you had any business in London," Mary challenged. She hated standing there in her underthings, but her dignity wouldn't let her scramble from the room.

"I do," he replied coolly, "when the occasion warrants."

He knows why I'm in London. The thought sent Mary's senses reeling. She'd been discovered. And she would have wagered what was left of her dowry that he wasn't here as a solicitous neighbor.

The rat!

But before she could order him to leave, Mrs. Peebles made her presence known by pointedly clearing her throat. She held her precious vase in one hand and primped her butternut curls with her other.

Suddenly, Mary remembered how lively Mrs. Peebles had behaved at Jane's wedding and the whispered rumors. The biddy had eyes for Barlow.

"Oh, yes, Aunt Alice," Jane said, remembering herself. "This is Mr. Tye Barlow, one of our neighbors from Lyford Meadows. Tye, this is my aunt Alice Peebles. I believe the two of you met at the wedding."

Jealousy replaced Mary's embarrassment. "More than 'met,' if what I heard is correct," she said derisively in a tone for Barlow's ears alone.

He ignored her. Instead, with a gallantry Mary didn't know he had, he took Mrs. Peebles's hand and said in a warm voice, "We danced at Jane's wedding. I'll never forget."

Mrs. Peebles giggled like a young girl and Mary wanted to gag.

"Howard," Mrs. Peebles said to her butler, her gaze still on Barlow as if he were a piece of marzipan she could gobble in an instant. "Why didn't you tell me we had a caller?"

"That had been my purpose for going upstairs until I was deterred . . ." He paused tactfully.

"I understand," Mrs. Peebles said. "Here, take this vase away. Bring sherry. Or perhaps you would prefer port, Mr. Barlow?"

"Port," he answered.

"Port it is," the older lady said. "Madame Faquier, you are dismissed."

"*Oui*, madame." The dressmaker bowed out, followed by Howard, who officiously hurried off as if they were entertaining the king.

Mrs. Peebles waved her hand to the sofa. "Please, Mr. Barlow, stay a moment and tell us about your business in town." She batted her eyelashes, a trick she'd unsuccessfully been trying to get Mary to do.

"Oh, please, my lady, after you," he said gallantly. Simpering with delight, Mrs. Peebles sat her buxom figure daintily on the edge of the sofa. She patted the cushion next to her, indicating where she wanted Barlow to sit.

"After you, Jane," he said.

Mary stood rooted to the floor dressed in her undergarments and Barlow's coat, watching this elaborate play of manners as if the world had been turned upside down and she the only one to realize it.

Mrs. Peebles broke through the moment. "Miss Gates, don't you believe you should excuse yourself from the room?"

And leave Barlow down here alone with Jane and Mrs. Peebles? "No."

"I thought you might want to *dress*," Mrs. Barlow pointed out in a loud whisper.

Heat rose in Mary's cheeks—but her sturdy linen undergarments provided better protection than the muslins and silks Mrs. Peebles had insisted she purchase—and who knew what untold mischief Barlow could cause if she didn't keep her eye on him? "I'm fine. Barlow and I don't stand on ceremony."

"No, we don't," he agreed, the corners of his mouth curving into a smirk.

Mary would have dearly loved to box his ears and throw him out the door. Instead, she strode over to the sofa with the arrogance of a Crown Princess and sat right between Mrs. Peebles and Barlow.

Her benefactor opened her mouth ready to object, but she was stopped by Barlow, who started laughing. It was a good-natured laughter, nothing smug or evil about it, and in a blink, Mary could see the absurdity too. She joined him and for a few seconds the two of them were in perfect accord, while Mrs. Peebles and Jane stared as if they'd lost all sense.

Fortunately, Howard entered carrying a tray with a steaming pot of tea and some cakes. He set it on the tea table, then turned to fetch a bottle of port and one of madeira from the liquor cabinet. Mary slipped her arms through Barlow's jacket, rolled up the sleeves and picked up the pot. Pertly, she said, "Tea?"

"No, no," Mrs. Peebles condescended. "A gentleman always prefers port." She poured a glass then handed it to Barlow by rising and crossing

around the tea table to him. She also took the opportunity to wiggle her way into the space between himself and the edge of the sofa, forcing
Barlow to bump Mary over if he didn't want Mrs.
Peebles sitting on his lap. The brazen woman
then placed her hand possessively on his thigh
and Barlow let her.

"Am I crowding you?" Mary asked with false
sweetness.

"No, not at all," Barlow replied. He knew Mrs.
Peebles was shamelessly after him . . . and he was
encouraging her for what reason Mary didn't
know. But she didn't like it.

For a second, she was tempted to pour the contents of the teapot in his lap. Instead, she batted
her eyelashes *à la* Mrs. Peebles.

Her action surprised a laugh out of him just as
he was taking a sip of port. He started coughing.

Mrs. Peebles said, "What is so funny? Did I
miss a jest?"

"No, Aunt," Jane said. She'd witnessed it all
and sent Mary a look, one warning her to behave.
Mary poured tea. "They are close friends—in
spite of their differences."

Mary could have corrected her but decided to
be on her best behavior for once.

"Madeira for me," Mrs. Peebles instructed.
Giving Barlow's knee a friendly little squeeze, she
said, "Tell me, Mr. Barlow, what business brings
you to London?"

"Yes, what business?" Mary echoed. She wondered what excuse he had concocted.

"Horse business," he replied.

"Then you should go home," Mary said, "because *your* business is concluded."

"I don't believe so," he said, handing Mrs. Peebles the poured glass of Madeira. "Although," he added, eyeing his jacket around her shoulders, "it might be *wrapped* up shortly."

She tightened her grip on the saucer she held, the cup shaking slightly. Why didn't Barlow move that biddy's hand from his leg? "Jane, tea?"

"Yes, please," her sister said, and took over the conversation. "Tell us how everyone is back home."

For the next few minutes, Barlow updated them on affairs in Lyford Meadows. Jane missed David fiercely and when Barlow talked of seeing him, her eyes grew misty. Studying the depths of her teacup, Mary felt guilty for her recent churlish behavior. Jane was making a sacrifice for her, and she hadn't cooperated as often as she should have.

"Will you be returning home soon?" Jane asked.

Barlow hesitated, and there was something in his hesitation that put Mary on her guard. "It depends on how long my business in London takes."

"You can leave today," Mary interjected.

"Mary," Jane warned. Mrs. Peebles become indignant, but Barlow laughed.

"I might be able to," he told them, his gaze smoothing over Mary's linen pantaloons and his jacket and she knew, knew, *knew*, he was here for one purpose only—and that was to thwart her plans. She wondered how he'd found out she was here to find a husband.

David.

Her guilt over Jane and David vanished. She'd have to throttle her brother-in-law when she returned home.

"So, you will be in town tomorrow night?" Mrs. Peebles inquired.

"Yes, I believe so," Barlow answered. "Although I'm not as anxious over my business interests as I was before I arrived in town."

Mary heard his veiled reference. What? Did he believe her unable to attract a husband? Well, she'd show him.

She was so miffed she didn't register the meaning behind the excited exchange of glances between Mrs. Peebles and Jane until her sister said, "Then you can come to the soirée tomorrow night in Mary's honor."

"No, he can't," Mary said.

"I'd be delighted," Barlow answered.

Turning on him, Mary said, "I'm not inviting you."

"But I am," Mrs. Peebles countered. "This will be wonderful. We needed an escort."

"Yes, that is what I was thinking," Jane agreed.

"And you will be perfect, Mr. Barlow." Mrs. Peebles leaned her ample bosom forward while familiarly rubbing his knee. "You and I will also be able to further our acquaintance."

Mary smashed down her teacup. She stood. "I don't want him there."

"Please, Mary," Jane started, but Mrs. Peebles came to her feet.

"Why, oh why, can't you behave?" she demanded. "This man is a guest in my house and you are embarrassing me."

Mary decided it was time for candidness. If she didn't say anything, Barlow would gull everyone. And Mrs. Peebles was acting like she thought he could become her next lover!

Dramatically, she announced, "You don't understand, Mrs. Peebles, I know this man. He is not here as a friend."

Barlow set his empty wineglass on the tea table. An expression of wounded misunderstanding crossed his face. "Here we go," he warned Mrs. Peebles, who simpered in sympathy. "She always attacks me in this fashion."

"And not without reason," Mary said. "This man is the worst sort of bounder!"

Jane rose from the sofa. "Mary, you are wrong to say such a thing about Tye and in front of Aunt

Alice, too. Truly, sometimes I grow impatient with you and this petty feud. Tye has done nothing to earn your ill will. In fact, Father's grudge against the Barlows was ridiculous."

"How can you say that?" Mary demanded, shocked by her sister's lack of loyalty.

"Because it is true! You know how Father was. What I don't understand is how you can continue to carry it on?"

Mary didn't know how to react. She took a step back, Barlow's jacket falling down off one shoulder.

He came to his feet. "Please, Jane, you don't have to defend me. Mary and I are blunt whenever we speak to each other. We're competitors. It's to be expected."

Mary narrowed her gaze. Why was he defending her?

"Competitors in what way?" Mrs. Peebles asked.

He answered, "Mary recently purchased a horse I wanted very much for my stables. She knows I am here to ask her to sell it to me."

"Which I won't. Ever," Mary vowed hotly. "And don't think I won't marry well," she added. "I'll do what I must to buy Tanner."

"Yes, I see that," he said, a double meaning coloring his words as he let his gaze casually drift over her unconventional attire—except this time his was not the burning look a man usually gave a half-dressed woman. It was nonphysical, dismissive, cold, even—and it made Mary all the more embarrassed.

Damn him to Hades. She tugged his jacket up over her shoulder, her pride getting the better of her. "You wait, Tye Barlow. I will set London on its ear. Men will be begging to marry me and they'll be willing to buy me anything I wish. You might as well return home now."

Something passed in the depths of his eyes, something she couldn't quite define. She knew it wasn't anger, and yet, there was an intensity, a hunger.

When he spoke, his words were controlled and slightly taunting. "Oh, no, I can't leave yet. Why, seeing all of London at your feet is a sight I wouldn't miss for a stableful of prime horseflesh."

A gauntlet had been thrown down between them. She had no one to blame but herself.

For a second, her mind flashed back to another time, another place. It was the summer she'd turned fifteen. He'd been eighteen. They'd kissed, and even now, she could remember the taste of him . . .

Mary brought herself back to the present with a shake of her head. She hated Tye Barlow. Hated him, hated him, hated him. And she'd never back down from a challenge.

"Well, then," she said proudly, "perhaps you *should* be our escort. I'll see you tomorrow evening." She turned on her stockinged heel and left the room.

Mrs. Peebles broke the silence first in the aftermath of Mary's departure. "What was that about?"

Still staring at the door, Tye felt stiff and cold inside. Damn Mary. She didn't have the sense God gave a blackfly or else she would admit defeat and let him have Tanner.

And what was that last moment between them about? Something had passed through her stubborn mind, something that had darkened her green eyes with passion and caused her to invitingly wet her lips. She was such a bull-headed innocent, he doubted she knew what she was doing, but his hot blood had responded. What else was he to do when she was standing there in little more than her chemise? Yes, her linen garments provided adequate protection, but he was no damned eunuch.

He forced himself to relax and face the women. "She's a stubborn lass," he said lightly.

Mrs. Peebles rolled her eyes in agreement. "It will be the devil trying to find a husband for her." She then launched into the story of having to chase Mary earlier.

Tye listened with half an ear. He noticed Jane was very quiet, her expression troubled. The polite interval of time for a call had passed. At the first opportunity, he made his excuses and rose to leave. Jane quickly offered to see him to the door before Mrs. Peebles could grab his arm.

Outside the parlor door, Tye said, "Thank you."

Jane smiled. "Aunt Alice is a handful." A beat of silence. "So is Mary. They don't mix."

"It was obvious."

In the front hall, Jane told Howard she would see their guest out. The butler returned to other duties. Alone now, Jane asked, "How much did David tell you?"

Tye shrugged, then admitted, "All."

"I want Mary to be happy," Jane said. "I know she wants the horse, but I think a husband is the best for her."

He gave her hand a reassuring squeeze. "It is." *Provided the man wasn't wealthy.*

Jane assessed his thoughts. "Because you want the horse."

"Because Mary deserves better." His response surprised him.

"You're right," she agreed sadly. She picked up his hat from a side table. Dusting a piece of lint off the brim, she said, "At one time, I'd thought the two of you would have made a fine couple."

Tye gave a sharp laugh that sounded brittle to his own ears. "Had you lost your mind? Hopefully, you've returned to your senses."

"I know more than people think I do." She offered him his hat. "There was a time when you and Mary were close."

Tye didn't know what to say. They'd thought they'd met in secret. However, he didn't deny it now. He knew he could trust Jane. "A long time ago . . . and I really don't know how close we truly were." He paused, memories of fervent, searing kisses crowding his brain, and added, "She made it clear I was beneath her station." Funny how those words hurled at him years ago when she'd told him it was over still had the power to hurt, while her successive taunts had little impact on him.

"Tye—" Jane started but he turned away.

"It's the past. Leave it." He reached for the door.

"Father beat her." Jane pushed the door closed. She leaned close. Tye didn't want to listen. She continued anyway. "I didn't understand why at the time. It was after Mother had died and Mary was all Niles and I had. I remember we were frightened. She couldn't leave her room for days. Later, I realized Father had found out about your meetings. He was a cold man, a hard one. Sometimes I fear Mary's feelings about him are very confused. Mine are clearer, perhaps because she protected me. But you are right. She was very young. Too young. And she had no choice but turn her back on you." She placed her hand on his arm. "Please don't judge her harshly."

For a second, Tye let himself remember that summer when he'd fallen in love. They'd met almost every day in the woods bordering their properties. Then, one day, Mary had just stopped coming. No note. No explanation. Weeks passed, and finally he'd risked her father's wrath to seek her out. When he did, she'd told him in the most cutting words possible her feelings for him were dead.

Jane's information didn't change things now. If Mary had come to him, he would have protected her—instead, she'd chosen another, something it seemed Jane didn't know.

"It's the past, Jane. And, no, I wouldn't ever want to be saddled with a strong-minded woman like your sister. I pity the poor bastard who weds her. The man will need spurs."

Jane leaped to her defense. "You know she hasn't always been like this."

"I can't remember when she wasn't," Tye lied. He put on his hat. "I'll see you tomorrow evening." He let himself out the door.

The next morning, Tye woke at his customary early hour feeling a bit at loose ends since he had no horses to feed or chores to perform. Few of the other tavern guests were up. He went out into the streets and watched dawn wake the city. Goods flowed in from the farms. Hawkers called their wares, and within hours shops selling everything imaginable would be open for business. It was all certainly fascinating in its way—but he wanted to go home.

The air smelled and the streets were dirty. Worse, as the day progressed a man couldn't walk anywhere without bumping into people. Noise from carts, animals, and people filled the air to the point where he could barely think.

In preparation for the evening ahead, he bathed in a local bath house and spent a good amount of time with the barber. He also paid to have his boots polished. He didn't want to appear too much of a yokel in front of London company.

He brushed off his good brown wool jacket, tied his neck cloth with extra care, and—shaved, clean, and feeling rather urbane—presented himself upon Mrs. Peebles's doorstep at the appointed hour. He'd even hired a coach for them to ride in that evening. Mrs. Peebles had sent a note informing him that as their escort, the conveyance was his responsibility. He hadn't liked the extra expense . . . but it was only for one night.

The butler answered the door, took his hat, and led him to the back parlor. Jane appeared a few minutes later.

She looked quite handsome in a flowing green gown with daisies embroidered around the hem and bodice. An emerald scarf held her curls back from her face. "David is a lucky man," Tye said by way of greeting and she blushed, pleased with the compliment.

"And how fine you look."

"Can you imagine what the good folks of Lyford Meadows would say if they could see us now?"

"And here we are going to our first London party." She lowered her voice to confide, "I am so nervous . . . and excited. I wish David could be here."

"Is Mary ready?"

The happy light faded in her eyes. "No. I'm worried, Tye. I told her to start dressing, but when I left the room she'd barely begun. Aunt Alice will have a fit if we are late."

"Perhaps you should go help her now."

Jane shook her head. "She doesn't want my help. She's been behaving in an odd manner since yesterday afternoon, quiet and secretive—completely unlike herself. She refused to attend any of Aunt Alice's last-minute lessons. She said she'd had enough of deportment and manners and chose instead to stay in our room."

"That sounds like the Mary I know."

"Yes, I know she has been difficult, but, Tye, she wants the horse. She should be at least dressing. I feared she was coming down ill but she seemed happy when I'd finished and left the room. What am I to tell Aunt Alice if Mary decides not to come down? She's gone to so much trouble on Mary's behalf and she's already nervous Mary will embarrass her in front of her friends."

At that moment, Mrs. Peebles swooped into the room dressed in lavender lace and tulle. Her hair was piled on top of her head and pinned in place with giant, curling ostrich feathers. Rouge colored her cheeks and lips. "Mr. Barlow, punctual, punctual! I do so admire punctuality in a gentleman—"

She skidded to an abrupt halt. The smile faded from her face. "You are not ready, sir?"

He was uncertain of her meaning. "I'm here. Ready."

Her frown deepened. "But you are . . . are . . . not dressed," she replied faintly.

Tye shifted his weight. Clearly he was wearing clothes. He glanced to Jane, who appeared as confused as he was. "But I am."

Mrs. Peebles's hands fluttered in distress. "I beg your pardon, sir, but this evening's soirée is after the dinner hour. We *dress* for dinner in London. And you have no gloves. A gentleman doesn't go to dinner without gloves."

"I have riding gloves." He pulled them out from his waistband to show her. He hadn't worn them because he hadn't thought them appropriate in the house.

"*White* gloves, Mr. Barlow," Mrs. Peebles said. Her lip curled with displeasure. "Your jacket can pass and perhaps your breeches, too, but a gentle-man doesn't wear *boots* to a dance."

They did in Lyford Meadows, but Tye bit back the words. Instead, he said stiffly, "Do you wish me to leave?"

Jane came to his rescue. "Aunt, please, Tye looks very handsome. Certainly people will under-stand he is from out of town? And we'll ex-plain his presence at Mary's debut was unexpected. Certainly we could not exclude a neighbor?"

Mrs. Peebles pulled on her elbow-length gloves, obviously annoyed. She didn't answer Jane directly. "I don't know how this evening is going to go. I've invited every eligible bachelor of my acquaintance. All my friends will be there. You realize, don't you, Jane, that I didn't know your sister well? I hadn't truly registered her presence at your wedding. I'd probably mistaken her from one of the young *men* in the village, what with her breeches. And I had thought in your let-ters you referred to a woman I hadn't met. I fear the outcome of this evening. I shall be ridiculed. My reputation is very important to me."

"I don't need to go," Tye said, concerned by the state the woman was working herself into.

"Oh, no. We need an escort," Mrs. Peebles re-sponded with a touch of alarm. "Especially since Mary is so—so—well, *old*." She forced a little smile. "Besides, Jane is right. You do cut a fine figure, proper dress or no. You'll have to do."

No one had ever told Tye he had shortcomings in any form. "Have to do" was not what he considered a compliment.

A footfall sounded behind them. Anxious, they all looked up, each expecting Mary and anticipating another problem. However, the vision they met was completely unexpected.

For a second, Tye could only gape.

Mary stood in the doorway, but not the Mary he remembered from yesterday. No, this young woman was a vision of feminine perfection.

He'd always thought her attractive, but now . . .

Her glossy hair was smoothed back into a simple chignon, so different and refined compared to the curly styles of the day. The classic lines of her cream-colored dress hugged her figure and left nothing to the imagination. The material seemed to cling to every curve, every valley. Not even the shawl of sparkling gauzy material concealed an alarming discovery—Mary had breasts. Full, bountiful breasts. The kind of breasts men prayed for.

The bodice was cut low. Too low. Breathtakingly low . . . and there were those beautiful breasts, begging to be admired.

She floated into the room, moving with such

ethereal grace he wondered if her feet even touched the ground. Her skin glowed with health and vitality. The innocent and yet seductive scent of honeysuckle lingered in the air around her.

She stopped in front of him and raised her green-eyed gaze. She held out her gloved hand. "Mr. Barlow."

Her voice had changed. Overnight. Mary's brash bray had sweetened to warm molasses.

He was struck dumb. He couldn't move—and yet a part of him, the very male part, was having a strong, immediate, and intense reaction to this new Mary.

And if *he* had this reaction, every other male would too—including the wealthy ones.

Chapter 8

Mary cleared her throat, making Tye aware that she still held her hand out to him. He bowed over her fingers—but not before he noticed a victorious gleam in her eye.

It brought him to his senses.

Mary was wily; but he could be wilier. He gave her fingertips a warning squeeze. She lifted a brow, a salute of sorts to let him know the battle had been joined.

Mrs. Peebles and Jane were still stunned. Jane found her voice first. "You look lovely." She crossed the room to her sister. "You're the very image of Mother. I'd forgotten how vibrant she was before she got sick. There won't be a man in the room tonight who will be able to take his eyes off you."

"Yes . . . yes." Mrs. Peebles repeated, dazed.

A lovely pale pink tinted Mary's cheeks. "Thank you."

Tye didn't like the fact the extra color enhanced the sparkle in her eyes. His surliness wasn't helped when a moment later, Mrs. Peebles clapped her hands together and announced, "We are ready to leave, save Mr. Barlow."

Mary tilted her head at Tye. "Is something the matter?"

"His dress." Mrs. Peebles sniffed. "It's not appropriate. He's not even wearing gloves."

Jane·quickly came to his defense. "Now, Aunt, you agreed a moment ago it was not so bad."

"I don't know," Mrs. Peebles allowed with an expression of long-suffering worry.

Mary walked around Tye, inspecting him carefully in the same vein one considered a horse. He was tempted to ask her if she'd like him to open his mouth so she could inspect his teeth.

Instead, he directed his comments to Mrs. Peebles. "I believe your concerns are nonsense. Every man I've met in London has been dressed this way."

"Oh, well," Mary said, "then that settles matters. Barlow is right and everyone else wrong, hmmm? London must be like Lyford Meadows, where Barlow's word is law."

Her gibe struck a raw nerve—and reminded him that beneath her new veneer, she was still

Mary. He turned, ready to set her in her place, but Jane quickly interceded, "The coach is waiting outside. Are we ready?" She separated Mary and Tye by stepping between them.

"Yes, yes," Mrs. Peebles agreed. "We must stop dallying around. Come!" She slipped her arm in Mary's and directed her toward the door, taking these moments to give last-minute advice and admonishments.

Tye offered his arm to Jane. "She may be your sister, but I hope she falls on her face tonight," he confessed, and was surprised when Jane laughed. "What is so funny?"

"Oh, it's not funny, but the two of you . . ." She waved her hand.

"The two of us what?"

"Can't you see? I mean, everyone else does."

"See what?"

She stopped. "Both of you get along so well with others, but when you are put into a room together, well, the tension is so thick you can cut it."

"Her insults would make anyone tense. You can't blame me for wanting to defend myself. If she were a man, I'd stomp her."

"If she were a man, I don't think you'd be feeling any tension," Jane observed, and went out the door.

"I don't know what you mean," he replied coldly.

"No, of course you don't." Her tone of voice let him know she meant the opposite.

He was forced to leave the matter be because they'd come to the coach.

The hired conveyance was a close quarters affair with bench seats facing each other. Tye waited for the ladies to settle themselves before he took a seat beside Mrs. Peebles opposite the sisters. There was barely leg room for the women, let alone for him. To his chagrin, he was seated across from Mary, whose legs were almost as long as his . . . and he was forced to straddle his legs around her knees.

His anger with her evaporated.

Especially when the driver snapped the reins and the lumbering coach started rolling and bumping across the cobblestones. Mary's knees brushed the inside of his thighs. He didn't move. He couldn't. There was no room, but also, no self-respecting, red-blooded male would have.

Her gaze swung to meet his.

He waited for her to say something waspish. Instead, a stubborn line appeared at the corners of her mouth. Her chin rose a notch. If she wasn't moving, he wasn't either.

Mrs. Peebles and Jane were unaware of the war of wills being played out beside them. Instead, they babbled with anticipation over the upcoming party, not really needing input from Tye or Mary.

Studying her delicate profile, Tye was reminded of the first time he'd noticed what long legs Mary Gates had. He'd come upon her riding in a pasture close to the property line. She'd ridden bareback, her legs straddling the horse, her shoes and silk stockings tossed aside and her skirts hiked up to her knees. He hadn't recognized her at first. Her cornsilk-blond hair had been loosed from its braid and flowed down her back. She'd guided the horse with her knees, her arms stretched heavenward like a meadow nymph beseeching the gods . . . and he had been unable to take his eyes from her . . .

Mary shifted in her seat across from him bringing his mind back to the present. Her leg brushed his and then forcefully, she brought the heel of her kid slipper down on the toe of his boot.

She didn't hurt him, but she made her point clear. He wondered how much of what he'd been thinking had shown on his face and laughed with the first genuine amusement he'd felt since she'd walked into the room.

Jane and Mrs. Peebles looked to them. "Is something the matter?" Jane asked her sister. "Am I crowding you?"

"No, not anymore," Mary replied with a pointed look at Tye. She gave him a cold shoulder, her attention turned to the passing scenery out the window. A few minutes later, she appeared lost in her own world.

Tye crossed his arms. Mary Gates needn't

worry about him. He could fantasize about wrapping her long legs around him—but that was all. Idle fantasies. Bedding her was out of the question. One of them would kill the other before the night was over.

Of course, what a night it would be. Yes, a very good night—

"Mr. Barlow?" Mrs. Peebles's shrill voice intruded upon his consciousness.

"Yes?"

"We have arrived," she stated simply.

"Arrived?" The coach had come to a stop and he hadn't realized it.

"Would you open the coach door for us?" She shot a glance at Jane as if questioning his mental faculties.

Feeling like a bloody idiot, he managed to avoid eye contact with Mary, and said, "I was wool-gathering."

"Obviously," the older woman said. "Would you open the door?" Jane ducked her head to hide a smile, but Mary sat silent.

Tye opened the door and jumped down to the walk. He lowered the step to help the ladies from the coach.

The house where the dance was to be held was ablaze with more light than he'd ever seen in one place in his life. It was one of several attractive row houses surrounding a small tree-lined park. He had the first inkling of misgivings. This affair would not be like the comfortable neighborhood evenings in Lyford Meadows. He debated over wearing the riding gloves or not.

Many guests had already arrived or were approaching. Some walked and others took either a coach or a sedan chair. They crowded the front door and formed a line down the stairs leading to the house.

Mary was the last to leave the coach. She'd hung back, making Mrs. Peebles and Jane climb over her. He held out his hand. She didn't take it immediately. He leaned into the coach. "Come along, Mary. We don't have all night."

In the moonlight, her complexion was flawlessly pale. She stared at him as if she hadn't understood him, a small line of worry between her eyes.

"Mary," he prompted, and waved his hand in her face.

Her gaze dropped to his fingers. She moved then, placing her gloved hand in his. However, as she climbed down, she didn't look at him.

Jane and Mrs. Peebles bubbled with excitement. Mrs. Peebles recognized several friends and started with introductions. In contrast, Mary seemed unusually quiet. However, Jane didn't appear concerned, so Tye dismissed his own worries.

Mrs. Peebles huddled them together and gave whispered instructions. "Mr. Barlow, Jane and I will enter first. You escort Mary. Count to ten before you follow us. No, wait, I'll give a signal, a wave of my hand. This way, I can start introductions and Mary can make an entrance." She sighed in anticipation. "Every man in the room will swoon over her. If we are lucky, she could have a good offer by the end of this week." She gave Mary a quick look over. "With her looks, mayhap sooner."

Tye shut the coach door a bit too hard. "Whatever you wish."

The coach pulled away. Mrs. Peebles took Jane's arm and charged up like a head mare taking control of the herd. She made quick introductions of Jane then set to work touting Mary's qualities.

Meanwhile, Tye and Mary waited. He was becoming keenly aware he hadn't dressed properly. The gentlemen entering the house were dressed in black and dark blue coats with white knee breeches and white waistcoats. They all wore white gloves. None wore boots.

Self-consciously, he pulled on his riding gloves.

Words like *husband* and *marry* floated down to where they stood. Necks craned for a better look at Mary. Eavesdropping guests also turned to stare. He shifted, uncomfortable for Mary. 'Twas as if she was stepping up to an auction block—

A soft sound was all the warning he received before Mary bolted. She turned sharply as if to climb back into the coach and, finding it gone, without a backward glance she took off for the park, the spangles of her shawl reflecting light from the house.

Tye glanced up to the front door, where Mrs. Peebles and Jane were busy with the other guests. They hadn't seen Mary leave. It was going to be up to him to bring her in line.

With a frustrated sigh, he turned and charged after her. She'd sped up a bit, an elegant figure weaving around an approaching group of guests. He thought she would stop at the park. She didn't. She kept walking.

Where did she think she was going? Did she plan to walk all the way back to Mrs. Peebles's house? He didn't know what flea itched Mary's fancy now, but he would find out.

His long legs ate up the distance between them. He reached her as she came to a street corner. There were no street lights and the beckoning warmth of the party did not extend this far. They were alone.

"Where are you going?" he demanded, keeping his voice low.

She didn't stop. He reached, hooking his hand around her arm. "Don't you hear me?"

She whirled on him, her eyes wide and shining in the dark, as if his presence surprised her.

"Mary?" he asked, wary. "Are you feeling well?"

She wet her lips. "I can't do it. I can't go in there. I can't stay."

He wasn't in the mood for one of her tiffs. "So where are you going? Marching to Lyford Meadows?"

"Yes, if I must." She took a step to turn but he held fast.

"Listen, I'd like nothing better than to leave, too, but I can't and neither can you. I don't care about Mrs. Peebles, but your sister has gone to a great deal of trouble on your behalf. She's introducing you now as if you were a princess of the realm. You'll embarrass her if you run off this way and she doesn't deserve that. If you want to throw one of your fits, do it on the morrow. But tonight, you are a guest and you will behave as one."

Her brows snapped together. He braced himself for an infamous Mary Gates tongue lashing, but then a shiver ran through her and she backed off. Almost urgently, she pleaded, "I can't do it."

This was not the Mary he knew.

A step sounded behind them. "Mary? Tye? Is everything all right?" Jane had come for her sister.

Mary ducked behind Tye for protection. "I can't talk to her right now. Please . . . I can't even breathe . . ." She grabbed hold of his coat with one hand and held fast like a child afraid of falling.

He took pity on her. "Everything is fine, Jane.

We are waiting a moment. Mary wants to make a grander entrance than Mrs. Peebles planned."

"A *grander* entrance?" Jane questioned. Her step slowed to a halt.

"Yes, she wants all eyes on her."

"Jane, where are you?" Mrs. Peebles called. "Where is *everyone*? It is time to go in. I waved and waved and no one did what they were supposed to!"

Jane's worried gaze met his. She couldn't see her sister, who cowered against his back, but she knew Mary was there. Jane pressed her lips together in indecision and then said, "I'm with Mary, Aunt Alice. She's waiting a few minutes and planning to make a grander entrance."

"Grander?" Mrs. Peebles made an impatient sound. "Oh, very well, but I'm not going to stand in the dark waiting for this entrance when I could be inside enjoying a glass of champagne. Jane, you come too. I don't wish to walk in alone."

Jane looked to Tye. He nodded, urging her forward. Mary still hid in the haven of his shadow.

"Very well," Jane said. He wasn't certain if she had sized up the situation or not, but she left.

Mary released the breath she'd been holding and leaned against him. "I'm glad she didn't stay. I would not embarrass her for anything."

He faced her. "Then come inside."

She stared at his chest, the seconds passing like

minutes. "I can't." Abruptly she started to walk away.

Tye let her go three strides and then called, "I thought a Gates wasn't afraid of anything."

Those were magic words. She stiffened, turned. "I'm not afraid."

"Yes, you are. You balked on those steps like any spooked filly."

Instead of the fierce retort he expected, her eyes suddenly filled with tears.

Tye drew back, alarmed. Other women might resort to tears, but not Mary.

Angrily, seeing he'd noticed, she swiped them away. "You don't understand."

Tye took a step forward. "Then tell me. Bring whatever 'tis out in the open and be done with it."

She turned from him.

"Are you afraid those people will laugh at you? Or notice what a country bumpkin you are? You needn't worry. I'm the one who will stand out."

She didn't respond but stared stonily at the brick corner of the building in front of her.

He tried again, his voice coaxing. "You've worked hard preparing for this night . . . and your work has paid off. No one will know you for anything other than what you are, a beautiful woman."

Again, tears threatened and she lifted her gaze skyward as if to avoid them.

Tye released a deep breath. He couldn't leave her this way, but damned if he knew what to say. "I know I'm not the person you would choose to confide in, but you don't want Jane, and I'm the only one there is."

A fat tear escaped the corner of her eye and rolled down her cheek. She blinked back the others, keeping her gaze averted from him.

"Come now, Mary, release it. Whatever is troubling you, let it go and be done with it. I won't tell a soul." He held up his hand. "God's promise. The feud aside, there must be some sort of loyalty bond between those of us from Lyford Meadows."

He'd added the last, intending for her to smile. Instead, when at last she looked at him, there was so much pain and fear in her eyes, it almost broke his heart.

"What is it?"

"I am afraid *he* is in there." Her voice was barely audible. "He lives in London. What if I go inside and there he is?"

Tye didn't need to be told who "he" was. Lord Jergen's son. He'd known immediately.

"You could have run into him at any time in London," he said almost brutally.

She nodded. "I know. I refused to go out and it's one of the reasons why I've behaved so badly to Jane and Mrs. Peebles—"

Her voice broke off. She looked around her,

wildly, as if all this was revelation to her, too. Her dress shimmered in the moonlight. "I shouldn't be here," she said softly. "I have no right to marry *any* man."

"And why should you say that?" he demanded.

"Because I'm not whole, not pure."

A numbing coldness crept through Tye's limbs, starting with the pit of his stomach. He'd asked the question without anticipating the answer.

The rumors were true.

Lord Jergen's son had had her. He'd lain with her.

Every gossip in the parish had speculated it was so, but Tye had not wanted to believe. After all, she would never have given herself to him and he would have offered marriage.

"Why?" he croaked out, the only word he could speak.

Mary crossed her arms against her chest, the spangles of her shawl moving merrily with her movement. She shook her head. "Papa wanted me to snare him . . . any way I could." She paused. Tye waited.

"He wanted John to come up to scratch before he left Lyford Meadows to return to London. It would have saved the cost of a Season," she added with a touch of bitterness. "Papa was still so angry over catching me with you and I wanted to make him happy. I also wanted to be-

lieve John when he said he loved me. I loved him
so much."

Betrayal struck hard and deep in Tye's gut. He
was surprised by the force of it. He'd known she
hadn't loved him. She was the one woman who
had spurned him. Still, one would think such an
admission would eventually lose its power to
hurt.

"I shouldn't have told you that," she said, reading his mind.

He forced a laugh. "What was between us was
years ago. We were children."

"Yes."

"I don't even think on it," he assured her.

She nodded quietly.

"We are fire and water. Never the two should
mix. Ever."

"No," she agreed.

Tye stood a moment, silent, giving himself time
to recover, but then—"How could your father
have let such a thing happen? How old were you?
Seventeen? You should have been chaperoned."

"As I was with you?" The moment she said the
words, she attempted to call them back. "I'm
sorry. I shouldn't have made the comparison."

"I would never have used you in such a way,
Mary."

"I know." Her gaze dropped to the ground. She
pulled her sparkly shawl closer around her. "I'm
not certain how it all happened. He—"

Tye held up his hand and took a step away. "You don't have to tell me this." He had no desire to hear a confession. Or details.

She held out a hand. "Please, I must tell someone. I've kept everything inside for so long. I know there was talk in the parish, but I've never said a word to anyone. Not even Jane. Now, I must, or I don't know what is going to happen to me." She touched the sleeve of his coat. "And maybe you are the person I owe an explanation to the most."

"You don't." And yet, he did not walk away. When she didn't speak, he said, "Jane told me about what your father did when he learned you'd been meeting me. About the beating. I suppose that is enough to put a girl off a lad."

Her fingers clenched around his arm, then she released her hold and pulled her hand back. "I learned never to disobey him."

He wanted to ask if she had any regrets. If she remembered that time between them the way it haunted him.

"And then I met John . . ." Her voice was barely a whisper.

"And became lovers," Tye said flatly.

Her gaze flicked to meet his and then away. "Yes. When John started calling, Papa told me to go driving with him. That's all. I was starry-eyed. I was alone with him." Her manner switched to fierce protectiveness. "I never let Jane have any time alone with any man. Not after what had happened to me."

"Then Jergen's son forced himself?" Tye demanded, wanting a reason to put his fist down the man's throat.

"No," she said sadly. "It wasn't his fault—not completely. I was too young. I craved love." Her gaze met his. "I don't mean any of this as an excuse. I've paid my price, Barlow. I've paid a bitter price."

Yes, he had to agree, she had paid. And he'd paid, too, because after Mary, he'd not trusted again. David had been right. The only women he ever let close were those who expected nothing from him.

"I should never have left Lyford Meadows," she said brusquely. "You can have the Stud. His price is too high for me." She turned on her heel and would have walked off, save he came to his senses quickly enough to pull her back.

He swung her around, placing his hands on her shoulders and looked her straight in the eye. "I don't want the Stud. Not this way. There isn't a one of us who is perfect, Mary."

"Yes, but some mistakes are worse than others."

"Bull." He let the truth of his words focus him. "It's the past, Mary, gone. You can't relive it. Furthermore, you can't keep hiding behind men's clothes and a gruff exterior. You have the right to attend a party, to smile, to dance, and to be wooed."

"Yes, but—"

He gave her a little shake. "No. You can't let Jergen's son or your father dictate your life. Not any longer. They are the past." He spoke to himself as well as her.

"But don't you see? I'm not worthy of any honest man. I'm soiled, Barlow. I've sinned."

"It's a sin as old as time," he replied impatiently. "Confess it and move on, but don't ruin your life over it. Besides, if I didn't go places where I feared I'd run into someone I'd slept with, I wouldn't be able to take a step out my door."

His declaration shocked her. "You're joking," she said.

He grinned. "I'm the Buck of the Parish, remember? I didn't gain the reputation by sitting home knitting."

A martial light returned to her eyes. "You really are conceited." This was the Mary he knew. *His Mary.*

"Yes, and I'm also right," he told her. "Your fears are groundless. Jergen's son won't be anyplace close to here. Can you imagine the likes of him running around with the likes of Mrs. Peebles or anyone she knows?"

The absurdity of his suggestion startled a

shaky laugh out of her. "She isn't his crowd, is she?"

"Not unless there is something about her we don't know."

"I doubt that." She smiled.

Tye tipped her chin up. "Courage, my girl. We villagers from Lyford Meadows don't frighten easily."

Her smile twisted ruefully. "Well, this is London."

"Yes, and I plan on winning a horse, a very fine horse, the best Stud in all England."

Her eyes flashed with challenge. "Not if I have my way, Barlow." She took a step toward the party, then stopped. "You know, you had your chance to steal Tanner from me."

"Steal? You said I could have him."

"Yes, but you didn't take advantage when you could have. Why?"

She appeared so regal, so beautiful standing in the moonlight, and he realized that the old ghosts had finally been banished between them—at least for him. The past was forgiven. He understood . . . and accepted. At last.

Perhaps he hadn't come to London for the horse, but for this moment.

Still, he was determined to win Tanners Darby Boy.

"I'm not worried," he replied.

"You should be," came her response, full of pride, spit, and vinegar. So very Mary. Head high, she marched toward the party as if going to battle.

Tye watched the determined sway of her hips and then lowered his head. He'd had his chance at the horse, and he'd let it slip through his fingers. God knew he was a fool.

He followed her toward the party.

Chapter 9

Mary's heart pounded in her ears as she walked over the threshold of Mrs. Willoughby's house. The bravada she'd used to charge away from Barlow evaporated, but pride kept her moving—especially when she heard Barlow's step close behind, a challenging, yet strangely comforting presence.

She was so very conscious of him, of his height, his strength, his assurance. And she couldn't turn tail in front of him, not a second time.

Her knees trembled as she stepped into the front room lit by hundreds of candles. The furniture had been moved back to prepare a dance floor. Several couples already moved through the steps of a lively contredanse while a woman played the tune on a pianoforte. She was accompanied by a male violinist.

The other guests stood around the edges of the room, laughing and talking. Paste jewels sparkled in the light. Ostrich feathers perched in dozens of coiffures waved and moved. There were a host of men, men who appeared elegant, polished, sophisticated.

But John, her old lover, was not of their number.

She didn't realize she'd been holding her breath until she released it.

Barlow touched her elbow. "Are you waiting for me to *carry* you in?" he asked, his tone slightly mocking.

"That won't be necessary." Using her temper as impetus, she entered the room.

Jane was the first to notice her, then Mrs. Peebles, who said in a carrying voice, "Here is our guest of honor."

Immediately, heads turned. Someone signaled for the music to stop. The dancing ended. Women whispered, smiled, nodded, but the men took their time, evaluating, judging.

Jane hurried to her side. "I was worried. Is everything all right?"

"Everything is fine," Mary said firmly.

Mrs. Peebles approached, holding the arm of a big-bosomed woman of diminutive height. "Mrs. Willoughby, I would like you to meet our guest of honor, Miss Gates. Miss Gates, this is my very good friend, Mrs. Willoughby."

Mary made a small curtsey and said, as rehearsed, "I thank you for your generosity in hosting this reception."

"It was nothing, nothing at all," Mrs. Willoughby trilled so loud everyone heard her. And Mary had to agree, since she had financed this affair. She tried not to think about the price of candles when compared to what she needed for grain.

"You are a lovely young woman," Mrs. Willoughby pronounced, and there were those who nodded agreement. "Both of you are," she added, including Jane.

"Let me introduce you to one of our neighbors," Jane said kindly. "This is Mr. Tye Barlow of Lyford Meadows. He's our escort this evening."

"In-deed," Mrs. Willoughby said, breaking the word into two syllables. She looked Barlow up and down and sniffed with distaste. She did not offer her hand. "Welcome to London, Mr. Barlow. You are *recently* from the country, no?"

If Barlow noticed the slight, his expression didn't betray him. He bowed. "Yes, and thank you for including me in the invitation." His voice was tight.

A young man with curly blond hair and ingenuous blue eyes nudged Mrs. Willoughby's elbow. He cleared his throat, wanting their attention.

Mrs. Willoughby turned. "Ah, Mr. Foster. I see you are begging an introduction with our guest of honor."

"If I may," he said.

"Oh, you may, you may," Mrs. Peebles repeated giddily.

Their hostess performed the introduction. "Mr. Foster, this is Miss Gates, daughter of the late Squire Gates of Lyford Meadows, a charming village. Completely charming. Her family owns a considerable piece of property there."

"Ah," Mr. Foster said, this piece of information apparently important to him.

Mary wondered where Mrs. Willoughby had gained her information, since as far as Mary knew the woman had never laid eyes on Lyford Meadows.

"Mr. Foster is a solicitor," Mrs. Willoughby said with a sense of importance. "His prospects are most excellent," she added in a low-voiced aside and, of course, he heard.

He blushed boyishly. "I fear Mrs. Willoughby is more than kind, but my prospects are good. Tell me, Miss Gates, are you enjoying London?"

Mary would have told them she'd rarely taken a step out of the house, her time being consumed by dress fittings, dance lessons, and deportment nonsense, but Mrs. Peebles rushed to answer.

"She is having a marvelous time. We've been here, we've been there."

"We've been everywhere," Mary added with a touch of irony, earning a pinch from Jane to behave.

"Yes, we have," Mrs. Peebles enthused.

A charming dimple appeared at the corner of Mr. Foster's mouth. His blue gaze met hers and he let her know he'd caught her small jest. Perhaps this husband hunt would not be as bad as she'd anticipated. "Will you dance, Miss Gates?" he asked.

"One moment, Foster," a tall, lean gentleman with dark hair and a long jaw interrupted. "I have yet to meet our delightful guest of honor, and I am not going to allow you to monopolize her. Mrs. Willoughby, please make introductions." The intensity of his gaze caught Mary off guard.

"Of course," she said. "Miss Gates, this is Mr. Charles Applebaum. Mr. Applebaum is with Whitehall."

Mary understood the importance of a position with the War Office. "Your work must be interesting."

Mr. Applebaum's secret smile assured her it was but before they could converse, another gentleman begged for an introduction, and then another and another. Slightly overwhelmed, Mary glanced at her sister. Jane smiled encouragement even as Mr. Foster took her hand.

"I believe this dance is promised to me," he said, not only to her but to the other gentlemen crowding around. She noticed he had short, stubby fingers that didn't fair well against the image of Tye's strong, well-formed, capable hands. She had no idea where such an irrelevant comparison came from.

Some of the gentlemen took a good-natured step back, but Mr. Applebaum laughingly made her save the next dance for him before he would budge. She agreed. She noticed he was too skinny by half, especially when compared to Tye's broad-shouldered figure.

As Mr. Foster led her out on the dance floor, she overheard Mrs. Willoughby say to Mrs. Peebles, "She's a find, Alice, a diamond of the first water."

"Yes, she is," Mrs. Peebles agreed.

They liked her. Everyone was pleased with her. It had been so long since she had been the belle of the ball. She hoped Tye noticed.

The dance was a reel, one of Mary's favorites. Mr. Foster was not a good dancer, but she didn't mind. Instead, she lost herself in the music and this golden moment of rediscovering something she had thought lost. Halfway through the dance, she laughed just from the sheer joy of being alive.

From a corner of the room, Tye watched Mary dancing with some pimply-faced chap whose stooped shoulders and skinny legs made him wonder how she could grin at the man, let alone dance with him—

"Here you are, Tye. I wondered where you'd gone off to." Jane came up to his side.

"It was getting too crowded where I was standing," he answered, referring to the way every male in the room had flocked to Mary once introductions began.

"Yes, she is a success, isn't she?" Jane said softly.

Those were not the words he wanted to hear. Especially since a group of men hovered by the dance floor eager to claim Mary for the next set. And he knew why. Mary was more than beautiful this night. She glowed! He'd not seen her eyes so alive with joy since years ago at the parish dances—

"Ask me to dance." Jane linked her arm in his.

Tye drew away. "I'd best not." He glared over her head to where the haughty Mrs. Willoughby was talking with her friends. Probably making up more lies about Mary, the better to sell her off. "I definitely have the feeling I'm unwelcome."

Jane squeezed his arm. "I'm sorry Mrs. Willoughby was so rude earlier."

He brought his gaze down to her. "I don't like London. I may be a respected man in Lyford Meadows, but in London, shoes matter. A man's coat matters. A man's look of wealth matters. The man himself is unimportant."

"Dance with me," Jane urged. "You'll feel better."

He kept his feet glued to the floor. He'd rather stick his hand in burning coals than dance with this crowd. The second set had started. Everyone around them were tapping toes. Tye's frown deepened.

And then Mary—from over the shoulder of her partner, that tall man from Whitehall—looked right at him, and she gave him a gloating smile.

The minx!

Did she think he was bested yet? Oh, no.

Tye grabbed Jane's hand. "Come, let's join the dancing."

Jane skipped to keep up. "But the set isn't finished yet."

"We'll join it," he announced, and true to his word, tagged the two of them on to the end of the line of dancers.

They were not welcomed by the couple next to them but Tye didn't care. Instead, he danced up a storm. When the music ended, he found another partner and was on the dance floor before she could blink. All told, he danced with a Miss Bord, a Miss Easterling, and a Miss Reece, not to mention every dowager in the room, including Mrs. Peebles. Oh, yes, he was for spreading himself around, and he noticed that not everyone was as snobbish as Mrs. Willoughby. Mary might be making conquests, but he was making a few of his own, too.

He made a point of ignoring Mary—although it was damn hard since he rarely had his eyes off of her. And he noticed a time or two, she sought him out with her gaze, usually right before she started laughing at something her partner was saying as if she was having the time of her life.

At last, when he decently could, Tye brought the miserable evening to a close by approaching Jane and saying, "We must be going."

"I'm ready, but I don't know about Mary."

"We're going," he replied tightly.

The hired coach was where he'd ordered it to be. With Jane's help, he rounded up Mary and Mrs. Peebles and hustled them all down the steps and into the vehicle. Mr. Foster followed them out. Tye enjoyed slamming the coach door in his boyish face.

"Was it not the most marvelous evening of your life?" Jane asked Mary. They sat across from Tye and Mrs. Peebles, all cozy and happy.

"Yes," Mary whispered with a hint of wonder, "it was."

Jane hugged her. "I've wanted this for you for so long. I wanted you to have a night like this."

Her words eased some of the tension in Tye's shoulders. His churlishness almost embarrassed him.

The women started discussing the evening, finding much to chatter and laugh over. Tye even managed a smile over some of the stories they shared. Before he knew it, they'd arrived back at the house and he found himself abruptly dismissed by Mrs. Peebles, who whisked Mary away without a backward glance.

Jane lingered. "She's a success."

"Hmmmmm."

"You were a success too," she added.

At his sharp look, she said, "Oh, come, Tye, you know the women were fawning over you. I think before the end of the evening, even Mrs. Willoughby was impressed."

He shrugged. He didn't have much to say on the subject.

"Mary noticed how popular you were too."

That piece of knowledge pleased him. He knew better than to let Mary Gates think she had too much of the upper hand. But he didn't say such to her sister.

Jane hesitated before heading toward the door. "Thank you," she said in her soft, quiet voice.

"For what?"

"Mary told me what happened before the party started. We spoke in the ladies' retiring room. She said she would have bolted if not for you."

He was astonished Mary had confessed. Jane rose on her tiptoes and kissed his cheek. "You are a true friend, Tye, and a very *noble* man. After the number of times Father tried to destroy you and your father, I am surprised you have forgiven us. Thank you for rescuing my sister. You could have let her go and then the horse would have been yours."

She started for the door. He stopped her. "Jane."

"Yes?"

Tye paused, uncertain. "What happens next?"

"With Mary? We wait to see if there is someone who loves her enough to marry her."

"Loves her?" he repeated. "Isn't that asking a great deal of one dance?"

"I met David at a parish dance and the moment I laid eyes on him, I knew. Just that quick. He felt the same about me."

"Did Mary meet someone tonight?" He hadn't noticed any obvious signs of love about her.

Jane laughed. "Worried about winning Lord Spender's horse, aren't you?" she teased. "No, I don't think she met anyone tonight. Sometimes love doesn't happen quickly. Sometimes it takes time. Still, who knows what the morrow will bring?"

"Yes, who knows?" he echoed.

"Good night, Tye," she said and walked up the steps to go inside the house.

Tye stood staring at the front door a good while longer. He wished he'd let Mary bolt.

He wished he knew his own mind.

He did not sleep easy that night.

The next afternoon at three, Tye rode Dundee to Mrs. Peebles's house with the idea of asking Mary if she'd like for him to rent a horse for her. Then they could take a ride in the park not too far away. He'd woken with the thought and it had been playing havoc with his reason ever since.

However, when he turned onto Mrs. Peebles's quiet street, he was surprised to see street boys walking several horses. He dismounted his own and a lad standing to the side quickly offered to hold Dundee for a shilling.

"Who owns those horses?" Tye asked the boy.

"Some gentlemen visiting that house there." The lad pointed to Mrs. Peebles's. He lowered his voice to confide, "An army of them, sir. An army."

An army of gentlemen?

Tye had not expected them. He told himself the boy exaggerated.

He strode over to the house, marched up the steps and was surprised to find the door half open. He let himself in—or, at least, as far as he could make his way because Mrs. Peebles's small foyer was packed with gentlemen Tye recognized from the party the night before and some he did not. They formed a line all the way up the stairs to the first-floor formal sitting room. Some held flowers. Their scent mingled with the smells of boot polish, Imperial water cologne, and men.

Nor were they any happier to see him than he was to see them.

"Get to the back of the queue," one told him rudely. "Fifteen-minute calls and you wait your turn."

Tye didn't have a clue what he was talking about. But then, Mrs. Peebles came down the stairs. Her eyes danced with excitement. She giggled and teased the men as she made her way down. Catching sight of her butler, Howard, who had just stepped out of a side room, she said, "We need more Madeira. Oh, yes, and biscuits. Tell the cook, more biscuits."

The servant hurried away, and Mrs. Peebles's eye fell upon Tye. She practically jumped down the last few steps to pull him aside into the dining room. "This is so exciting. *Everyone* is here. Mary is a success. Beyond a success. She is a phenomenon!"

"So why are you making everyone stand here?" he groused.

She shook her head with exasperation. "They are making *formal* calls, Mr. Barlow. They don't know her well and there are very strict rules about how one goes about these things."

"Really?" he said dryly.

She rolled her eyes. "I forget you are from the

country. Yes, really. Therefore, we are admitting only three gentlemen at a time, no call over fifteen minutes."

"Do you mean these men are going to cool their heels for what—" he glanced at the line and made a quick calculation—"two hours to see Mary?"

"If they wish to continue calling, they must," Mrs. Peebles said with complete seriousness.

"Why would they *want* to see her that much?" he demanded. Yes, Mary was a lovely woman and had made an impression, but to *wait* for her? Were these men or mice?

Mrs. Peebles made a little humming noise and then pulled him closer. "Well, she is new, a novelty," she said, then added, "I admit I elaborated a bit about her prospects. I mean, you have to provide a little honey to bring the bees to the flower."

"They think Mary is wealthy," he repeated blankly, and then the irony struck him. "She's hoping one of them is rich and they think as much of her?"

She bristled at his conclusion. "These gentlemen all have excellent prospects. They are well to do."

"Bull," he answered. He surveyed the line up the stairs and almost felt sorry for them. Outside of their evening clothes from the night before, none of these gents dressed better than he did.

And "well to do" wouldn't provide the money Mary needed.

Mrs. Peebles grabbed his arm. "Don't you ruin this for her, do you hear?"

"I hear," Tye told her crossly. "You are hoodwinking them."

"I'm doing no such thing! If one of them falls in love with Mary, he will be fortunate to have her as a wife."

Love. There was that cursed word again. Were all women hopeless romantics? And was Mary as pitiful?

He glowered as another suitor presented himself at the front door and, as instructed by the others, docilely took his place at the end of the line. *Tye's* place, where he should have been standing if he'd queued up.

Real men didn't wait their turns, Tye surmised. And *he* was a real man. This was Mary and if he wanted to see her, he'd just go up and see her.

He marched out into the hall and started up the stairs. "Where are you going?" Mrs. Peebles demanded. "You can't jump ahead of everyone!"

"Yes, man," one of the line standers said. "Get back there." The other gents grumbled their protests but one scowl from Tye was enough to convince them not to challenge him. Besides, being almost twice their size, he had the muscle to put them in their places.

Really, these London men were pathetic sods. Mary would see right through them.

He reached the top of the stairs, Mrs. Peebles bustling behind him. She attempted to slide by and reach the sitting room door before him, but he was quicker. With a twist of the handle, he entered.

When the door opened, everyone in the room turned. Tye frowned. The cherub-faced Mr. Foster sat on the settee alongside the dark-haired White-hall man and then there was some lanky, long-nosed chap. All three of them wore starched neck cloths tied so high and tight they could barely move their heads. They reminded him of three frogs crowded on the same lily pad.

Jane acted as chaperone. She sat on a straight-backed chair, her hands folded primly in her lap.

The only person who appeared comfortable with the situation was Mary, and she was basking in her glory. She wore a dress of robin's egg blue that emphasized her pale blondness. She was so elegant and poised that he understood why all those lads had queued up the stairs.

She arched one delicate eyebrow. "Why, Barlow, this is a surprise."

Did she think him a fool? He could see the laughter lurking in her eyes. She was enjoying herself. She'd proabably been waiting for him to appear so she could gloat.

He would have slammed the door shut except for Mrs. Peebles pushing her way in.

"I explained the rules," she informed the room at large. "But would he listen? No. So here he is, barging in, pretty as you please. I'm so sorry. So dreadfully sorry," she apologized to the suitors.

Jane stood. "Please, Aunt Alice, you are growing overwrought. Sit here."

"And you don't need to apologize for me," Tye said with a growl. He turned to the suitors. "Mary and I go back a long ways together."

"Some would say *too* long," Mary murmured.

Ah ha! There was the old Mary. His nemesis. His sparring partner.

He was ready to flash back a retort but she gracefully dismissed him by turning to the other men and prompted, "Mr. Applebaum, you were sharing with us an amusing story about your experience at Whitehall?"

"Oh, yes." The officious gentleman cleared his throat and started in on some nonsense about losing a piece of paperwork and finding it on the bottom of an admiral's shoe. Everyone twittered as if he'd told a fine jest. Even Mary, who usually snickered at such pap.

Something inside Tye snapped. He didn't like seeing other men behave like lap dogs. He didn't like the feeling of being ignored. "Isn't their time up?" he questioned Mrs. Peebles.

"Yes, it is," answered the voice of one of the other suitors from the other side of the door.

The whole experience smacked of a circus to Tye's thinking.

Mary rose and held both hands out for the suitors to bow over. "I am so sorry you must leave," she said in a submissive voice that didn't even sound like her own. "I do hope to see you again."

"And I you," the cherub said.

"Likewise," the jokester of Whitehall echoed.

"Myself, also," long nose agreed.

Tye opened the door and motioned them out. Jane frowned at his blunt hint. Mrs. Peebles made an exasperated sound. Mary smiled serenely.

He waited until the last one was gone and then shut the door before the next three could enter. The men outside didn't take kindly to his gesture. They pounded on the door. He turned the key in the lock. "Wait your turn," he ordered, and faced the women.

All three were upset. Mrs. Peebles was so affronted all she could do was sputter. Jane said gently, "Tye, please."

But Mary opened fire. "What do you think you are doing?" She placed her hands on her hips.

"I'm bringing common sense in the world."

"Have I informed you yet to stay out of my affairs?" she said, her gaze narrowing. "If I haven't, let me say it now."

"Ah, Mary, come to your senses. You can't marry someone you barely know— for a horse."

"Why not?" she demanded.

"It's heathen."

Mrs. Peebles butted in, "Women contract arranged alliances to enhance their station in life all the time."

"Some women," he admitted, "but not Mary." He turned to her. "You can't tell me you would be happy with any one of those fops? Especially if they let me bully them the way I have?"

He had her there. She stopped a moment—and then changed her mind. "What do you take me for? A fool?" She shook her head. "I know what you are trying to do. You want Tanner. Well, go back to Lyford Meadows, Barlow. Lick your wounds and go home."

"The devil I will," he answered. He reached for his temper. It was safe. He understood it instead of the range of emotion suspiciously like jealousy that had been bombarding his senses from the moment he saw the horses out in the street. "Have you not been paying attention? Those men are bankers and clerks. Losing a sheet of paper, my arse. Important men don't chase paper. And not a one of your so-called suitors has the money to buy a horse like Tanner."

"They do—" Mary started and then stopped. The color drained from her face. "They don't," she said, realizing the fact the first time.

"They bloody well don't," he said with satisfaction.

"Tye," Jane said with distress even as a knock sounded on the door.

"It's our turn," a male voice called out.

No one in the room paid attention to him. Instead, Mary turned to Jane and Mrs. Peebles. "Is this true? Does one of them have the money to afford Tanner?"

Mrs. Peebles attempted to bluster her way out of the matter. "They are all very marriageable with good prospects—"

"But are they rich enough to help me buy the Stud?" Mary demanded sharply.

Jane said, "Mary, we want to do what's best."

"We want a husband for you," Mrs. Peebles reiterated.

"But I need a *rich* husband," Mary said.

"Oh poo," Mrs. Peebles corrected. "You need a husband, plain and simple."

"We want you to be happy . . ." Jane said, but her voice faded off as if she knew this wouldn't be enough.

His temper released, Tye felt a stab of guilt. Perhaps he shouldn't have forced the issue. At least, not here.

Mary took a step back from the two women. "I will be happy when I own Tanners Darby Boy."

Jane entreated, "We will be happy, too—but first, we must find a husband—"

"You *know* that's not how I wanted it," Mary said, cutting her off.

A knock sounded on the door again, punctuating the tension in the room.

Mrs. Peebles reacted with a sound of exasperation. "This is ridiculous! All this talk about a horse is nonsense."

"He's the greatest Stud in England," Mary said proudly.

"He's a horse," Mrs. Peebles countered. "Nothing more, nothing less. You need a husband and you'll be lucky if we can find one. You're no fresh beauty, my girl, and your dowry is little more than a pittance. Even the house in the country you offer doesn't have enough land to it to even tickle the interest of a rich man. Anything of value in your family will be going to your brother. Oh, no, your fortune is in your face and you should be thankful if you have any offers at all!"

Mary whirled on her sister. "Is this the way you feel? Have you brought me to London merely to get married? Don't you want me to have Tanner?"

Jane clenched and unclenched her hands in the folds of her skirt. "I . . ." She paused, her expression tight. Then with a deep breath she admitted, "I want you to have someone in your life. I want you to be happy—"

Mary sliced the air angrily with her hand. "Stop saying that! Tanner is my happiness. He's all I want. All I've ever *let* myself want!"

She didn't wait for an answer but ran to the door, threw it open. The suitors gathered there started to step forward, some offering flowers, but she pushed them aside and charged down the stairs.

In the wake of Mary's leaving, Mrs. Peebles stamped her foot impatiently. "Oh, this is ridiculous." She looked at Tye and then to Jane. "It's just a horse."

The front door slammed shut and the questions the gentlemen asked of each other about her abrupt departure could be overheard.

Helplessly, Jane looked to Tye. "I wanted her happy. That's all. She deserves *more* than a horse."

Stunned by what his temper had created, Tye said, "You don't understand." He went after Mary.

Chapter 10

Blindly, Mary ran out into the street without hat or gloves. She didn't care. She wanted to tear off her stupid kid slippers that weren't good for anything and throw them aside. Then, she wanted to rip off her clothes that had cost her a small fortune, stamp her feet, and scream.

Ruined! She was financially ruined and for what? She'd squandered a good portion of her dowry on this ill-advised husband hunt, and even if she brought one of those earnest young men up to snuff, he wouldn't have been able to buy the horse.

Worse, Jane had known all along.

Mary had seen the guilt in her sister's expression. She'd known then Barlow's accusation had been right. There wasn't a one of her suitors with the money to purchase the Stud.

Heedless of who watched, she yanked the pins out of her carefully styled hair, ready to lose herself in a fit of madness. Her hair fell freely down her back. The residential neighborhood was empty save for the street lads walking horses. They stared at her with wide eyes, some taking a step back and leaving their horses standing.

Mary held the pins in her clenched fists. "What's the matter?" she demanded. "Haven't you ever seen a fool before?"

"Mary!" Barlow's sharp voice cut the air.

She stiffened. He stood on Mrs. Peebles's front step, his broad shoulders filling the doorway. Behind him, her erstwhile suitors timidly peeped out. She shook her head. She had no desire to talk to anyone right now—especially *Barlow*. Why, if he'd stayed out of her affairs, she would have left London last night and been saved the humiliation of this day.

A horse nickered, its ears pricking up with intelligence and Mary instantly recognized Dundee, Barlow's gelding. The other horses were hacks, but Dundee was prime horseflesh. He could carry Mary out of London and all the way back to Lyford Meadows if he'd a mind to.

She whisked the reins out of the surprised urchin's hands, and without the aid of a leg up, climbed into the saddle with an ease borne of experience. She sat astride, her skirts hiking up her leg. Her elegant slippers had little heel and felt strange in the stirrups, almost as if she rode barefoot—but Mary felt herself again.

'Twas good to have a horse beneath her. To be able to look down on the world. She could think clearly.

She didn't belong in London. Those suitors lined up in Mrs. Peebles's sitting room could never give her what she wanted. Not a one of them . . . and she wasn't just referring to the Stud.

Dundee pawed, anxious to be off and away.

Barlow had reached the bottom step. His gaze met hers. He understood. He knew. "Don't do it, Mary."

"Do what?" Jane asked anxiously. She'd squeezed her way through the gaping suitors.

Perhaps, if those callow young men hadn't been there, Mary would have listened to Barlow. Instead, sick of being confined for weeks and heady with recklessness, she put heels to horse and charged off.

She heard Barlow swear and Jane cry out behind her.

Mary didn't stop. She didn't know where she was going and didn't care. Barlow called out Dundee's name but Mary kicked him hard and the horse listened to her. She was free.

The world beyond Mrs. Peebles's genteel neighborhood was busy. She had to rein Dundee in or run over a street vendor marketing fruit on a corner. People on foot, in carts and carriages, or riding in sedan chairs moved with purpose, going about their afternoon errands.

Several stopped conversations or slowed their step to ogle a lady astride a horse.

Mary shifted in her seat, aware of how vulnerable she was. Perhaps she should return—?

A horse blew out a snort of protest behind her. She turned to see Barlow pursuing her on the back of a sway-backed nag owned by one of her London suitors. She almost laughed. His tall frame was too large for the horse and the animal was not pleased with his rider.

Dundee's head swerved in his master's direction but Mary wasn't ready to be brought back. Not yet.

She pushed Dundee out into the stream of traffic. Barlow's hack had trouble keeping up. For the next twenty minutes, Mary played cat and mouse with him, moving in and out of the traffic. Slowly, her temper started to cool.

Coming to the gates of a park, she rode in. The hour was too early for the fashionable world to be crowding the driving paths, but there was still some activity. Several nursemaids walked their charges. Three old ladies rode in a landau pulled by two matching grays. The hood was down so they could enjoy the air and they were involved in an animated conversation.

Further in, a small band of militiamen practiced maneuvers. They marched with rifles. Not far from them, beneath the spread of an aged oak, a young boy of no more than three or four received riding instruction from his well-dressed mother. Her military-styled riding habit was embellished with gold braid and was in keeping with the golden ribbon she used as a lead line for her son's fat, shaggy Shetland.

Self-consciously, Mary tugged her skirts down over her knees, acutely aware of the contrast between herself and the fashionable mother.

Not too far from the oak tree, a maid stood guard over a blanket spread with fruit and sweetmeats while a groom in the same blue and gold livery waited with a gig. They weren't watching the mother and her son, but discreetly made eyes at each other.

Envious, Mary watched them flirt. They were obviously in love. Giddy, silly, mind-boggling love.

Then, the young boy on the trotting pony spread his arms to show he didn't need his reins. He called to his mother to look at him. An expression of panic crossed the woman's face, but she tempered her emotions. Mary could see she forced herself to relax and applaud his antics. And, as quickly as possible, she reined in the animal so she could lift her son in her arms and bring him back to safety. Then, and only then, did she relax. She heaped praise on him for being such a fine, brave rider. His small arms hugged her neck. His eyes sparkled with pleasure. They rubbed noses, laughing.

Mary was riveted by the sight.

A maternal instinct she would have denied existed overwhelmed her.

Barlow's hand reached out and grabbed Dundee's reins. His growl brought her back to reality. "What the devil do you think you are doing?"

He was hatless and his dark hair fell over his forehead. His eyes snapped with anger.

"Going for a ride," she announced, grandly. She glanced at the bony nag he rode. "Move your steed over, Barlow. You're crowding my horse." She nudged Dundee to walk on.

He let go of her reins and followed. "*Your* horse?"

She smiled. "I must admit, this is a prime bit of horseflesh you have here. I didn't realize he was such a sweet goer. Collects himself well. Who was his sire? Your old stallion?"

Instead of answering her question, he demanded, "Are you aware of how ridiculous you look?"

"No," she said breezily, but tugged down on her skirts again.

"For your information, women, *gentle*women,"

he clarified, "do not ride willy nilly through the streets like some Lady Godiva."

"I'm not naked," she shot back, although she noticed the old ladies in the landau frowning with disapproval in her direction.

"Nor are you leaving much to the imagination." He edged his horse to come between her and the landau. "They probably think you are some Cyprian."

"They probably think I am *your* Cyprian," she flashed back and suddenly gave a laugh. "*That* would be funny. You and I," she explained when he didn't seem to see the humor.

"I understood the jest. I didn't think it was amusing for you to compare yourself to a trollop."

She reined in. "You don't like my humor. You don't like my dress. Why are you here?"

"You are on *my* horse?" he suggested.

"And is that the *only* reason?" she asked archly. "You knew I would come back eventually."

"Actually, I didn't know any such thing. Not after the way you tore out of the house. Besides, Jane is upset."

"Jane's upset?" she repeated incredulously. She shook her head. "For all that it matters, Barlow, let her be stark-raving mad. She doesn't care whether I buy Tanner or not. This was all a scheme on her part to marry me off to the first man who would take me."

"No," he contradicted, "she wants something more important. She wants your happiness."

"My happiness is buying—"

"Damn, Mary, sometimes you are so thick."

Her temper rose. "I am not stupid."

"That's not what I meant. You're being as dense as that oak tree over there. You can't see beyond what is in front of your nose." He sat back on his horse and with a shake of his head added, "I'm surprised. I thought women were more in tune with the finer emotions—you know, those things that people say men don't understand."

"Now you are accusing me of *not* being a woman?" she demanded coldly.

He raised his eyes heavenward. "That's not what I said, either."

"It certainly is."

An open carriage drove by them. Mary could feel the interested stares from the carriage's occupants, an older man and woman, both dressed to the teeth with their *correct* hats and *correct* gloves with all the *correct* frills.

Barlow blocked her view. His blue eyes dark with frustration. "You are the most stubborn, pigheaded woman."

"No," she replied, "an *independent* woman is the kind I am. A woman who doesn't wish her freckles would disappear and become slavish to creams. A woman who doesn't care what people gossip about her! And yes, I'm sitting astride! I like riding astride. But if I wanted to ride side saddle, I'd still be able to outride any man!"

Instead of being horrified at her lack of restraint, Barlow actually laughed. "Oh, you care," he said with a shake of his head. "You care more than you want anyone to know. That's why you're so wrapped around the axle all the time over being so independent. Why you stubbornly refuse to conform."

"I am not stubborn—"

"Mary," he warned.

She closed her mouth, then admitted, "I am stubborn . . . but so are you."

"My pride is my worst fault . . . and I let it get the best of me this afternoon. If I'd kept my mouth shut, none of this would have happened. Come along. Let's turn here. It's more private." He directed them down a side path looping away from the soldiers and the carriage.

Without urging from Mary, Dundee mindlessly followed his master just as the rest of Lyford Meadows and the world always seemed to do what Barlow wished. For once, Mary was content to go along.

"You only spoke the truth," she told him.

"Sometimes, the truth isn't necessary. Jane didn't mean to hurt you," he answered. "She believes she is doing what's best."

"Well, she isn't."

"Then why don't you do the best thing for her?" he countered.

Mary didn't understand where he was going with his argument. She reined in. They were sheltered here from the main drive by a row of vines tangled in lilac bushes not yet ready to flower. Dundee stretched his neck to take a nibble of the young leaves. She pulled him back. "What are you talking about? I have always done what is best for my sister."

"David and Jane want children."

She shook her head. "Well, I can't help her there," she replied dryly.

"They've been trying but with no luck. David believes it is because Jane worries about you being alone. He says she can't seem to rest easy until she knows you are happy."

"Oh, what a pother," she said impatiently. "I *am* happy. Why doesn't she understand?"

"Because you are not married."

She sent a level look his way. "You are not married either. Are you unhappy?"

His mouth flattened. He didn't like having the conversation turned on him. "I'm male."

"Are you saying you don't deserve some happiness, too?"

"It's more acceptable for me to be in charge of my own life. And for the sake of argument," he added, before she could refute his claim, "I have . . ." He paused for the right word. ". . . *relationships*. I'm not as *alone* as you are."

"Oh yes," she snapped tartly, "I'm sure you've found meaningful, loving relationships with Brewster's barmaid or that widow in Oxbury."

He laughed easily, unoffended. "How do you know about the widow?"

"I'm not the only one the village gossips over. The Buck of the Parish fuels the conversation at more than a few afternoon social calls, especially between matchmaking mothers and their daughters."

He frowned his irritation at the mention of matchmakers.

"It's your own fault, Barlow," she informed him, pleased to ruffle his feathers. "If you hadn't become such a successful breeder, no one would pay you attention—and I didn't mean that in a risqué way," she added quickly at his raised eyebrows. "I was talking about horses."

"Ah, yes, always horses. You are too single-minded, Mary."

"And you aren't?"

Actually, her assertion that all he had to offer was his success wasn't true. He was the kind of man physically and in spirit few could ignore, even if he'd been a pauper. When he had stormed into Mrs. Peebles's sitting room, where in all honesty Mary was being bored to tears by Mr. Foster and his friends' conversation about weather, she hadn't been able to stop herself from comparing Barlow to the other men. The London dandies had come across as weak and effeminate—and what was that silly story of Mr. Applebaum's about losing a piece of paper? Real men didn't spend their days fidgeting with paper.

"Well, some women," he was saying, "want more out of marriage than *money*." He filled the last word with disgust—a direct reference to her search for a wealthy husband.

"If so, why haven't you married? You've had ample opportunity and all of your friends already are." With the devil's own conscience, she added slyly, "Besides, time is passing. Why, you are longer of tooth than I am. How old are you now? Thirty-one?"

"Thirty," he replied tersely.

"I bet the fresh, young ones are already whispering you are old," she said, relishing the grim set of his mouth.

"Thirty is not old."

"It's not young, either," she replied coolly.

"Well, you should know. You're close enough to it yourself."

His barb hit its mark.

Mary would have ridden off, but he reached for her reins, holding her in place. "I'll tell you something else, Mary Gates, old or not, if I wanted to make you jump over fences, I could. I saw you last night. You're not as independent as you pretend to be. You were as wide-eyed and giddy as any girl at her first dance when a gentleman approached."

"Perhaps," she admitted candidly. "To every man save you."

"Or are you just afraid of me?" he challenged. "Afraid of what a *real* man could make you do, could make you feel? A man who understands what a woman wants and can give it to her?"

For a second, Mary went speechless, hit with two very counter emotions—lust and outrage.

Who did he think he was, speaking to her this way? And at the same time, she wondered, could he make good his boast?

Nor was he unaffected.

His gaze dropped to her lips. He leaned closer. "There was a time," he said, his baritone vibrating through her, "when we were not adverse to each other. When we were very compatible."

"We were children." She echoed the excuse he'd used the night before, but when had her voice turned so husky?

"Not . . . really."

No, not really.

Her breasts tightened and pressed against her gown. His calf brushed hers, his knee touched hers, his thigh against hers. Neither pulled back . . . and there was a dizzy humming in her ears. Dundee shifted his weight beneath her and yet she could not pull her gaze from Barlow's.

In the depths of his eyes, she saw her reflection and something else, something that drew her closer, deeper. "I don't—" she started to protest, and then forgot what it was she didn't want . . . because all her senses were wanting something.

"You don't know what you want," he answered for her. "But I want this."

He kissed her.

Their lips connecting seemed like the most natural thing in the world.

Mary held very still, savoring the contact. They'd kissed before. Long ago. She'd almost forgotten what it had been like.

A shimmer of something unexpected, indefinable, went through her. The humming grew louder and before she realized it, she relaxed and let herself enjoy.

As if reading her mind, Barlow's arms came around her, pulling her closer. His lips moved and she responded in kind. Was this how it had been between them, this delicious anticipation? Yes.

She remembered now.

Memories beaten from her mind by her father's brutal force came hurtling back. Dear Lord, they had been such innocents then, and he'd been so gentle, so gallant.

His tongue tickled her. Her lips parted and—

The kiss changed—taking on a new heat, one not of her remembrances.

Innocent was not the word she would use to

describe it. Nor was it anything familiar. No, this was new, exciting. Hesitantly, feeling her way, she opened to him and he took full advantage.

For a second, she couldn't think. All she could do was feel . . . and, yes, he really did know what she wanted.

Mary lost herself in the kiss. The world, her problems, even the horse beneath her seemed to fade into oblivion. This kiss was her reality.

His arms circled her tighter. She'd dropped the reins, raising her hands, not quite knowing what to do with them. His tongue teased hers. With a small, satisfied sigh, she placed her hands on either side of his face, the better to hold him dear. Her fingers brushed his hair; his shaved skin was a rough texture beneath her palms. Her breasts brushed against his chest and she thought she would melt with desire. It wouldn't matter. Barlow knew what to do. He would guide her. 'Twas as if he could drink the very soul from her—

Gunshots rang through the air. The horses startled, but held their place.

Both Mary and Barlow broke apart. They looked around, confused. Both edged their horses back to the road, looking to where the militiamen had been drilling. In formation, the small party of soldiers lowered their weapons even as a woman's scream cut through the sudden stillness.

"The baby! My baby!"

The shaggy pony had been frightened by the

gun blasts and bolted. He now galloped madly across the park, the golden ribbon that had served as his lunge line flying in the air behind him. The boy clung to his pony's mane for dear life. The footman and the nurse stared, slack-jawed. The mother gave chase on foot but she'd never catch the pony.

All this Mary perceived in the blink of an eye—even as she put her heels to Dundee's flank and charged after the runaway pony.

Chapter 11

The pony moved with amazing speed. Mary feared the boy would lose his hold. His face was white with fright and his thin legs had already lost their grip.

Behind her, Barlow attempted to follow, but his hack was unable to compete with Dundee's powerful stride.

Several of the militiamen jumped into the pony's path, waving their arms in an attempt to capture him. The fools didn't realize they were frightening him more. With the sure footedness of his breed, the Shetland veered off in another direction.

Mary thought she could overtake him—but then Tye shouted a warning.

The landau carrying the gossiping old ladies

rolled right into her path. The vehicle had turned off a side lane and neither the driver or the occupants were aware of the drama unfolding in front of them.

There was no time to stop. Collision was imminent. Then, Mary felt Dundee's muscles bunch. The horse was going to jump the carriage.

Mary's mind screamed for the animal to stop. The jump was too high, too risky—but they had no choice. She put her weight back in her heels, gripped Dundee's mane, and trusted the horse.

The animal leaped and for a moment, they were flying, suspended in air. Dundee soared over the carriage. The old ladies and their driver shrieked but also had the good sense to duck.

Dundee hit the ground heavily on the far side, stumbled, and then righted himself.

In three galloping strides, he blocked the pony, who had the good sense to halt. In fact, the Shetland almost seemed relieved to have been stopped. He hung his head, licking. The child remained seated, his arms around the pony's neck.

Mary slid off Dundee's back and hurried to the frightened boy. He had wide eyes and blond curls, and when she reached for him, he wrapped his arms around her as if he'd never let her go. His whole little body shook, but he didn't cry. From the corner of her eye, she saw the militiamen slink off. They obviously didn't want to take responsibility for what could have been a tragic accident.

"Everything is fine," she assured him. She could still remember the first time a pony had bolted on her and how frightened she'd been to have no control. "You stayed on. I've never seen a more excellent rider."

Her praise struck a chord. He pulled back slightly to look in her eyes. "I was scared," he confided as if telling her a big secret.

Mary's heart caught in her throat. He could have been killed. "You had every right to be."

He nodded, agreeing.

Then he heard his mother's voice. The elegant young woman ran up to them. Her stylish hat was held on by the ties around her neck. Her dark, curling hair had fallen down around her shoulders. "Charles, my baby!" She held out her arms.

Charles reached for his mother. Mary didn't want to let him go. His weight felt good in her arms . . . and yet, she had no choice.

The mother held her son close and rained kisses all over his sweet face.

Again, Mary felt a maternal pull she'd not experienced before deep within her . . . especially when Charles laid his head against his mother's neck with a soft sigh. 'Twas something special—

"You could have gotten yourself bloody well killed!" Barlow's heated voice broke through the moment. He dismounted. The landau had blocked his path and he'd just arrived. The occupants of the carriage and the landau craned their necks in curiosity but did not instruct their drivers to stop and offer assistance, nor did they apparently see themselves as playing a role in the drama. Such was life in the city, Mary thought sourly.

Barlow gained her attention by taking each arm and looking her in the eye. "When you jumped that carriage—" He shook his head as if he couldn't find the words to describe his feelings. He had to take a step away, and then, he found some. "Stupid, dangerous, ill-advised—"

"And magnificent," Mary finished for him. She turned to Dundee and hugged the horse's head. "He was incredible. Did you see the way he took that jump, Barlow? He didn't hesitate but flew over the carriage. I was flying!"

"You could have killed yourself. Have you no sense? How would I explain to Jane how you broke your neck?"

"Oh, poo, I wasn't about to do anything of the sort. Not on the back of this animal. Who was his dam?"

He practically snarled, he was so enraged. "I'm not going to discuss breeding with you. Not right now. Riders better than you kill themselves all the time, and they weren't wearing skirts or silly noheeled shoes. What if your foot had slid into the stirrup?"

His high-handedness brought out a flash of her own temper. "I have an excellent seat, flat shoes or no."

He raised his hands as if ready to shake sense into her, and then his mood changed. He dropped his arms. "I feared for you. If something had happened, I wouldn't have forgiven myself."

Barlow in full temper, she understood.

This man, a man who attempted to explain himself . . .

She shifted and then realized how close they stood to each other. 'Twas as if they practically breathed the same air. She could even make out the texture in his eyes, seeing brown mingled with the blue. The memory of their kiss rushed back to her—

"Take that animal away," Charles's mother ordered. She'd directed her command to her footman, who came running up, the maid in tow.

The pony, now docile, lowered his head and stood patiently. He knew he'd been bad.

"I want him destroyed," the mother said. "I never want to see the beast again."

Mary quickly grabbed the pony's reins. "No, absolutely not. You can't do such a thing."

Charles started crying.

The footman might have attempted to fight Mary for the animal, but Barlow took a protective step forward. The footman looked askance at his mistress.

Mary pleaded her case. "This animal is not skittish. When the soldiers fired their guns, which startled *all* of us, the pony ran for safety, which is a perfectly reasonable reaction."

"But your horses did not run," the mother said, defending her position. "My son could have been injured. He's my only child and my husband's heir."

"The pony was going for safety. He was trying to save his rider," Mary reiterated.

"What? Did he think to run back to his barn? He'd have a long distance to go," the mother replied stonily.

Barlow stepped in. "Dundee is a well-trained horse, my lady, and the nag I'm riding is more afraid of me than rifle fire. If that pony had wanted to harm your son, he could have done so. Instead, even though he was running, he took remarkable care of such a young rider."

It was the boy himself who decided matters. He squirmed and pushed away from his mother until she had to set him down. He ran to his pony. "Beaters is sorry, Mother. He's never hurt me before."

Being a smart animal, Beaters did his best to appear contrite.

The mother crossed her arms in indecision. She looked at her son, then to Barlow, and finally to Mary. She released her breath. "I worry." She smiled sadly. "Charles is growing up too fast. I must protect him."

The pony nuzzled the back of Charles's neck. Now dry-eyed, the boy giggled, quite recovered from his ordeal.

"They are always like that with each other," the mother admitted.

"Then you can't be angry with the animal," Mary said.

The mother sighed. She glanced at the maid and the footman as if realizing they were intently listening to everything being said. "Marie, Rawlins, gather our things."

"Yes, Your Grace," they said in unison.

Your Grace? This woman was a duchess? She was too young! Mary dropped a sloppy curtsey. She'd never laid eyes on a duchess before and could not help staring. Of course, when news of her latest escapade reached Mrs. Peebles, the older woman would be drinking her Madeira straight from the bottle without the pretense of a teacup.

"Take the pony with you," the duchess commanded.

The boy revealed a strong will. "I'm going with Beaters. He's mine. Papa gave him to me. I'll take care of him."

His mother said, "Oh, Charles." When the child didn't move, she relented reluctantly. "Very well, go along with Rawlins. See that Beaters is tied to the back of the gig. Help him," she added pointedly to the footman.

"Yes, Your Grace."

Charles insisted on leading the pony himself and he was allowed to do so. Before he left, he very seriously told his mother, "I want to see if Beaters can jump a carriage the way her horse did." He pointed at Mary.

The duchess's face paled.

Reading her mind, the child insisted, "I *will* jump a carriage, Mother."

Barlow took charge. He knelt to Charles's level. "My lord, Dundee is the one horse in a thousand who could have made such a jump."

"Then I shall have my father buy him for me."

His mother made an exasperated sound. But Barlow said calmly, "And I shall be happy to sell him once you've mastered this pony."

"It won't take me long," the boy informed him with the confidence of youth.

"I have no doubt it won't, my lord," Barlow answered.

Satisfied, the boy let the footman lead him and his pony away.

The duchess waited until her son and servants were out of earshot and then heaved a sigh of relief. "Thank you," she told Barlow fervently. "My husband lives for horses and our son wants to be so like his father. I'm not a good rider. The creatures frighten me. That is why I was here practicing with Charles. I was hoping I could overcome a bit of my fear working with the pony. Then, of course, Charles insisted on riding."

"There is nothing wrong with being afraid of riding," Mary assured her, tagging on a "Your Grace" as an afterthought. She gave Dundee's neck a pat. "I am always conscious a horse has a mind of its own and a bad fall can injure or even kill." Out of the corner of her eye, she caught Barlow rolling his eyes.

"Yes," the duchess said softly. "My brother broke his neck on a jump. I remember the day it happened. Then, this afternoon . . ." Her voice broke off, her expression distressed.

"But your son doesn't have those memories," Barlow reminded her quietly, "and if he wishes to ride, you must let him, else he'll never be a man—not in your husband's eyes."

The truth of what he'd said, and his empathy, startled Mary. She would not have credited him with such insight . . . but then, she was learning this man was not as bullish as she'd surmised over the years. She raised a finger to her lips, remembering their kiss.

His gaze passed the duchess and honed in to where her finger touched her lower lip. A possessive light appeared in his eyes. For a second, she could have sworn neither of them could breathe.

The duchess's voice interrupted the moment. "Yes, you're right, of course," she said with uncertainty.

Both Barlow and Mary blinked. He came back to the present first, answering, "Right? Yes! Well, with all due respect, Your Grace, I'd advise you to hire the best riding instructor you could for yourself and a good gentle horse who will help give you confidence. It would be best if you left your son's instruction to His Grace. Sooner or later, your fears will spill over to him."

She was not happy. "I don't know," she hedged. "My husband is a good and honorable man, but he seems to believe the best instructors are the ones who shout and intimidate their students. They seem to enjoy dressing my son down in front of others. And Charles is a sensitive boy." She looked to Mary. "Then those may be my own fears. I hate hearing them yell at Charles. I wish I was like you." Her gaze dropped to Mary's slippers and followed the line of her dress that was looking very much the worse for wear.

Mary raised a distracted hand to her hair, wishing she had kept pins in.

"You are so bold," Her Grace said with surprising admiration. "So brave . . . so *modern*."

Mary shifted uneasily, but when Barlow developed a coughing fit, she yearned to box his ears. What was wrong with being modern?

As if answering her question, Her Grace lowered her voice to confide, "Several of my friends and I have been reading the works of Mrs. Wollstonecraft." When Mary didn't recognize the name, she explained, "She was a great free thinker about women and their place in the world. Why, if she had seen you jump that carriage and rescue my son, she would be as full of admiration for you as I am."

"Please, Your Grace, it was nothing."

"And so modest, too!" the duchess exclaimed.

Embarrassed by the unexpected praise, Mary was thankful when Barlow interrupted. "I don't mean to interfere, Your Grace," he said, "but I have friends among the horse world in London. I would be honored if you would let me ask around for a good, firm, but less domineering instructor for your son. One that would meet with His Grace's approval."

The duchess gifted him with an appreciative smile. "I would be in your debt, sir," she replied, "as if I am not already to both of you. But, please, I've just remembered we have not been introduced. I'm Georgina, duchess of Ethridge. My son is Viscount Henley."

Mary's legs almost collapsed beneath her at the knowledge to whom they'd been speaking. The duchess of Ethridge was the talk of all London. The young, beautiful woman set fashion. She epitomized good taste. Her word was law among the ton.

And Mrs. Peebles worshiped her.

Fortunately, Barlow had the wit left to introduce the two of them. Mary started a shaky curtsey, but the duchess stopped her. "Please, let us not stand on ceremony. *Égalité.*" She extended her hand.

Mary froze. She didn't think one was supposed to shake hands with a duchess.

Her Grace prompted her. "You have saved my son's life and I am in your debt, Miss Gates."

"No, please, Your Grace. 'Twas nothing," Mary said.

"It was *everything*," the duchess corrected her. She took Mary's hand and gave it a shake. "Furthermore, I insist we advance our friendship. I want His Grace to meet you. He believes my interests in philosophy and education are ridiculous. He likes docile women," she admitted, as if confiding a great secret. "But if he met you and was favorably impressed—and why should he not be? You have saved our son's life!—then he will be more open to my wishes to expand my thinking."

Mary sensed Barlow was as surprised by this turn of events as she was. "I'm not certain, Your Grace . . ."

"Please! Besides, we must talk to His Grace about the riding instructor."

How did one refuse a duchess? Especially one who took your hand and said, "My husband and I are hosting a small dance party tomorrow evening for a few close friends. I pray you and Mr. Barlow can join us."

Mary's mind went blank at the honor of the invitation. Barlow murmured something about Jane and Mrs. Peebles, although Mary wasn't certain what he'd said, and then he was giving the duchess Mrs. Peebles's address.

The footman drove the open-topped gig up to her and Mary saw what she should have noticed from the beginning, the ducal coat of arms on the door. Charles bounced on the seat next to his maid. Beaters was tied to the rear.

Georgina gifted them with one more perfect smile. "Please don't forget to provide your recommendation for a riding instructor," she reminded Barlow and climbed into the carriage. "I will look forward to seeing you both tomorrow evening and introducing you, Miss Gates, to my friends."

They watched her drive away. Both the duchess and her son waved farewell.

Slowly, Mary turned to Barlow. "Could you believe such a thing happened?"

"Not if I hadn't been present."

"If I had met the king, I couldn't be more impressed. Georgina is more beautiful than they say she is."

"Why, Mary," he said, "you sound almost respectful."

"And why not? *She* thinks I'm modern. *She* wants to be like *me*."

He snorted. "I think if her husband has any sense, he'll tie her up and refuse to let her visit with those friends of hers. Equality. What non-sense. She's a duchess! Come, let us go."

Mary balked. "I thought her very wise. I ad-mire independent women, too."

"I believe a wise woman doesn't usurp her husband's authority. Nor does any man, duke or not, want an independent wife. He wants a woman who will comfort him and be a pleasure in his life."

She tilted her head, not certain she'd heard him correctly. "Are we discussing a wife or a concubine?"

"Both," he replied. "A man likes to know when he says something, he will be obeyed. No ques-tions asked, simple obedience. It's why he's the head of his household."

She'd heard her father say those same words—and, at last, like a clap of thunder, she under-stood what Jane had been talking about when she criticized their father. She finally saw him as he really was. The pieces she'd denied, the confu-sion, the guilt—all fell into place. He'd controlled her with his fist, and his method for instilling fear had been so effective it had held long past his death.

Now, here was Barlow spouting the same non-sense.

Her common sense immediately refuted the comparison. No, she didn't think he'd ever use force, 'twas not in his makeup, but for a moment she confused both in her mind. The hot, yearning memory of the kiss turned sinister. His kiss had held the power to envelop her to the point she'd been about to forget everything about him that irritated her so much. And there was quite a bit!

"What is it?" he demanded. "You are looking at me like you'd like to wring my neck."

"Or stuff something in your mouth." She shook her head. "I don't know why I let you kiss me. I must have had goosedown for brains."

She started toward Dundee but he called her back. "Whoa." She paused in surprise. He demanded, "What was wrong with that kiss?"

"Did you say 'whoa' to me?"

Annoyance crossed his face. "It was a figure of speech."

"No, it is what you say to horses and I am not a horse," she informed him with exaggerated patience.

"What is the matter with you?"

"First, tell me why you kissed me," she countered.

His gaze narrowed suspiciously. "You were there. You know."

"Know what? That you reached out and grabbed me? That you demanded a kiss and I ooobbbeediantly"—she stretched out the syllables to mock the word—"behaved? Well, I hoped

you enjoyed it. You'll not be getting another one."
She reached for Dundee's reins.

He blocked her way, his arm on his horse.
Leaning forward until his lips almost brushed her
ear, he accused, "You *liked* that kiss."

Oh, she'd more than liked it, but she'd not admit
it to him. Barlow was arrogant enough without her
paying compliments. "It was passable."

He reacted to her snub as if she'd slapped him.
His eyes turned cold. "You are obviously more *experienced* than I am."

There was a dangerous tone to his voice that
she didn't trust. She knew what he was doing. He
was using her confession about John against
her . . . and it hurt. Cut her to the quick. Of
course, she should have known better.

She moved to protect her pride. "How dare
you speak to me in such a manner? You who
have tomcatted his way through the parish. Well,
I'm proud of independence. I'm proud of the way
I am."

His jaw hardened. "Well, excuse me, Your
Highness, but I'd thought you a willing partici-
pant in our kiss. And for a woman so proud of her
independence, you are certainly willing to sell
yourself in marriage."

She didn't even deign to answer. Her feelings
were too confused and jumbled in her head as it
was. Her eager participation in their kiss now embarrassed her.

And to think she'd begun to admire him!

"Move back and I'll be gone," she said tightly.

He shook his head, his smile far from pleasant. "Not on this horse. You ride the nag. And do me a favor, ride him side saddle, or at least give the appearance. I'm tired of having people stare at us."

She frowned her answer, but did as he asked, even letting him help give her a leg up, because she was tired, too. Very tired. She almost regretted starting a fight with him. But it was for the best. Especially when a little jolt of electricity seemed to go through her at the brush of his fingers against her ankle. He jerked back as if he'd rather not have contact with her.

'Twas the last insult. She kicked the nag forward.

The park was starting to grow more congested. They drew stares because of the way she was dressed, his lack of hat, her hair around her shoulders, but they brazened it out, each lost in his or her own thoughts.

And, no, she couldn't stop thinking about the kiss—Including wondering jealously where Barlow had gained his experience? He hadn't kissed like that when they were younger.

Why was independence in a man to be admired and the same in a woman to be condemned? Perhaps she should read some of the writings of Mrs. Wollstonecraft. Mayhap this woman could explain. She would have to ask the duchess when next they met.

Mrs. Peebles opened the door before they'd climbed the steps to the house. "Mr. Foster tired of waiting for you to return his horse," she greeted them in acid tones, her gaze on Mary.

"I'll see the horse is returned to him," Barlow replied.

Jane appeared behind Mrs. Peebles and widened the door so Mary and Barlow could enter. "Thank heavens you found her, Tye," she said, ushering Mary into the back parlor like a worried mother hen. "You shouldn't have run off like that, Mary. I know you were upset and I'm so, *so* sorry for my part in it." She took Mary's hands. "I plead arrogance. I'd hoped finding the right man would make you happy. I can see horses mean much more to you."

"Oh, yes, *horses*," Mrs. Peebles said from the doorway. She crossed to the liquor cabinet and poured herself a healthy draught of Madeira and a dram of whiskey in another glass. "This is for you, Mr. Barlow. I'm certain you need it after rescuing Miss Gates from her own hoydenish antics."

Barlow accepted the whiskey with thanks and mockingly toasted Mary.

In truth, Mary felt a touch of guilt over her behavior. "I'm sorry," she said softly, speaking primarily to Jane. "I was angry and not thinking."

"Yes, I understand that kind of anger," Mrs. Peebles interjected sourly. She drained her Madeira as if she drank water and set the glass down with a thump.

Mary did not trust the older woman's mood. "You might be surprised to learn the most fantastic tale to tell."

"First, *I* have something to say," Mrs. Peebles announced. "Jane, Mr. Barlow, *Miss* Gates." She cleared her throat. "While making excuses to some of the finest young men of my acquaintance for the callow, rude, unpredictable behavior of my current protégée—"

Mary sighed. This was not going to be an easy lecture.

"—I reached a conclusion. Jane, as much as it pains me, I must ask you and your sister to leave."

"What?" Jane said. "But, Aunt Alice, we can't leave yet."

"You must. I don't believe my reputation can last through another one of your sister's scenes."

"But—" Jane started but Mary cut her off.

"She's right, Jane. We should go back to Lyford Meadows. Who cares if the duchess of Ethridge has invited us to a dance party?"

Mrs. Peebles was too involved in what she was going to say next to pay close attention. "I must ask you to pack your bags and take tomorrow's stage home—*what did you say?*"

"Nothing," Mary replied innocently. "Come along, Jane, we must pack. There is room in the inn where you are staying, isn't there, Mr. Barlow? I wouldn't want to miss the duchess of Ethridge's rout before I returned to the country. We'll have to give her Mrs. Peebles's regrets."

She started for the door, but the petite woman raced to catch her and draw her back. "What are you talking about? What do you know about the duchess of Ethridge?"

"We met her in the park," Mary said. "She took a liking to Barlow and me."

"Noooooo," Mrs. Peebles droned as if such a thing was unthinkable. "This could not be true." She cocked her head like a robin eyeing a worm. "Something terrible has happened. Am I right?" She didn't give them time to speak but said, "Please tell me the greatest patroness of fashion in all London, in all the world, didn't see you riding a horse with your skirts hiked up. Please say it isn't so."

Mary pressed her lips together. Jane was as anxious for an answer as Mrs. Peebles. Barlow remained solemn and silent, seeming preoccupied with swirling the whiskey in the glass in his hand. She stifled the urge to stick out her tongue at him.

Instead, she answered proudly, "Yes, she did see me that way."

Mrs. Peebles's response exploded from her, "Merciful heavens! We are ruined!"

"But we are not," Mary hastened to say. "She has invited us to a dance."

"Do you expect me to believe that?" Mrs. Peebles demanded. She reached for the Madeira bottle with a shaking hand. "What am I going to do? What will my friends say?"

Someone knocked on the front door. The sound echoed down the hallway.

Everyone in the parlor went still. The women maneuvered close to the door so they could see down the hall to the entrance.

Howard emerged from the dining room to answer the knock. He opened the door, blocking their view of the visitor. Nor could they hear what was being said, although Mrs. Peebles inched closer and closer. Howard shut the front door. He turned and in his hand was a vellum invitation sealed with red wax.

The butler started to put the invitation on the silver salver, but with surprising swiftness, his mistress raced out to the hall and snatched the invitation from his hands.

She walked back into the parlor, staring at the seal. She looked up at the others. "It's from the duke of Ethridge."

Mary took a step forward since she was certain the invitation was for her, but Mrs. Peebles was

already ripping it open. She pulled out a hand-
written card.

For the space of several heartbeats, all was
quiet as they watched her read, her lips moving
slightly. At last, she looked up, "The duke and
duchess of Ethridge request the honor of our
presence at a dance tomorrow night."

Then she swooned.

Jane picked up the invitation. She quickly
scanned its contents. Tears welled in her eyes
even as she laughed. She walked toward Mary
and threw her arms around her sister. "This is the
most wonderful news."

"Well, it will be quite an experience to tell people back in Lyford Meadows," Mary agreed.

"No," Jane said, pulling back to look in Mary's
face. "Oh, my dear, dear sister, don't you understand? At last, you will have the chance to meet
men wealthy enough to buy your horse and *anything else you wish*."

Barlow dropped his whiskey glass to crash into
splinters on the floor.

Chapter 12

The next evening, Mary stood in front of her looking glass. She wore the same cream ball gown and sparkling shawl of the other night . . . but she was even more nervous, if that was at all possible.

Few people received a second chance in life. This was hers. She prayed she kept her temper in check and managed the evening without making a fool of herself or arguing with Barlow.

Jane entered the room and came up behind her. Their gazes met in the mirror. "You look beautiful." She turned her around so they faced each other.

Holding her gloved hands, Jane said, "I have such a good feeling about this, Mary. Things don't happen without a reason. The play of events over the last two weeks have all been leading to this evening."

"What do you mean?"

Jane gave her hands a small squeeze. "Tonight, you are going to meet *him*, the man you are going to marry. I can feel it inside me. When we arrive at the duchess's, he'll be there waiting for you."

Mary laughed shakily. "You were always the fanciful one."

"Because I believe in love," Jane said firmly. "I believe that in this life there is someone you are destined to be with forever and ever, and you'll know who that is the moment your eyes first meet."

Mary thought back to her first meeting with John. She could remember everything, even down to the scent of the candle wax burning in the room. Most of all, she recalled the special tingling she had when he'd asked her to dance.

She shook her head. "You are an incurable romantic, Jane. Life is rarely the way you imagine it."

"Oh, Mary, you are wrong. I know how you feel. I feared there was no one for me and then one day, there was David. Even though we lived in the same village, it was as if I'd never seen him before until that special moment." She closed her eyes and confessed, "Now, he is everything in my life. I miss him so."

Mary ran her thumbs over the yellow kid

gloves covering her sister's knuckles. "Well," she said carefully, "if your premonition is correct then we shall not be in London much longer."

Jane opened her eyes. "You don't believe me. You think I talk stuff and nonsense but, Mary, I promise, after tonight, your life will have changed. I feel it here." She tapped her heart.

"I'd settle for living through the evening without one embarrassing incident. Pray for that."

With a quick grin, Jane confessed, "I have been."

A knock sounded on the door. Howard said, "Mr. Barlow is waiting in the back parlor."

"We'll be right down," Jane called.

A second later, Mrs. Peebles knocked and sang, "Time to go! Time, time, time!"

"You would think she was about to have an audience with the Prince Regent," Mary said.

"The duke and duchess of Ethridge are more important than the Regent," Jane corrected. "At least, in Aunt Alice's mind." She opened the door.

Mrs. Peebles stood waiting in her finest dress, with so many ostrich feathers in her hair she almost looked like a bird herself. "Come, come. Wait, Mary, turn around, let me see you. Ah, yes, you look lovely. And you, too, Jane." She reached out and took Mary and Jane's hands. "This is the grandest night of my entire life. I can't thank you enough for giving it to me."

"We appreciate your letting us stay under your roof," Jane replied.

A tear appeared in Mrs. Peebles's eye. "You are so dear to me."

In perfect accord, the three women went downstairs to meet Barlow. He was to have arranged for another hired coach. As they came to the last step, Mrs. Peebles confided that she had some doubts about the advisability of having him escort them. "He was not at all the thing at Mrs. Willoughby's."

"His name was also on the invitation," Mary replied loyally.

"Yes," Mrs. Peebles said, "but the way he was dressed? I was trying to think of a way to explain his presence to the duchess as that of a servant, or some other menial. I fear what she will think of us."

"The duchess has already met him," Mary reiterated with exasperation. She strode straight for the back parlor. Truly, Mrs. Peebles had to be the most shallow woman. Yes, Barlow might embarrass them with his country dress, but he was a member of their party and therefore they should make the best—

She entered the back parlor and skidded to a halt right in her tracks. Jane and Mrs. Peebles were no less surprised. They both ran into her.

Barlow was not in the room. Or, at least, not the Barlow they remembered.

The person standing by the hearth waiting for them could have passed for a Corinthian of the first stare . . . an out and outer . . . a gentleman.

Even Jane gaped.

Barlow was dressed in midnight black, relieved only by his dazzling white waist coat and starched shirt and neck cloth. The style emphasized the muscle in his legs and the breadth of his shoulders. He'd cut his hair. The shorter style suited him. It played up the strength in his jaw. His eyes appeared sapphire blue in contrast to the severe black and white of his attire.

This wasn't the Barlow she was used to. No, this man appeared more worldly, more capable . . . more intimidating. She could merely stare, seeing him with fresh eyes—and she sensed the change was more than a suit of clothes, but she couldn't quite explain her uneasiness.

Mrs. Peebles was the first to gather her senses. "You look handsome, Mr. Barlow."

His expression self-conscious, he shrugged. "I thought I ought to dress better . . . for tonight. I bought this from a tailor. The gentleman he'd made them for never paid or picked the clothes up. He was a touch smaller than myself. The jacket is tight."

"Not that anyone can tell," Mrs. Peebles said, coming forward. She ran an experienced hand across Barlow's back. "No, no one could tell at all," she said approvingly.

"Aunt Alice is right, Tye," Jane said. "You will cut a dash."

"You all look lovely, too," he said. Mrs. Peebles and Jane preened at the compliment but Mary couldn't move. She could barely breathe. Something about the change in him made her uncomfortable. Women usually flocked to him, but now—why, they'd be undressing in the duchess's foyer! They'd all set their caps for him. She noticed he'd barely given her the slightest glance.

She decidedly liked him better in his old dress, his old manner.

Mrs. Peebles and Jane were ready to leave. This time, Mrs. Peebles took Barlow's arm and had him escort her to the waiting coach. Chattering with excitement, Jane took Mary's arm. However, Mrs. Peebles was the only one to answer Jane's comments. Both Mary and Barlow were quiet.

Inside the close confines of the coach, Mary once again found herself across from him. His long legs had to straddle hers just as they had the other night.

Except this time, Mary didn't fidget. She studied his white gloved hands he rested on the top of his legs, too shy to meet his gaze. She didn't know why.

He didn't move either, not so much as a finger . . . and yet, she was very aware of his presence. But then, she'd always known the moment

Barlow entered a room—even back in the church in Lyford Meadows when it was crowded with every parishioner for miles around. She'd told herself it was because he was so arrogant he commanded that sort of attention. Still, this was different, and she feared she wouldn't be comfortable around him again until he returned to being himself.

As they drew nearer the duke of Ethridge's London home, everyone fell silent. Even Jane appeared nervous.

At last, their hired coach moved into a queue of vehicles waiting to unload their passengers at the front door. Mary said two quick prayers. The first was that she could watch her temper; the second, that she would not disgrace herself or her family.

The duke and duchess of Ethridge lived in the most fashionable section of town in a house that, in the moonlight, appeared to be carved out of marble. A line of liveried footmen stood along the steps leading to the front door and the lights shining from the windows were three times brighter than those at Mrs. Willoughby's.

"They entertain like this at least once a week," Mrs. Peebles said in awed tones.

When their coach reached the bottom step, Barlow jumped out and started to offer a hand to Mary, but a footman beat him to it.

Another footman came up to them. "Mr. Barlow, Miss Gates?" he said, and Mary recognized him as Rawlins, the footman in the park. "Please, will you and your party follow me?"

He didn't wait for an answer but started up the stairs. After all, he was a duke's footman. Obviously, it was their place to obey him. Mrs. Peebles rushed in front of Mary in her excitement to see everything. They were all conscious the other guests had noticed the honor they were being accorded.

At the front door, the footman whispered to a butler, who asked them to follow him in the same polite, well-trained tones. He led them through a crush of people waiting for a receiving line.

Mary had never seen so many fashionable and richly dressed people. Jewels—emeralds, rubies, sapphires—sparkled in their hair, at their throats, in the folds of their neck cloths. Why, any one of their jewels would have paid for Lord Spender's Stud three times over.

The room itself was magnificent. Greek statues depicting the muses graced alcoves in the walls. The ceiling rose to a dome and was painted with the constellations. In the center, around a skylight, was the motto of the duke of Ethridge printed in Latin. It was too high up for Mary to read—at least, not without gawking.

The butler bypassed those waiting to be announced and moved into the next room, where the duke and his duchess received guests.

This room was not a sitting room turned into a

makeshift ball room. No, this room was designed for entertaining. Lit by thousands of candles, it was twice the size of Mrs. Peebles's house and already crowded. Musicians sat up in a loft playing light arias until the dancing could begin. Servants moved through the guests with trays of iced champagne.

Mrs. Peebles appeared ready to swoon again, just from the sheer joy of being present in such esteemed company. The glow in her eyes said she recognized several important personages. Mary envisioned her spending the rest of her life bragging about this evening to her acquaintances. And she felt a bubble of pride that in spite of being, in Mrs. Peebles's words, "hopeless," she had been the one to deliver such an evening to her benefactress.

The butler stopped by a tightly knit group of people. "Your Grace, Miss Gates, Mr. Barlow, and their party have arrived."

The other guests stepped back to reveal the duchess, beautiful in ice blue silk, and the duke, who was shorter by a head and twice the age of his wife. Mary felt a trill of disappointment in meeting her first duke. Especially since his wife was so lovely.

"Miss Gates, Mr. Barlow," the duchess said warmly. "I am pleased you could join us this evening. This is my husband, Robert, duke of Ethridge."

Barlow bowed and Mary curtsied, conscious that all eyes in the room were on them.

"I'd also like you to meet my mother, Lady Chester," the duchess said.

Lady Chester was as graceful as her daughter. She took Mary's hand. "Thank you for saving my grandson's life."

Around her, several of the guests whispered questions to one another and there were answers, so Mary knew the story of her rescue was becoming common knowledge.

Barlow introduced Jane and Mrs. Peebles, who was so overwhelmed that she almost bowed to the floor when she curtsied to the duke. Even Jane's eyes were as wide as saucers.

Accepting their subservience as his due, the duke addressed Barlow. "Your man presented himself today. I agree, he is a very capable riding instructor. Not only will Her Grace proceed with him but I shall also have him instruct my son. I've also made some inquiries and have learned you are a horse breeder, Mr. Barlow. One of considerable repute."

"As is Miss Gates," Barlow said.

The duke cocked a doubtful eyebrow. "Indeed? *This* is Miss Gates." A note in his voice said she had been an object of discussion between them.

"She is a superb horsewoman," Her Grace said as if justifying Mary's presence.

His Grace hummed his answer. He was unimpressed.

Mary didn't know how to respond. But Barlow said smoothly, "Miss Gates is a remarkable woman in many ways."

"Such as?" His Grace asked.

"She is a shrewd manager of her brother's estate and one of the pivotal personages of our small village."

"She also," Lady Chester said in ringing tones, "saved the life of your son."

Both Mary and Her Grace shot a thankful glance in Lady Chester's direction, because those were the words needed to unthaw the duke.

"Yes, and for that I am in your debt, Miss Gates." Then the proud duke of Ethridge did a wondrous thing; he bowed to Mary.

All up and down the receiving line, people whispered, repeating what had been said. They stared at Mary with undisguised curiosity and, yes, with admiration.

Her Grace's smile was radiant with pleasure. "Please, Miss Gates, I want you to meet everyone this evening. You are our guests of honor."

Mrs. Peebles started to tremble, she was so excited.

The duchess turned to Lady Chester. "Mother, would you do the honors of introducing our guests? Ethridge and I must stay here until it is time to start the dancing. Introduce Miss Gates as my personal friend."

Lady Chester was more than happy to honor her request. For the next hour, Mary met people whose names typified the very cream of Society. The tale of her rescuing the viscount was repeated over and over. The gentlemen appeared particularly interested in her story. She sensed their masculine interest, knew they found her attractive . . . and thought of Jane's premonition. Mrs. Peebles's face was flush with excitement and even Jane seemed to glow.

Barlow was quiet. He stayed by her side. She searched for a moment to offer an olive branch and thank him for easing her interview with the duke, but there was no opportunity.

She was also conscious of an amazing number of covetous glances sent in his direction by the ladies. Gentlemen may have been begging introductions to her, but even more women were seeking him out.

The dancing began. No less a personage than a marquis requested her hand, but to her surprise, Barlow stepped in. "I'm sorry, she is promised to me."

The marquis bowed and begged for the next dance.

Barlow held out his hand. Carefully, she placed her palm on his. His fingers tightened around hers. His touch felt good. He led her to the floor.

The music started.

It was a stately pavane. Barlow knew the steps and led her through them. She was very conscious of how tall he was and how well he fit into these surroundings whereas she felt like a gauche country girl in dress-up.

The steps brought them together. "Everyone is staring at you tonight," he whispered. "They are stunned by your beauty."

Surprised, Mary looked to him. The memory of their kiss, the heat of it, returned full force. Her throat went dry. He was so handsome, he fit right in with their noble company. "Thank you."

A frown formed on his forehead, the expression in his eyes unfathomable. "It appears you'll win the Stud."

Mary didn't know what to say or why she felt a twinge of disappointment when he referred to the horse. "I hope so," she managed softly.

"Mary . . ." he started, and then seemed to change his mind. The dance took them apart.

She waited impatiently for them to come together again. "What were you about to say?" she prodded.

He wavered, apparently considering, and then with a tight smile, said, "Nothing."

The musicians finished the set. Barlow mur-

mured a terse, "Thank you," then led her to the
marquis. Mary watched him move away from her
through the crowd with an unsettling sense of
loss.

After that, she had no more time to consider
what had happened—or more rightly, *hadn't* happened—between herself and Barlow. She was
tempted to search him out but instead was inun-
dated with gentlemen requesting the favor of her
company. She danced every dance and found herself surrounded by admirers. They complimented
her hair, her eyes, her nose, even her feet.

Mrs. Peebles approached around midnight to
tipsily inform her in excited tones that no fewer
than fifteen gentlemen had asked for her address,
including the handsome marquis, in order to pay
their respects to "the ravishing Miss Gates," and
the night was still young. "We can get one of
them up to scratch before the end of the week,"
she assured Mary with her usual optimism. "Especially with your name on everyone's lips."

Mary didn't know how she felt about such information. She searched out Barlow with her
gaze. He appeared busy. He danced. He laughed.
He drank. Beautiful women flirted with him. The
men included him as one of them. He was as
much of a success as she was and yet, there
seemed about him an air of aloofness.

Once or twice their gazes met. She always
looked away first. After all, she had her pride.

Guests kept arriving, even into the wee hours. The smell of perfumes, burning candle wax, and the crush of people started to give Mary a headache. However, neither Mrs. Peebles or Jane appeared ready to leave.

She began to long for a breath of fresh air and said as much to her current dance partner, Lord Dabney, a jelly belly lord who had stepped on her toes often during the last set.

"Let me escort you to the terrace," he replied, and took her arm to guide her toward a set of double doors.

Outside, Mary drank in the cool night air with a sigh of relief. She could think again.

The terrace was lit with paper lanterns. Here and there, other couples lingered, stealing a moment of privacy.

Lord Dabney led her over to the far corner away from the noise and music of the ballroom. Mary hesitated, uncertain of his intentions.

"I thought you wanted fresh air?" he asked. He had piggy eyes, the sort a wise women wouldn't trust. She knew he was after something more than taking the air.

"I do, but the dancing has left me parched. A glass of punch would be nice."

"But the punch is inside," he argued.

"Yes, and it would be so nice to sip it out here in the moonlight." She batted her eyelashes *à la* Mrs. Peebles and he changed his mind.

He leaned close, his voice next to her ear. "I will be back before you can say my name," he promised. "Don't go anywhere."

"I won't," Mary assured him but the moment his back was turned she rubbed her ear as if to remove even the touch of his breath.

Her plan was to slip back into the ballroom and hopefully lose him for the rest of the evening but the scent of honeysuckle wafted through the air.

Honeysuckle. Her mother's scent.

Mary moved toward the far corner and there, on the other side of the stone balustrade lining the terrace, was a honeysuckle bush climbing the roses along the terrace. It was just beginning to bloom.

She reached over the wall and lightly touched the feathery flowers on the vine. For a moment, the scent of the rose and honeysuckle comingled, delighting her senses. They reminded her of Edmundson, of the roses that would be budding along her porch, of the honeysuckle vines growing wild along the hedgerows, and of seeds that needed to be planted in her fields.

The wave of homesickness almost brought her to her knees.

She couldn't marry a London man. She couldn't leave Lyford Meadows. The village was part of the fabric of her life.

And yet, she'd committed to buying Lord Spender's horse. She wanted the horse. Edmundson needed it. Her honor was at stake . . . and yet, the price was too high.

Barlow had been right.

"You know, Mary, you look lovelier than ever."

She froze. She knew his voice. She'd never forgotten it. Funny how when she'd finally relaxed her guard, he should appear. Her heartbeat quickened.

Slowly she turned to face John, Lord Jergen's son . . . and the only man she had ever loved.

Chapter 13

John hadn't changed very much over the past years. Yes, he was older, but he'd always had a youthful face and it carried him well into his adulthood. He had to be thirty.

The same age as Barlow.

His golden brown hair curled carelessly over his forehead. His lips were well-formed, his jaw strong—and yet, for some reason, his boyish looks made her uncomfortable. 'Twas as if the years had passed and life had taught him nothing. He lacked Barlow's rugged individuality and strong masculinity.

She edged back into the corner, then forced herself to stand still, her arms hanging uselessly at her side. The other couples who had been enjoying the terrace had gone inside. They were alone.

"Hello, John." Her voice was even. Good.

He offered one of the glasses of champagne he held in his hand. "I saw Dabney. He told me he was bringing you refreshments and I assured him he need not worry."

"Oh." Awkwardly, she accepted the glass, but did not sip. She could barely move, let alone think. "Thank you." John came around to sit on the balustrade beside her. His teeth gleamed white in the darkness. "Ethridge told me a goddess was his guest of honor tonight. A woman so beautiful, every man in the room panted to dance with her." He leaned toward her. "He compared you to Diana, the Huntress. Everyone says you saved his son's life when his pony bolted."

Mary ran her thumb along the rim of her glass. She couldn't visualize the dour duke speaking in such sweeping superlatives. These were John's words, fabricated for his own benefit. She kept still.

He reached over and took the glass from her hand. She let him, raising her eyes to meet his, silver and opaque in the moonlight. She wondered what he was thinking.

"I knew before he said your name you were here," he whispered. "There is only one woman with the seat to do what you did."

Mary found her voice. "You couldn't have thought it was me. You didn't imagine I was anywhere close to here."

"I wanted to *believe* it was you," he restated. He set their glasses aside on the balustrade. She waited, heart in her throat.

"Did you ever think of me all these years, Mary?"

She stiffened. "How could I not?" She paused, then added in a small voice, "You left me."

The pain of his desertion came reeling back. Suddenly, she could no longer stay in his presence, fearing she would do something foolish. "I must go in."

She started for the door but he caught her arm. "Mary—"

"Please, John, the past is a closed door between us."

"I didn't mean to hurt you—"

"But you did." She faced him. "You knew how I'd felt. You left without a word."

For the space of a heartbeat, her words hung in the air between them.

His gaze shifted from hers. He stared unseeing into the distance. "I wanted to come back to you."

"Why didn't you?" she said, each word painful to speak.

"Father." He shrugged, finally looking at her. "He wouldn't let me. Your father had told him about us, expecting me to come up to scratch, but my father wouldn't let me."

"My father told—?" She leaned back toward the balustrade, raising a hand to her head. Her father had gone to his demanding marriage? "I'd not known." She took a moment to absorb the information. "But you'd said you loved me. You'd made promises, promises I believed. What difference would my father telling yours have made?"

"None to me. I would never have left you given my choice. I wanted you, Mary. I wanted you like I've never wanted any other."

This was too much. She couldn't believe that he was saying these words, that she wasn't conjuring them out of her dreams, her frustrations . . . her pride.

"Then why did you leave?" she said faintly. She wouldn't have. She would never have left him. In her mind, she'd returned to the girl she had been, the one who had so fervently wanted to believe in love, who had sacrificed all.

"I didn't *want* to." He ran a careless hand through his hair. "But it's different among my class. I had obligations, dictates that I had to fulfill, and we were both so young. Father refused to hear my suit. Ah, Mary, you must understand." He reached out, pulling her to him. His lips brushed her forehead. She sensed the velvety touch without feeling.

She studied the pavestones at her feet. "Did you love me?" she whispered. She had to know. For so long, she'd feared she'd been deceived. That his words of love had been little more than lip service.

She needed to know her sacrifice had been worth the cost.

"Yes," he answered. "I cared for you very much."

For a moment, Mary was overcome. Closing her eyes, she struggled to hold at bay tears of relief.

He had loved her.

"And you are still so very beautiful," he murmured. His lips brushed her eyes, tasted her tears. His hands came down around her waist and pulled her to him.

She let him hold her, lost in the relief of knowing her girlhood trust and love had not been a mistake. Yes, she'd been foolish, but her motives had been pure.

He had loved her.

He found her mouth and urged her lips to part for his.

Gratefully, Mary opened to him.

"Have you seen Mary?" Tye asked Jane.

"Why, no, I haven't." She half rose from her chair and searched the room. She'd been sitting with several other young matrons and had been involved in a spirited discussion when he had approached. Now, the women stared at him with undisguised interest.

Tye frowned, taking a step away. He was discovering the ton were a predatory group. He'd had five offers to leave—with *married* women, no less—in one night. People didn't behave in such a way in Lyford Meadows. Or at least, *he* didn't.

"I saw her dancing earlier with Lord Dabney and I know she was promised to Lord Fountaine." She shook her head. "I can't find anyone in this crowd. Perhaps we'd best walk around the room."

She made her apologies to her new friends and took his arm. "I'm certain she is here someplace," she said.

Tye didn't answer. He had to duck the flying hand movements of a grand dame who'd had too much champagne. She almost whacked him with her fan. She whirled on him in irritation as if he'd done something wrong and then, seeing him, her manner changed. Boldly, she did all but undress him with her eyes. "And you are?" she invited.

He didn't reply. He kept moving. Mary wasn't on the dance floor. He directed Jane toward the supper room. "I'm ready to go home," he admitted.

"To Lyford Meadows," Jane agreed wistfully. "I miss David." She patted his arm. "But then, you could leave, couldn't you? I mean we have needed your support as our escort, but there is nothing truly holding you here . . . and yet you stay." She stopped. "Why is that?"

Her question made him uncomfortable. He had no answer save one. "I'm here to protect my interests concerning the Spender Stud."

"Are you?" Jane frowned. "I wonder."

"What do you mean?" he questioned.

She pretended to ignore him and sidestepped his question by searching a near empty supper room. "Well, Mary is not in here. There are some card rooms down this hall."

He blocked her path. "What did you mean?"

"About what is keeping you here?" she repeated.

"Yes."

Her lips curved into a secret half smile. "You and Mary are both as tenacious as bulls on the subject of the horse. At the same time, I can't help but wonder if there is something more."

"Like what?" he demanded.

"Like Mary."

He went silent a beat, then, "I don't know what you are talking about." He started down the hall.

"Oh, I think you do," she said, trailing behind him. "I recognize the signs."

"What signs?" he threw over his shoulder. He peered into the first card room. No Mary.

"The way the two of you bicker."

"Because we don't like each other," he was quick to point out. "Mary and I don't rub along well."

"Hmmm," Jane answered.

He stopped dead in his tracks and confronted her. "What does 'Hmmmm' mean?"

"It means I think you feel something more for my sister than just friendship."

"We're *not* friends," he declared stoutly.

"Even more interesting," she replied.

"I don't know what you are talking about," he said dismissively. He started up the hall toward the next card room.

"I've always thought the two of you would make a handsome couple," Jane called after him.

He laughed. "You must be joking. Mary and me?" He shook his head, firm in his denial. "Never. We can't walk down the street without having an argument, let alone live under the same roof. Or sleep in the same bed." She wasn't in the second card room either.

"You might surprise yourself about sharing a bed," Jane said. "I'd think you'd be a good match."

Tye looked around, hoping no one had overheard this absurd statement. "What nonsense, Jane." What damn, heady, mad, erotic nonsense. In truth, his mind might reject the notion of sleeping with Mary, but his body didn't.

As if reading his mind, she said, "Every time the two of you argue, you stand so close another person couldn't get between you edgewise. I noticed that the day you came to Edmundson and attempted to persuade her to sell you Tanner."

"I was angry."

He would have started for the third and final card room except that she said, "Tye, don't fool yourself. You're a breeder. You should recognize the signs. You've been doing some sort of mating dance around my sister for years."

He backed her up to the opposite wall. "I have not."

"You have too," she replied with a stubbornness reminiscent of her sister. "You and Mary are itchy around each other, just like any stallion and mare."

Startled by her bluntness, he said, "The devil you say! Jane, watch your tongue."

"Tye, I'm a married woman. I've learned a thing or two about men." A militant sparkle gleamed in her eye. "You want Mary and nothing will satisfy you until she's yours. That's why you are so grouchy right now. You just can't admit it to yourself."

For a second, Tye couldn't speak. His mind had gone blank. First, he rejected her premise—even as he recognized the element of truth.

"I want the horse," he insisted.

"And a marriage between the two of you would give you both what you want," she replied reasonably.

"Mary and I would not suit," he restated. But he knew that wasn't true. They'd suited very well in the park the day before. The taste of her was burned into his memory.

Jane sighed. "Perhaps you are right," she conceded. "David claims I am a terrible matchmaker. But I've had this feeling—"

She broke off her thought with a shake of her head. "Come, let us retrace our steps and search the ballroom again. We must keep missing her." She started back down the hall.

He didn't move. "What feeling?"

She considered him a moment. "This feeling that tonight is a momentous one for Mary. That she'll meet the person she should be with. When I saw the two of you standing together in all your finery at Aunt Alice's, well . . ." She ended with a small shrug. "As you said, I am fanciful." She continued toward the ballroom.

Tye watched her a moment, his common sense and intelligence rejecting everything she'd said as romantic flummery. If there was any man walking the face of this earth who could meld Mary into a biddable enough creature to wed, he was welcome to her.

But it wasn't going to be him.

And his pursuit of the Stud wasn't an excuse to stay in London the way Jane claimed it to be. Period.

However, in the ballroom as he scanned the crowd of dancers, he knew Mary wasn't here. He sensed it all the way to his bones. He would have felt her presence even if he hadn't been able to see her.

In his mind were two questions. The first, where the devil could she be?

The second, why was he so aware of Mary above and beyond any other woman he knew?

On the terrace, Mary was ready to quit kissing long before John. Funny, but when she'd been younger, she'd lost herself in his kisses.

Now, she wanted to talk.

This kiss did not move her. In fact, reflecting on memorable kisses, the ones that came to mind were not his, but those innocent ones she had once shared with Barlow—and that brazen, soul-searching one they'd shared in the park.

The thought was startling, upsetting.

She shifted her weight from one foot to the other, a signal it was time for John to come up for air.

He broke off the kiss and leaned into her, his brown eyes sultry with emotion.

Mary took a step back and bumped into the wall of the house. He leaned one hand on the bricks by her head and loomed over her with that strange, intent expression of his.

"Why are you staring at me like that?" she said.

"Because I can't seem to stop looking at you. You're more beautiful than you were at sixteen." He lightly touched the line of her cheek. "I remember everything, Mary. You were exquisite. So passionate, so giving."

And so needy, she remembered, startled by her own thoughts. She had been lonely back then. She closed her eyes, paralyzed by dark memories.

John boldly traced the line of her bodice, his finger rising over the curve of her breasts and lingering in the valley between them. "I still want you, Mary."

She opened her eyes. His words echoed through time. He'd said them before.

His hand covered her breast. "We were good together. Do you remember?"

For a heartrending moment, it was all she could think of—but her memories were not sweet. Instead, she envisioned hot, sweaty hands pawing at her, the thrust and push of flesh, his grunts of passion. She'd locked those remembrances away. Now, they came raging forth.

He leaned down to kiss her again. She turned her head, and his lips found her neck.

She attempted to sidle away, but he placed his other hand on her waist and held her in place. She hesitated.

He took her hesitation for acceptance and pressed himself closer. She could feel his arousal pressed against her stomach.

This, she remembered—her misgivings while he pressured her to please him.

"Did you know my father passed on?" His voice was by her ear. "He died last year. I'm the earl now." He playfully nipped her ear. His hand at her waist started to pull up her skirts.

Mary shifted and yanked her skirt back down. "I'm sorry for the news," she said, stiffly.

"It was his time." He rubbed his thumb lightly over her nipple. "Now I carry a great deal of influence."

Uncomfortable, she pressed back against the wall. "I don't think this is wise."

He laughed and slipped his leg between hers. "I want you, Mary. I want you *now*." When she tried to edge away, he pinned her to the wall with his weight. He wiggled, rubbing his erection between them. "Let's go. I know a place where we can be alone."

Mary brought her hands to his waist and attempted to push him away. "Are you asking me to marry you, John?"

He laughed, the sound easy and carefree. "I'm already married. And, if I am to believe the gossip among the other men, you may be soon yourself."

"You're married?" she repeated, uncertain if she'd heard correctly.

"Of course." He nibbled beneath her chin and Mary came to her senses.

She slipped out of his grasp and faced him. "Married?" she repeated.

"Yes, yes, married," he said. He reached for her breast. "Why should that stop us?"

She slapped his hand away. "You don't love me."

He let his hand drop to his side. "I care for you."

"But you don't *love* me," she said. "You never did."

He made an impatient sound. "I'd forgotten how provincial you were."

Something snapped inside Mary. 'Twas as if shackles fell away from her. "Provincial? I was sixteen, John. Sixteen and in love. When you left, it destroyed me."

"You appear recovered now," he countered. He waved a dismissive hand. "Oh, come, Mary. What was between us was years ago. I can't go back and make amends now. We can't relive the past." He moved so close to her their toes touched and her breasts could brush his chest. He placed his hands on her arms. "All we have is the future."

He leaned forward to kiss her, but she ducked, sliding out from his hold, and he kissed air.

"Go home to your wife, John."

"I can't," he replied lightly. "She's having a go

at it with her lover. It's our evening away from each other."

It took a moment for his words to register, and when they did, the immorality of them robbed her breath.

She backed away as if he were the devil incarnate. "No," she managed. "There is nothing between us."

She would have run to the door, but he caught her arm and swung her back around. "You don't walk away from me." His grip tightened. "And I'm not finished yet."

Roughly, he attempted to kiss her. She twisted her face away and he brought a hand up to pinch her cheeks and hold her in place. He was strong. He wanted to have his way and her desires did not matter.

So, she kneed him.

John released his hold, doubling over as the air left his body.

Mary backed away. "No one makes me do anything I don't want to do," she said. "Not anymore." She turned and walked toward the ballroom. A few pins had come loose in her hair. She paused to make herself right—

Forceful hands jerked her violently back. He spun her around and shoved her toward a corner using the brute strength of his body. His eyes glittered dangerously.

"You she-devil," he hissed. "Did you think to

neuter me? Or do you just like to play rough?" His lips came down on hers, demanding and spiteful.

Mary struggled to free herself. His hold tightened. His teeth bit her bottom lip while he backed her into the shadows against the wall.

His anger gave him strength, but what frightened her most was the ugliness inside him, the desire to hurt her—

Suddenly, he seemed to lift up off the ground.

For the space of a heartbeat, she thought he was flying and then she saw Barlow. He easily held John by the nape of the neck. The ballroom door was open and several interested faces peered out to see what was happening.

"Jergen," Barlow said, his deep voice acknowledging John's presence as if they'd met on the street.

"Do I know you?" John asked, his expression confused as if he didn't understand what was happening.

"Tye Barlow, Lyford Meadows," Barlow said. "I've been wanting to do this to you for a long time."

His fist came forward with such force that when it connected with John's jaw, he really did fly. He hit the balustrade, lost his balance, and ignobly tumbled into the bushes on the other side of the terrace.

Chapter 14

Tye stretched out his fingers and gave the hand he'd punched Jergen with a shake. He'd bruised the tops of his knuckles but, damn, it had been worth it. Several people who had witnessed the scuffle ran over to the edge of the terrace.

He turned to Mary, the image of Jergen forcing himself on her burned in his mind. "Are you all right?"

She nodded. Her eyes appeared large and overbright, her complexion pale, her lips bruised and swollen. Jergen had torn her gown at the bodice, revealing the curve of her breast. She made no move to repair it. Instead, she asked, "Did you kill him?"

In answer, there came a groaning from the

bushes. One of the gentlemen from the ballroom leaned over the balustrade and offered a hand to help Jergen up.

Tye decided the time had come for them to leave. Taking off his jacket, he put it around Mary's shoulders. Only then did she realize her dress was torn. Color, hot and red, stole up her cheeks.

"Don't worry about it now," he said. "Let's go." He didn't wait for an answer but directed her toward the door.

A young woman and her escort came out on the terrace. Noticing the others gathered by the railing, they wandered over. "Did he fall?" Tye heard her ask the others.

"Don't know," came a gruff reply from a man holding his hand out to Jergen, who was still too brain-addled to help himself.

"Must have had too much to drink," another fellow said with a laugh and then hiccupped—a sign he'd been tippling too much also.

The blood had stopped pounding angrily in Tye's head and sanity was returning. *What had he done?* Surely there would be a scandal. He had to protect Mary. He needed to remove her from this house before anyone noticed her dress—or before Jergen started caterwauling.

They slipped back into the ballroom, where the party had not ebbed. The hour had to be close to three and still guests were arriving. The musicians played with equal fervor and the champagne flowed.

He searched for Jane and Mrs. Peebles, but couldn't stop himself from saying in a low undervoice, "What were you doing out there with that bastard?"

"I didn't go out with him," she replied tightly.

"What? Did he drag you from the ballroom?" Tye had not meant the words to sound as cynical as they did.

"He—?" she started and then her pride caught hold. "Never mind. I can see no matter what I say you'll blame me. Let us get out of here and I will answer any question you wish."

"I will look forward to the tale. Meanwhile, you move toward the front door. Keep your head down so no one establishes eye contact and tries to stop you. I'll find Jane and Mrs. Peebles."

She nodded.

They were about to part, when a man's voice rang out over the top of the music. "Barlow." At first, Tye thought he'd misheard, then the man shouted his name again and the music stopped. People looked around in confusion. He waited, pulling Mary behind him. The crowd parted, forming a line between Jergen and himself.

His lordship appeared the worse for wear. His nose ran and his eye was swelling. His perfectly combed hair stood this way and that with a few boxwood leaves as adornment. But his eyes blazed with fury. "I demand satisfaction."

Mary started forward as if to confront him, but Tye yanked her back. This was men's business.

The duke stepped forward. "What seems to be the problem here?" He frowned. "Jergen, you appear as if you have been rolling in the bushes."

"I have," the man snapped. He straightened the knot in his neck cloth and ran a self-conscious hand through his hair. "Barlow attacked me."

"Attacked you?" the duke repeated in surprise.

"Your Grace, may we speak of this in private—" Tye started, but Jergen would have none of it.

"Absolutely not, Barlow," Jergen said. "The court of public opinion has the right to hear what I have to say."

A warning clanged in Tye's head. Jergen had some other plan in mind. He again appealed to the duke. "Your Grace—"

"Lord Jergen attacked me!" Mary said, righteous indignation strengthening her voice.

Tye wanted to groan in frustration. He turned to her. "Not here. Please, I want to protect you as much as possible."

"You did protect me. You were brave and noble and wonderful." She looked to the duke. "Your Grace, Lord Jergen viciously assaulted me on the terrace."

"I did no such thing," Jergen flashed back.

"You didn't?" Mary answered. "Then how did

my dress get torn?" She shrugged out of Tye's coat and exposed one bare shoulder. The crowd moved their heads collectively from her, back to Jergen. "Or ask Lord Dabney," she continued. "He'll tell you that when he started to bring refreshment to me, Lord Jergen waylaid him."

"For what purpose?" the duke asked.

"To be alone with me, Your Grace," she answered. "So he could attack me."

Jane had come to stand beside her sister. She helped Mary ease the coat back up on her shoulder. The duchess had also come forward. She stood by her husband.

A murmur ran through the crowd. Tye wished he'd gotten her out without a scene. He knew Mary thought she was doing the right thing, but she wasn't. Her impulsive naïveté was about to ruin them both.

Jergen turned to his contemporaries. "I did nothing unwelcomed."

Mary gasped in stunned outrage. "That's not true. I tried to go inside and you wouldn't let me. I had to fight to defend myself."

"Oh, come now, Miss Gates," Jergen said in exaggerated tones. "Defend your *what*? Certainly not your virtue." He addressed the crowd. "Judge for yourself, my friends. Miss Gates and I have a history." He smiled. "Is that not so, Mary?"

The announcement caught her off guard. She turned to Tye, the expression in her green eyes changing from stunned surprise to the agony of betrayal. He wanted to throttle Jergen all over again.

Instead, he placed a protective arm around her shoulders. "Your Grace, we wish nothing more than to leave. We want no part of the scene Lord Jergen is creating."

"I can understand why," His Grace said with distaste. He motioned to a footman. "Signal their coachman."

The servant hurried off and Tye would have taken the women with him, but Mary shook him off. She took a step toward Jergen and said in a low voice trembling with emotion, "I can't believe I ever loved you. I hate you now."

Her testimonial was powerful and dramatic. Again, opinion swayed against Jergen—a situation he could not allow to continue.

"Do you hear her?" he asked his friends in a carrying voice. "She admits we were lovers." He shook his head. "Poor girl, she chased me relentlessly. It was embarrassing and quite a village scandal, I'm certain, eh, Miss Gates? So much so, no other man would have you." He surveyed the room, catching and holding the gaze of every man he could. "The rest of you may wish to court her for a wife. I assure you her charms in bed are not to be denied. But then, with some women, one doesn't have to marry to sample." He turned and left the room.

Mary stood as if carved from stone. People stared in astounded silence. She seemed oblivious. The duke motioned to Tye. "Mr. Barlow, I believe it best if you gather your party and leave. I regret the unfortunateness of this incident."

"I should have killed him," Tye answered succinctly.

Those were not the words the duke had been expecting. He frowned his disapproval but Tye was beyond caring what the duke thought. Mary was his concern.

Jane's soft voice said, "Come, Tye. Let us gather Aunt Alice and leave."

He nodded. Mary had not moved. He took her arm at the elbow and gave her a squeeze. "Courage," he whispered. "Show them you have courage."

His admonishment got through to her. The color returned to her face and her eyes regained their purpose, their intelligence. Her chin lifted with well-known Gates pride. "Yes, let us leave."

While Jane went in search of Mrs. Peebles in one of the card rooms, Tye escorted Mary through the crowd. As they passed the duke and duchess, they heard him say to his wife, "And this is the woman you wished to emulate?"

Bright spots of color appeared on Her Grace's cheeks.

Tye would have gone on, but Mary paused in

front of her benefactress. "Thank you for your hospitality."

The duchess lightly touched her hand. "I wish it could have been different."

"So do I," Mary agreed. She took Tye's arm and together they left the ballroom. People shuffled out of their way. One old biddy actually pulled her skirts back from Mary's path. She had been the one who had whispered an invitation to him earlier. The hypocrisy made him ill.

In the empty marble foyer, the butler handed Tye his hat and whispered that the hired coach had not arrived. There was nothing they could do but wait. Mary let go of his arm and moved a little distance away from him.

He worried she blamed him. And now that he knew the full story, and of course, the aftermath, he blamed himself. He shouldn't have let his temper loose.

"You don't have your spangled shawl," he said, more as a way to make conversation than anything else.

She stirred and he wondered if she'd heard him. Then, she said, "I lost it outside. With Jergen." She paused and then added quietly, "Thank you, Tye. I've never had anyone champion me before." For the briefest of seconds, her green-eyed gaze met his and she smiled, a smile that quickly faded.

Seeing her like this broke his heart. She was right—men like Jergen should be horsewhipped.

Jane entered the foyer towing a tipsy Mrs. Peebles, her ostrich feather headdress headed in every which direction. "I don't know why we must leave so soon," the older woman complained. "It's not even dawn and I've had the best run of luck at the card tables." She had obviously not learned of the catastrophe in the ballroom and for that, Tye was grateful.

"We must go, Aunt," Jane repeated firmly.

"Your carriage is ready, sir," the butler told Tye.

At the same time, Mrs. Peebles saw someone she knew peeking around the corner at them with undisguised curiosity. "Good-bye, Lady Blythe. I'll see you on the morrow," she trilled. "Lady Blythe is so nice," she confided to Jane in a carrying voice. "We met over cards and had such a lovely time."

"Yes, that is nice, Aunt, but now we must leave." Jane directed Mrs. Peebles toward the door.

"Yes," her aunt said and then added happily, "This was the best night of my life. My place in Society has been sealed. I shall be the envy of all my friends!"

Mary glanced at Tye, a small frown between her eyes. He motioned her to the door. "I have no regrets on her score," he whispered as she passed.

She didn't answer.

Outside, they were ready to climb into the waiting coach when a footman approached. "Mrs. Peebles?" he asked tentatively.

The older woman straightened her ostrich feathers. "Yes?"

"I have a message from Lady Blythe," he said.

"Oh, tell me," she said, her watery eyes bright with expectation.

The servant said in a quiet voice that Tye could overhear, "She said you are uninvited to tomorrow's event and she wishes you not to pursue the acquaintance."

"She what?" Mrs. Peebles repeated in disbelief.

"That is all she said," the footman responded. He backed away as if fearing her temper, bowed, and left.

Mrs. Peebles looked from Jane to the front door where the footman had disappeared and back to her niece again. "Why would she uninvite me?" she asked.

"Climb into the coach, Aunt," Jane said soothingly and, like a child, Mrs. Peebles did so, but not before asking why Mary was wearing Tye's coat. He didn't catch Jane's muttered answer, but it seemed to appease her aunt.

This time, Jane settled in next to Mrs. Peebles and Tye and Mary shared a seat. He took off his hat, climbed in, and signaled with a knock on the roof to the coachman they were ready to go. The coach lurched and they were on their way.

Mrs. Peebles continued her questioning. "I know Lady Blythe can't be angry at me. I let her win every hand at whist. There was no reason for her to be so churlish."

No one answered. In the coach's flickering lantern light, a rapidly sobering Mrs. Peebles looked from Jane to Tye and then to Mary, who leaned against the far side of the coach, her head bowed. She'd removed her gloves and seemed intent on staring at the tips of them.

"Perhaps you know something, Miss Gates?" Mrs. Peebles asked.

Jane answered, "Oh, Aunt, you know how fickle the ton are. Who knows what whim the woman decided to follow? Perhaps she must leave town."

"She doesn't want to *further* the acquaintance. That isn't a whim, Jane."

Mary looked up. "Mrs. Peebles, there will be no invitations on the morrow or the next day or the next."

"What happened?" she asked as if fearing the answer.

"Mary," Jane said, "you don't need to talk about this, not this minute."

"Yes, it's best we leave the matter alone," Tye agreed.

"Talk about what?" Mrs. Peebles demanded, more alarmed.

Mary said, "About how Lord Jergen attacked me out on the terrace."

"Good heavens! *The* Lord Jergen, the Non-pareil, the Lion of Society? Why should he do such a thing?" Mrs. Peebles asked.

"Why indeed?" Mary echoed. She answered brutally, "Because I was once his mistress and he wanted me back again."

"You were *what*?" Mrs. Peebles asked faintly.

"Mary, please," Jane said.

Tye kept his own counsel. He knew Mary well enough to know he could not stop her. Her lip was still swollen and a bruise was forming on her cheek. He should have killed Jergen.

"You heard me," she said to Mrs. Peebles. "In my defense, I will tell you I was too young to be left alone with such a rogue. And too naïve."

Tye noticed she no longer claimed to love Jergen.

"What happened tonight?" Mrs. Peebles said.

"Jergen attacked me, I struggled, Tye punched him—"

"You hit Lord Jergen?" Mrs. Peebles said to Tye.

"He sent him sailing into the bushes," Mary answered for him. "And the duke asked us to leave."

Dead silence met the end of her tale.

At last, Mrs. Peebles said to Tye, "You can apologize. I'm certain if you are pleasant enough,

Lord Jergen will forgive you and realize this is all a misunderstanding."

"There was no misunderstanding," Tye answered.

"Absolutely not," Mary agreed.

"Jergen should be the one to apologize," Jane said.

Mrs. Peebles waved her hand at them as if erasing their objections. "You are being oversensitive. Mary admits she has already let Lord Jergen in the barn, so to speak. I don't see the difficulty with giving him a little giggle. At least he would have been quiet about it. Now all is ruined. Mary will never make a decent match."

Her brusqueness evaporated as a new prospect dawned on her. "And you've ruined me, too. I've been dragged down with you." Tears came to her eyes. "Why, a juicy bit of scandal like this could be in all the papers. Everyone will be talking about it on the morrow. I won't be able to show my face anywhere." She broke down into noisy sobs.

Jane reached for her hand. "My dear aunt, please don't take this to heart."

Mrs. Peebles flinched and pulled away from her. "Don't call me *aunt*. You are no *blood* relative, either one of you. I'm now worse off than I was before you came. I wish I'd never laid eyes on Mary. I want both of you out of my house on the morrow. Both you and your hussy sister."

"Mary is not a hussy," Jane said, her eyes flashing. "I will not let you say such a thing about her."

"Oh, yes?" Mrs. Peebles questioned. "Let me tell you right now, *no man* will want her. She is soiled goods. She's been had. Any woman stupid enough to let a man have his way with her before marriage deserves to be whispered and gossiped about—"

"I will not sit here and listen to you say these things about my sister!" Jane shot back.

"No man will marry her," Mrs. Peebles taunted. "Not one."

"Enough." Tye's voice filled the coach. "I will marry her."

For a moment, there was stunned silence.

The coach, having reached Mrs. Peebles's house, rolled to a halt, but no one moved.

Jane found her voice first. "Tye, that is the perfect solution."

"It's madness," Mrs. Peebles said. "They can barely abide each other."

"I think I know my sister better than you do," Jane said.

"If you knew her so well, you would never have brought her to London," the older woman flashed back. The two appeared ready to come to blows.

Then Mary spoke. "I won't marry Barlow. I won't marry any man."

"*Don't* be stupid," Mrs. Peebles warned.

"Yes, Mary, please be reasonable," Jane started.

In answer, Mary opened the door on her side and jumped out. "You don't understand. I make my own rules and lead my own life." She started walking off into the night.

The coachman, who had tired of waiting, opened the door on the side facing the house. Tye pushed him out of the way. He threw his coin purse and his hat at Jane. "Settle up, will you?" He went in pursuit of Mary.

She knew he followed. He could tell by the quickening of her step.

"Leave me alone," she threw over her shoulder and started running.

He caught up with her in less than a minute and grabbed her by the arm. She whirled on him, flailing her fists to push him away. He ducked but she smacked him hard right on the nose.

Tye had had enough. He lifted her high, tossed her over her shoulder as if she weighed less than a sack of grain, and headed back toward Mrs. Peebles's house.

She attempted to kick, to squirm, claw, and bite.

That was Mary. When she fought, she gave it everything she had.

But for once, she'd met her match. He was bigger, stronger, and more stubborn.

Mrs. Peebles met them at the front door. "I

meant what I said. I want Miss Gates and my nephew's wife out of my house."

Tye walked right by her.

"We'll be happy to leave," Mary yelled down at her as he climbed the stairs.

From the top landing, Jane seconded the declaration. "I'll start packing now."

"Pack a second valise for Mary," Tye ordered. "We'll elope for Scotland by the soonest way possible."

Mrs. Peebles charged up the stairs after them. "Good!"

Mary lifted herself up. "Don't listen to him, Jane. I'm not going with him."

"Duck," he answered.

"Duck?" she repeated, having the good sense to do so as she spoke and saved her head from being walloped on the top of the doorjamb leading into the parlor.

He kicked the door shut right in Mrs. Peebles's angry face, walked to the middle of the room, and dropped Mary to the ground none too gently. She gained her balance, doubled her fists, and punched him hard. He captured both her hands at the wrists. She strained to break free.

All the pins were gone from her hair and it hung like a thick curtain down her back. In spite of his coat, a good portion of her breast on the torn side of her dress was exposed to view.

Seeing he overpowered her, she switched to overly dramatic defiance, as if she were some slave girl being held by a conquering infidel. "So what are you going to do now, Barlow? Hold me prisoner until I agree to marry you?"

Instead of answering, he kissed her.

Chapter 15

Mary was so shocked to have Barlow's mouth covering hers, she couldn't breathe. She couldn't think. She opened her eyes so wide they felt as if they bulged like a fish.

Barlow didn't care. He continued kissing.

She wanted to resist, to defy him, but he held her wrists and she was powerless, or so she thought . . .

His hands were at her waist, pulling her closer—and she discovered the arms she had believed held captive embraced his neck. The kiss picked up heat, starting at the point where the kiss in the park had left off and building with rapid intensity.

Dear Lord, kissing him appeared to be as natural to her as breathing.

His tongue stroked, then claimed her. With a grateful sigh, she relaxed against him. Deep within her a yearning was building with a force she'd not experienced. She lifted up on her toes. His arousal rose strong, hard between them—a testimony to what he wanted . . . if she'd give it.

Mary pressed closer, feeling the length and need of him.

'Twas the answer he wanted.

He lifted her, fitting her against him, backing her toward the closed door. Her back bumped the doorframe. He held her in place with his weight. His breath brushed her ear, sending her senses soaring to the ceiling and turning her legs to jelly.

Barlow kissed the corner of her mouth, her chin, her cheeks, her eyes. His other hand ran down along her thigh and then began pushing her skirts higher. His fingers stroked the bare skin above her garters. She opened her legs.

"Dear God, I want you," he whispered. And she wanted him. Deep inside her . . . with an urgency essential to her very being—

Mrs. Peebles banged on the door. "Mr. Barlow? Miss Gates? What are you doing in there?"

Jane's voice scolded, "Leave them be. They have much to discuss."

"It doesn't sound like they are discussing anything," Mrs. Peebles countered.

"Go to bed," Jane ordered with surprising force. "Leave them alone."

"Oh, I will, and when I wake you and your sister had better be gone!" Heavy footsteps trounced away from the door.

Barlow broke off the kiss but did not release her. He rested his chin on top of her head. Her ear was against his chest and she could hear the mad drumming of his heart, a drumming that matched the pace of her own.

Slowly, common sense reasserted itself.

He broke the silence between them first. "We will leave for Scotland as soon as possible."

She placed her palm over his heart. The beat was returning to normal, but he was still aroused. She shook her head. "It will take more than a kiss to make me change my mind." Or so she told herself.

"I didn't kiss you to convince you," he shot back. " 'Twas the only way I could think of to get your attention."

"A shut-up kiss?" She leaned her head back against the door and looked up into the blue depths of his eyes. "It worked."

"Then why are you still arguing?"

His retort surprised a small, slightly hysterical bubble of laughter out of her. Looking down, she realized the torn dress indecently exposed her breast to him, the nipple tight and hard. His gaze dropped. His lips parted. His head started to bend—

Mary slipped out from his hold. She backed

across the room from him, pulled his coat tight around her. If she had let him touch her, she would have been lost.

He took a space of time to collect himself. She sensed he was as embarrassed by their lack of control as she was.

"Marriage is the best course," he announced.

"Why is that?"

"It will stop wagging tongues and both of us will get what we want."

"Which is?" she asked tightly.

"Tanners Darby Boy."

She had to think a second to place the name. With all the upheaval, she'd almost forgotten the horse. Worse, the thought of owning him no longer was her first priority.

The revelation shook her to the core.

Barlow took a step forward. "Mary, are you all right? You've gone pale."

She held up a hand, warding him off. "I'm fine." His presence filled the room. She found it difficult to concentrate. She searched for her old passion, for the drive she'd once felt to own Tanner—but it didn't move her, not like it had in the past.

In truth, she no longer knew what she wanted.

But she couldn't marry Barlow. She didn't understand her reasons; she only knew her instincts.

"I can't marry you," she said.

"Or you won't?" There was tension in his voice.

Mary sank onto the goose feather pillow of one of the sofas. She didn't want this confrontation. Not until she understood her own mind better.

Barlow moved to stand in front of her. His fists clenched, he prompted, "Mary?"

"I won't," she whispered. Immediately, her chest tightened. She forced herself to breathe. "You don't understand. I don't want any man in my life. Everything foolish I've ever done has involved a male. Look at this evening."

He knelt. "Mary, the only thing you did was fall in love. You committed no crime save to trust the wrong man."

"Love?" she repeated, and then gave a small cynical laugh, a lump burning in her throat. "I don't know what love is. I never did." She looked at him. " 'Tis not good to love, Barlow. The cost can be more than one is willing to pay."

He took her hands, giving them a frustrated squeeze. He was so warm and she felt cold. "Then marry me," he said. "You know we don't love each other. There will be no expectations. And yet, you saw what happened a moment ago. I want you, Mary. You want me. It's enough. Ours will not be a love match, and therefore it will be free of all the baggage love brings with it."

She bent her head, hiding her face behind the curtain of her hair. Her body still craved his touch, still begged for release. His taste was still on her lips. And she feared what he could make her feel. He might rise from their bed unaffected . . . but she didn't think she would.

She captured his thumb with her hand and held it in place. She remembered a time when she had thought she was in love with him. Back when all was innocent and she had trusted.

"Look at what we've both become . . ." She let her voice trail off.

He understood. " 'Twas a long time ago, Mary. We've learned many lessons since then."

"Perhaps if I had been older?"

He stood, carrying her hand with him. "Forget the past. Think of the future. We'll have Tanner."

"And mayhap someday you will fall in love with another woman and regret this arrangement between us. What will you do then, Barlow, when you find yourself saddled with a wife you don't want?"

"I'm not Jergen," he said grimly.

"I don't compare you."

"Yes, you do. He was a bloody bastard. I'm not." He pulled her up. Her breasts pressed against his chest. He held her firm, his arms around her waist. "Feel the heat between us, Mary. We'll do well together."

Yes, they would. Already she wanted to melt

against him. And it would be nice to have another shoulder to bear the responsibilities of Edmundson. He'd been right when he'd said they shared the same values—family, horses, land.

As if reading her mind, he said, his voice low, "You aren't the only one ready to marry. I've yet to fall in love, and at my age I probably never will. But why shouldn't I marry for something I want?"

Tanner.

A wife for a horse.

She had been willing to do the same.

Her passionate nature, the one she struggled to control, wanted more. In the back of her mind had been the hope that perhaps on this venture to London she would have met someone to love— just like Jane had hoped.

Of course, she'd always wanted more than what she could have. Her father must have bred it in her and it had been her downfall ever since.

She shifted in his arms and he released her. Thoughtfully, she circled the room. She stopped.

"I will want control of Tanner's breeding schedule," she said, coming to her decision.

He frowned. "Sole control? Absolutely not. Our stake in this horse will be equal."

"Then you must promise you will not make any plans for him that I don't agree with." She squared her shoulders. "And you must accept me as I am."

He didn't like that. A wariness crept in his eye. "What do you mean?"

"I mean that I will maintain my independence. Our marriage will be a business arrangement."

"Of course." Grimly, he asked, "But you aren't planning any of your old tricks?"

She felt her spirit return. They were back on familiar ground. "I know, I know. I haven't always given you cause for trust. But if we are to be partners, we must learn to trust each other. A clean slate, so to speak." When he still didn't move, she added, "Come, Barlow, I know I can be a bit devious when I want something bad enough, but this experience over Tanner has taught me a lesson. Besides, if I cheat you, I cheat myself."

He frowned. "What is the trick?"

She held up her hands to show they were empty. "No tricks."

He still didn't trust her.

With an impatient sound, she said, "You are the one who has suggested we marry. I'm merely outlining my terms. And must I remind you that Lord Spender sold the horse to me? He's holding it for my return. If you want him, we must reach a mutually satisfactory agreement."

He raised a suspicious eyebrow. "But you have no money."

"I have some . . . and how much did you spend on this trip to London?"

"Touché." He considered her a moment, then said, "Very well. You can be independent, Mary, as long as your actions are for the good of the horse and our business."

" 'Tis fair. But I'll wear breeches when I feel like it."

"And sleep in my bed."

For a second, 'twas as if all the air had been sucked from the room. Very carefully, she nodded.

"Good," he said, but he did not color the word with emotion.

They stood, inches from each other and yet so very far apart. She didn't know what to say. It seemed they should seal their agreement in some way or another.

She held out her hand. "*Égalité*." Perversely, she knew it was the one word that would irritate him, and it did. She waited, half expecting him to call the matter off—and not knowing if she'd be relieved or disappointed.

His hand covered hers. "Done," he said firmly. A current passed between them, one she couldn't define as anything other than lust. Yes, she wanted to be in his bed too. Then, perhaps, she could think clearly again.

He released his hold. Compared to their earlier passion, they both suddenly acted awkward, shy even.

He took a step back. "The hour is late and we

both need to pack. Jane, too. We'll see her on the stage for Lyford Meadows. I must return to my lodgings and make plans for Dundee."

"What will you do?"

"Hire a rider to take him home." He looked around the room. "I don't see a clock. What say we meet again in an hour? A mail coach must be leaving for the north close to dawn." He paused. "I hope you don't mind going by mail. I think it best we conserve our money."

"Yes," she agreed. A beat of silence and then, she added, "I will be happy when we are home."

"Me, too." Unexpectedly, he added, "I want children."

She nodded.

"Very well, then." He crossed to the door and opened it. The hallway was dark. "I will be back. Soon." He left. She heard him go down the steps. The front door opened and then closed.

He was gone. She sat on the sofa. *Children.* An image rose in her mind of her holding a babe in her arms. She saw herself in church, at a christening and having the other women gathered around her to admire her baby. Tye would give her strong, healthy, *wonderful* children.

Jane appeared in the doorway, her eyes brimming with excitement. "I heard," she whispered. "You're going to marry Tye."

Mary nodded and Jane let out a whoop of joy.

She charged the sofa to envelop her sister in a huge hug.

"I heard all," Jane confessed.

"All?" Heat burned Mary's cheeks.

"Nothing I shouldn't," her sister amended wisely.

"Did Barlow see you when you left?"

"Tye," Jane corrected. "His Christian name is Tye and you must become accustomed to it. No more barking 'Barlow' the way you usually do. And, no, I ran and hid when I heard the door start to open. I didn't know how my future brother-in-law would feel about my eavesdropping."

Tye. "Barlow" gave her distance. Tye made it all seem more real. Dear God, what had she just agreed to? "Perhaps you could come to Scotland with us."

Jane grinned slyly. "What? And serve as a buffer between you? Oh, no. You're on your own now, Mary."

Outside on the front step, Tye paused. He heard Jane's glad shout and knew Mary had given her the news.

Mary. He was eloping to Gretna Green with Mary Gates.

Brewster, Blacky, and even David would be shocked to their cores when they heard the news. And why not? He still wasn't certain what he was doing. He did know one thing—he wanted Mary with a passion that was unholy in its desire. He would have struck their bargain even if the horse hadn't been the stake.

He started for his lodgings.

Chapter 16

Mary and Jane were both packed and waiting for Barlow when he arrived in a hack to take them to the posting inn. They were leaving with three times the luggage they'd arrived with. Mary would have preferred wearing her breeches, but Jane had refused to let her bring them to London. So, instead of being comfortable, Mary wore a blue striped dress and straw bonnet. She wondered irreverently if Madame Faquier the dressmaker would consider this proper elopement attire.

At the last moment Jane insisted on penning a quick note thanking Mrs. Peebles for her hospitality.

Impatiently, Mary said, "We *paid* for her hospitality, Jane." What was left of her money, she had placed in a valise along with a change of clothing and a few toiletries for the trip to Scotland. Jane would take the rest home with her.

"Yes, Mary, but it is always good to leave on a happy note," Jane said complacently.

"She wasn't happy when we last saw her. She forbid you to call her aunt."

"But she *is* David's aunt and I'm his wife, so I must attempt amends."

"Better David's aunt than mine," Mary muttered, and received a look of agreement from Barlow. It comforted her a bit, that look did. In spite of her doubts, she and Barlow might be able to build something together—and she discovered she wanted to do that.

When she returned to Lyford Meadows, she would be a married lady. The other girls, the ones that had married years before her and who had gossiped behind her back over her disgrace, would be spinning like dervishes when they realized whom she had married—Tye Barlow, the Buck of the Parish.

Of course, squeezed in next to her in the hack, he didn't look like any fine buck. All three of them were blurry-eyed and tired from lack of sleep. She stifled a yawn and he echoed it.

"Did you see to Dundee?" she asked.

He nodded.

Not exactly auspicious beginnings for an elopement.

The yard at the posting inn was busy chaos even at this hour before dawn. The air rang with the noises of shouting coachmen, stamping horses and smelled of manure, hay, soot, and freshly baked buns. Mary's stomach growled so loudly, both Barlow and Jane heard it and they all laughed.

He arranged for their fares, managing inside seats for the three of them. He booked he and Mary on the northbound mail coach and Jane on a stage. They decided to use Mary's valise for the two of them. He stuffed a clean shirt and his shaving kit on top of her things. The elopement started to take on the air of reality.

Barlow handed them each a hot bun he'd thought to purchase, tucking two extra ones in her valise for the road. He gave Jane an extra one, too. "We must hurry," he warned them. "Both our rides leave at any moment."

"But we must see Jane safe," Mary protested.

"There's no time," Barlow said. To punctuate the words, a blast of a mail guard's tin horn sounded, a sign they were departing.

"Go on," Jane said. "I shall be fine."

Mary was suddenly unwilling to let her sister go. Jane accepted a small hug then pushed them apart. "Go, Mary, please. You must. I will make my way back to Lyford Meadows safe."

"But—" Mary started to protest and Jane interrupted.

"Go meet your destiny."

"Come, Mary," Barlow said, and she let him pull her away. He hustled her to the mail coach.

"You almost didn't make it in time, mate," the guard called down at him from his perch in the back of the coach on the boot. The seats on top of the coach were already filled to what looked like overflowing. Mary feared a passenger would certainly tumble off and was thankful Barlow had paid the extra coin for an inside seat.

"But we are here," Barlow said. He helped Mary inside.

"Yes, well, if you dally at any of my coaching stops like this, we'll be taking off without you," the guard warned darkly.

Barlow didn't respond. Instead, he shut the door. "Here, Mary, make yourself comfortable."

That was going to be hard. The inside of the mail coach was even smaller than the hacks they had been riding around town. The bench seats on either side of the coach couldn't be any longer than a yard, and there were already two other passengers on board—a slight gentleman with greasy hair and a good-sized lady with impossibly red hair. She was dressed in velvet from head to toe. They were already asleep.

Mary took her place but didn't see how Barlow would fit with his long legs. She rested her feet on top of their valise. He packed himself in, though, removing his hat and setting it in his lap.

Untying the ribbons of her bonnet, she looked out the window and saw Jane climbing into her own vehicle. Panic threatened—and Mary realized she'd never been away from her family before. Jane had always been close at hand.

She leaned out the window. "Jane!"

Her sister looked up, smiled with confidence, and then climbed into her coach. And Mary was alone—for the first time in her life.

Another blast from the guard's horn, a crack of the whip, and the mail coach was off, heading north toward Scotland.

Barlow leaned close, resting his arm on the seat behind her. "Here."

Mary turned to see he offered her a linen kerchief. Only then did she realize she was crying.

She shook her head, embarrassed.

"Take it," he ordered. "Or are you going to challenge me on every little thing? If so, we'll be living in hell."

Temper replaced tears. "If you don't like it, Barlow—"

"*Tye.* My name is Tye." He sat back, annoyed. "Let's leave it, Mary. We're both too tired to think. With our dispositions, we'll be at each other's throats in no time, and I don't have the patience for that right now." He offered the kerchief again.

"We all cry at one time or the other. There's nothing heroic about pretending you don't."

This time she accepted it. He was right. They

were both exhausted. She blew her nose noisily. "Thank you." She offered it back.

"You can keep it," he said wryly, and she realized he wouldn't want it back after she'd made use of it.

"Sorry." The word came out more flippant than she'd intended.

He frowned. She attempted to explain herself. "I didn't mean to sound the way I did."

"I know." He leaned back. "Go to sleep, Mary."

For once, she didn't argue. She curled up as best she could and, clutching his kerchief in a tight ball, fell asleep.

Mary woke to the sound of someone smacking lips. She had a crick in her neck and for some reason she was rocking back and forth. A horn blew again and she realized it had woken her and not the lip smacker, who was the red-headed lady chewing a chicken leg.

Stretching awake, Mary found herself blocked in by a large, immovable form. Barlow.

He shifted, frowned in his sleep and settled in with a deep sigh. A dark whisker shadow covered his jaw and his neck cloth had been loosened so his shirt was open at the neck. His hat had tumbled from his lap to rest between his leg and the door. He appeared decidedly uncomfortable but out to the world.

"Men. They always sleep well," the woman

said, patting the head of the man snoring open-mouthed in her lap.

Mary nodded, still too disoriented to talk. She lifted the flap covering the window and dust blew in the coach. She dropped the flap quickly but she'd been able to see the day was well advanced. "How long have we been traveling?" she murmured, her throat dry.

"Not long enough." The woman pushed the chicken bone out the flap on the other side and reached for a pottery jug. She took a healthy drink and then offered the jug to Mary. "Would you like some?"

"No, thank you," Mary said with a shake of her head.

"Ah, just as well," the woman said. "Sixty hours to Edinburgh and they only give us three stops on the mail. I'm Mrs. Katy. This is my husband, Mr. Katy." She ruffled his limp hair as she spoke.

"I'm Miss Gates." She nodded to Barlow. "And this is Mr. Barlow."

"Oh," Mrs. Katy said, drawing out the syllable with interest. "I thought you were together."

"We are." Mary's stomach growled and she reached down to the valise at her feet, opened it, and felt around for the extra buns. She found one.

"Is he a relation?" Mrs. Katy pried.

Mary buried her thumb in the bun and split it in half. "No, he's my intended."

Excitement leapt to Mrs. Katy's eye. She sat forward, readjusting her husband's head in her lap. "You're eloping?"

"Yes." Mary bit into the bun.

Mrs. Katy laughed with undisguised delight. "I always wanted to elope, but Mac and I were married right and proper."

"We will be married right and proper," Mary said.

"Yes, you will." Mrs. Katy sat back with a smile. "Of course, it isn't very romantic, eloping in a mail coach."

"Well, we wanted the pleasure of your company," Mary answered, and then smiled. Barlow's dry humor was rubbing off on her.

"He is a big one, isn't he?" Mrs. Katy gave Barlow a critical once over. "A nice brute of a man. That's the way I like them. But I do love my Mac, too." She lowered her voice to confide, "He's a Romeo."

Mary could think of no answer to such a comment.

Apparently, Mrs. Katy hadn't expected any because, her gaze still on Barlow, she continued, "Yes, yes, a strapping fine man you are about to marry." Her gaze lowered. "*Very* strapping."

A rush of heat rose to Mary's cheeks when she realized what the woman ogled. Of course, she'd noticed herself how well endowed Barlow was.

Unfortunately, at that moment, he chose to wake.

"Mary?" he said groggily. She blinked and raised her eyes to his face, but it was too late. He sat up. "What were you staring at?"

"I was thinking," she said quickly. "Not staring." She changed the subject. "Good morning."

He frowned. "Good morning." His deep voice rumbled in his chest. His whiskers made him appear dangerously handsome.

She offered him half her bun. "Hungry?"

He looked at the meager meal with sleepy contempt and then took it from her. Turning toward the window, he cracked the flap to see the passing landscape as he ate.

So, Barlow wasn't communicative when he first woke. She wasn't either. This was a good thing.

He finished his bun and brushed his fingers off. The gesture struck her as intimate. It was a small thing but the sort of movement you only noticed through familiarity with another person.

And she realized that although she'd known him most of her life, there were many things she didn't *know* about him.

But soon, she would. She would know whether he drank tea or coffee in the morning or preferred ale. She would know if he snored or talked in his sleep. His shoes would be under her bed, his face across from her at the meal table. She would learn his likes and dislikes more than any other person on earth . . . and Mrs. Katy was right—being married to such a well-built man would not be such a bad thing—

"What are you thinking?" His voice startled her.

"Nothing," she replied quickly.

"Your face, you're all flushed. Do you feel well?"

"Fine," she said faintly. "I'm fine." Then her gaze met Mrs. Katy's. The older women lifted a knowing eyebrow and a smile spread across her generous features.

She'd known the direction of Mary's thoughts.

Mary said, "Barlow, this is Mrs. Katy. She and her husband are traveling north."

Barlow grunted a response, obviously not feeling up to striking a friendship.

Mrs. Katy met Mary's gaze—and winked.

He caught the gesture and frowned. She smiled back at him with unrepentant pleasure then pulled from her reticule a card deck. "Does anyone want to play a few games to pass the hours?"

Two days later, they got off the mail coach when it stopped to change horses in Carlisle, the last posting inn before the Scottish border. From here, they would have to make their own way.

Mary was heartily sick of traveling, especially

in such a confined space. She and Barlow both appeared the worse for wear. Her dress was hopelessly wrinkled and the growth of beard on his face gave him the appearance of a highwayman instead of a respected horse breeder.

Nor had they had one moment to themselves since the trip started. Mrs. Katy had paid avid attention to every word and nuance that passed between them. She and Barlow had not had the opportunity to discuss their plans or matters of importance. Instead, they'd slept—most of it uncomfortable—and played cards.

Mrs. Katy had assured them they could learn a great deal about each other from playing whist. She acted as if the game was a preparation of sorts for marriage.

Mary already knew Barlow liked to win but wouldn't cheat to do it. And she was pretty sure he was already aware she wanted to win at all costs—even if she had to tweak the rules to her advantage.

Mrs. Katy had clucked her tongue when they argued over who won a trick—a sign she didn't think a marriage between them held much hope for the future. Barlow and Mary both agreed Mr. Katy was henpecked. And Mary secretly had to admit she'd rather have Barlow belligerent and headstrong than submissive and subservient—at least, until the next time she was in danger of losing.

Now they stood in the village inn yard along-side a busy road, wondering what to do next. Chickens scratched in the dirt. Several dogs barked at some geese. The innkeeper and his lads had changed the mail coach's team in less than three minutes and then had disappeared inside the barn to feed the horses.

An ostler approached, scattering chickens out of his path. "I hear tell the two of you are bound for Gretna."

Barlow stepped protectively in front of Mary. "That's right."

Hooking his thumbs in the waist of his pants, the ostler said, "I could drive you there for a cost. I'm off in that direction with that wagon." He nodded toward the bow-shaped vehicle piled high with hay and pulled by two lumbering oxen.

Mary asked Barlow, "Can't we hire horses?" It would take forever to travel five miles with those beasts.

The ostler answered. "You could, if the inn had any other than those for the stage. They only keep teams here. The innkeeper says it's too much trouble to hire out individual horses."

"I'll check for myself," Barlow answered. He entered the inn, but returned quickly. "How much do you want?" he asked the ostler.

"Twenty shillings."

Mary leaned close to Barlow and lowered her voice. "It's robbery."

"His price is fair and it's the only way we can get there, unless you prefer to walk."

A dismissive note in his voice didn't sit well with her, especially after two days of travel. She frowned, then turned to the ostler. "I'll pay half your price."

"And I'll not be taking you," he answered.

"And you'll be the poorer for it," she said with a careless shrug. "This road is busy. Sooner or later someone else will come along."

"Not in the spring. There's too much work to be done."

She started to walk away, hoping the ostler would call her back.

He didn't.

Barlow was clearly annoyed. "I hope you enjoy walking."

She made a face at him and started for the inn door. "Well, if I must walk, I'm going to do it after eating a decent, leisurely breakfast and not one I've had to wolf down for fear of the mail coach leaving without us."

The ostler called, "Wait."

She stopped, her spirit lifting. "Yes?"

"Fifteen shillings."

"Twelve," she countered.

He glanced at Barlow, who kept silent. "Fifteen," he repeated.

"Done," Mary said. "But I'll have my breakfast first and a chance to freshen up."

The ostler shrugged. "I'll be leaving within the hour, with you or no."

Mary understood his meaning. She waited until the man had turned his back and then gave Barlow a triumphant grin.

Instead of his usual frowning response, he smiled back. "Good job."

For a second, Mary lost sense of time and place. When he looked at her like that, 'twas as if the two of them faced the world together and, yes, he was the one person she would have chosen.

As quickly as they'd come, she tucked these feelings away. No good ever came out of falling in love . . .

She whirled away from him, shocked by the direction of her own thoughts and needing to deny them.

He sensed her change of mood. "Is something the matter?"

"No, nothing," she lied. She walked into the inn without further comment.

An hour later they'd both eaten good, hot food and had taken a moment to freshen up. Barlow had shaved and she'd tied her hair back into a simple braid.

There was no place for them in the ostler's wagon except on top of the newly mowed hay, and they stretched out and relaxed. The day was beautiful and the countryside green from rain. The past several days of cloudy skies gave way to the promise of June and made a soul happy to be alive, even if the oxen pulled the cart at a painfully slow speed.

"Comfortable?" Barlow asked as they rode out of the inn yard. He'd safely buried both of their hats in the loose hay.

Mary nodded. She studied the sky a moment, the scent of hay making her homesick. "I wonder how my horses are doing?"

He lay beside her. "We'll see them soon enough."

"You're right, Barlow," she said with a contented sigh. The day was too perfect to worry.

A low growl was his answer. Blinking, she turned. "Did you growl?"

"I did." He came up on one elbow. "What is my name, Mary?"

Tye. But for the life of her, she couldn't say it. But "Barlow" in a defensive tone of voice came easily.

He sat up with a muttered curse. "You could drive a saint to madness."

"Because I won't use your Christian name."

"Because you don't trust me enough to use it."

His unerring insight put her on guard. She frowned. "Maybe I don't like your name. Besides, I've always called you Barlow."

For several long moments, he scowled at the road behind them. She sat up, uncomfortable with the silence. He wouldn't look at her. She crossed her arms and rested them on her knees, watching him with a cautious eye. He saw too much. It was as if he knew what she was thinking . . . sometimes before she'd had the thought.

"Do you want to call the marriage off?" she said at last.

He turned, his expression inscrutable. She shifted uncomfortably.

Behind them, the ostler burst out into song, singing for his own pleasure and no one else's.

"Barlow?" she asked.

He shrugged. "Ours will be a hell of a marriage."

They rode in silence, neither looking at the other.

Long before she was ready, the ostler shouted back to them, "We've reached the Esk." He nodded to the calm ribbon of water. "Gretna is there over the bridge, right beyond those firs."

Chapter 17

The lumbering hay wagon made its way over the bridge. Tye pretended a nonchalance he was far from feeling. He studied Mary's straight back and wished he could understand her.

He'd known Mary a long time. Back then, he'd been drawn to her because she was the most lovely girl in the parish . . . and he'd been curious, too. After all, the old squire had done everything in his power to destroy Saddlebrook.

But Mary had not been what he'd anticipated. While her mother lay dying, she'd nursed her, at the same time caring for Jane and their baby brother. Their stolen daily rides together had been her only release. She and Tye had found common ground. His own mother had died of consumption. He remembered the fears and the sense of loss, and he could share her pain. The Mary he'd known all those years ago had been on the cusp of womanhood—shy, in many ways forced by circumstances to be old before her time, and hungry for love. They had quickly grown close, a closeness that had included friendship.

With the benefit of time and distance, he realized that one of the reasons he'd felt her rejection so keenly is because she'd also rejected their friendship. To him, that had not been fair.

Jane's information about the beating explained some of Mary's behavior. She had wanted to believe the best of her father even back then. He was the only parent she had left.

But that didn't explain Mary's behavior now. Her stubborn refusal to use his given name irked him. Why could she not give an inch? Or trust him? All through this trip, she'd fight him before she'd agree with him. They'd seesawed back and forth. Sometimes she'd been right . . . but he didn't understand why she must constantly challenge, solely because she had a bad affair with Jergen.

Furthermore, did he truly want to be married to such a difficult creature?

The ostler drove them to a tidy inn settled in amongst the stately firs. A creek ran alongside, rushing its way to Esk. As their driver set the brake, a thin, cheerful woman in a mob cap and apron came to the door.

"Ah, Tommy, did you bring us a pair of love-birds?" she greeted him in a soft burr.

"Aye, Mrs. Donaldson, they are." Tommy jumped down from the wagon.

Tye hopped out too. He held out his hands to help Mary but she stayed where she was. She suspiciously eyed Tommy and Mrs. Donaldson. "The two of you know each other?"

"Tommy brings us many a young couple like yourself wishing to pledge their troth," Mrs. Donaldson replied. "But please, come in, come in," she said, opening the door wider.

Mary didn't budge. "How do we know we are at the right place?" she asked Tye. "The ostler didn't tell us he was known to these people. Something is not right here."

"Everything is fine," he assured her, but still she hung back.

And suddenly, he saw Mary as she was. He finally understood. Her suspicions hadn't grown just from her experience with Jergen. Or with himself. Everyone had betrayed her at one time or the other. Even her mother had died leaving her to raise Jane and Niles. Certainly her father had been too selfish to think of the children.

And she'd done it. Jane and Niles were happy people because Mary had borne the brunt of their father's temper, of the family's obligations and responsibilities.

But her sacrifice had left her scarred. She protected herself with her pride and her arrogance. 'Twas all a sham. Her stubbornness, her pride, her frustrating arrogance was her refuge.

Instead of snapping at her as was most often his wont, he rested his arms on the side of the wagon. She eyed him cautiously. In a low, calm voice, he said, "I don't know if Tom lied to us and spends his day waylaying eloping couples or really is a hard-working sort. I can't tell you what awaits inside the inn. We could find a bishop or a gaggle of highwaymen." He could see her slowly relax.

He continued, "However, at some point, Mary, you will have to trust me. It's not going to be simple. I can't erase the past, but I'll be damned if I'm going to spend the rest of my life having it thrown in my face. I'm not Jergen. I'm not your father."

"I know," she said faintly.

"Then tear down the walls you've built inside you," he begged quietly. He spread his arms like a magician showing he hid no tricks. "I understand you've been alone. Frugality and independence are hard traits to give up when they've been honed out of necessity. But I'm standing here, Mary, willing to offer you everything I have. Everything."

She listened, pale and silent.

He ached to brush a stray tendril of her hair that had come loose from her braid. He ached for the girl he'd once known who had been carefree, whom he had loved. He wanted to make things right, to make her whole again.

"You don't have to be alone," he whispered. "Not anymore."

Her eyes were bright with unshed tears. A small line of worry he'd come to know, and, yes, to adore, appeared between her brows. "I don't know if I can trust. I don't know how."

"There's no trick to it. You take my hand." He held his out.

She didn't move. "Sometimes, I don't know why I act the way I do. Why I accuse first and then question second." Her gaze dropped to his outstretched hand and then back up again. "You may not be receiving the best end of this bargain."

"I'm willing to take the risk. Will you?"

She didn't accept right away. He knew she couldn't. Faith, trust—both those elements took time to build. They could only be earned. There was no elixir, no magic potion, no incantation. The habit of doubt had been taught to her at her father's knee and then effectively justified over the ensuing years.

He waited.

Her sigh carried the weight of the world. She reached out and placed her hand in his.

He wanted more. He would have preferred a joyous declaration, a hug, even a smile. None came. She'd given him all she could.

Disappointment tightened like a band around his heart. "Very well, then, let's be married."

Solemn and ill at ease under the interested gazes of the ostler and the inn woman, Mary let Barlow help her from the wagon. Her legs wobbled a bit unsteadily.

"Och, come now," Mrs. Donaldson said, hurrying over to put a comforting arm around Mary's shoulders. "You dinna have to be afraid." The burr of her accent was strangely reassuring. "All brides are a wee bit nervous on their wedding day—if they have any sense."

She led them into the inn. Tommy followed.

The interior was dark, the walls colored by centuries of peat fires. Their footsteps echoed on the dull wood floor. A cheery blaze burned in the grate.

Barlow had to duck to enter the low-hung doors and even then his head appeared in danger of brushing the ceiling in the inn's main room. He carried their valise.

"He is a tall one, isn't he?" Mrs. Donaldson asked rhetorically. "And handsome, too." Mary nodded, while wondering if she'd be spending the rest of her life listening to other women admire her husband.

But then, what did one expect when she agreed to marry the Buck of the Parish? Her fingertips were cold with nerves.

There were no patrons save for a gray-haired man stretched out between two chairs taking a nap. A book rested on his chest, rising and falling with his snoring.

Mrs. Donaldson leaned over and shook his shoulder. "Mr. Rivaling, do you have a moment to witness a wedding?"

He came awake with a start. His hair stuck out every which way in corkscrew curls. His jaw was lined with a gray beard as if he'd not shaved in days and he was the furthest thing from a vicar in Mary's mind.

"A what?" he demanded gruffly, aggravated at having his sleep disturbed.

"A marriage," Mrs. Donaldson repeated. "Tom has brought this young couple who wants to be married."

Mr. Rivaling digested this information, then picked up the book that had fallen from his lap. With great care, he relocated his lost place, folded over a corner of the page, and closed the book with a snap. "Well, I'm ready then." He stood.

Barlow spoke. "What arrangements should we make?"

"Arrangements?" Mr. Rivaling said, then gave a sharp bark of laughter. "You have arrangements enough. I'm here and you've two witnesses, Tom and Mrs. Donaldson."

"And you are with what church?" Barlow asked. Mary was glad he'd asked the question.

Mr. Rivaling picked a pewter tankard up off the floor and walked over to the bar to refill it from an ale keg. "You don't need a vicar in Scotland. All you need is witnesses like myself, Mrs. Donaldson, and Tommy here."

"Is it legal?"

"In Scotland and recognized in England, but if you don't believe me, you can ask." He pulled a sheaf of parchment from a cubby behind the bar. "This is the marriage certificate. I say the words, you take your vows before witnesses, we all sign it, and you are married right and tight." His Scots accent rolled his *r*'s.

Mary didn't know how she felt about not having a church wedding. This didn't seem proper. She took a step away but stopped. Tye still held her hand . . . and she remembered what he'd said about trust. The tight knot of anxiety inside her eased a bit. She would let him make the decision.

Barlow considered the certificate a moment, then said, "Very well."

"The price is fifty guineas," Mr. Rivaling said. "That includes payment to the three of us and the use of a room for the night."

"Twenty," Mary heard herself say without thinking and could have kicked herself. Barlow had been right, the habit of frugality did die hard.

"Twenty-five," Mr. Rivaling said.

"Done," Barlow said before Mary could speak.

He turned to her. "Some things you don't barter over."

Properly chastised, she wisely decided to keep her peace—although she had saved them twenty-five shillings.

"And do you have a ring?" Mr. Rivaling asked.

"No," Barlow said.

"Well, you must. Here now, Mrs. Donaldson, show the gent what we have to offer."

From behind the bar Mrs. Donaldson pulled out a small jeweler's chest. Inside were gold bands of every width and size. "Pick one you like," Mr. Rivaling said. "The price is extra."

Mary leaned forward to inspect the bands. Barlow dumped the rings on the counter and sifted his way through them. They were of different weights of gold. She waited for him to ask her opinion. She preferred a thick band, solid and smooth, but thin, narrow bands were probably more practical. In spite of what he'd said out by the wagon, their marriage was really more figurative than substantial.

His hand hovered over the rings. She watched carefully. His hand lowered and he chose the one ring she would have chosen for herself, a thick band.

"This one," Barlow said.

"Fifteen guineas," Mr. Rivaling said.

Mary opened her mouth. Barlow eyed her as if

daring her to argue. She closed her mouth. If he was willing to spend fifteen guineas on her, then she'd let him. He slipped it upon her finger. The ring was a perfect fit. Its weight felt good.

"Here now, let me have the ring back," Mr. Rivaling said, "and we'll be on with it." Tom took his place beside Barlow. Mrs. Donaldson moved to stand beside her while Mr. Rivaling remained on the other side of the bar. He reached for a slim leather volume tucked in beside the ale keg. It was a *Book of Common Prayer*. He opened it to the wedding ceremony.

This was it. She was about to be married in almost the same amount of time it took to snap two fingers together—

"I need a moment," Mary blurted out.

Barlow pulled back, his brows coming together. She knew what he thought. "Just a moment," she pleaded with him.

He looked away.

"Of course, you need a moment," her ally, Mrs. Donaldson, said. "You haven't even had a chance to freshen up. Come with me. Pour a tankard for our bridegroom, Mr. Rivaling."

Mary picked up the valise and followed Mrs. Donaldson down a narrow hallway to a private room in the back. "I'll return with a pitcher of water," the woman said as she opened a window to air out the room.

The room was clean and neat. A double bed

covered with a colorful quilt dominated much of the floor space but there was a table, two chairs, and a wash stand. She went to the mirror over the washstand and took a critical look at herself and was shocked.

Two days of traveling had taken their toll. Tye Barlow was not getting a bargain. There were far prettier women and, certainly, much younger ones. Nor was she the sweetest of personalities.

I'll take the risk. Will you? The words he had spoken to her outside the inn echoed in her mind.

She faced her reflection in the mirror. Barlow would never leave her like John. Barlow was a good, honorable man, and they shared an equal passion for their horses. Such was enough on which to build a marriage.

And someday . . . maybe . . . he might learn to love her.

There was that pesky idea again, always lurking in the far corners of her mind. Love. She'd claimed she didn't believe in such a thing and yet, at this moment, she wanted to believe very much.

But if that was going to happen, he was right— she would have to change.

Today was her wedding day. 'Twas a better time than most for a new beginning.

She began untying the laces of the blue-striped muslin she'd worn for the last two days. Her hair appeared as if the mice had had a tea party in it.

She'd have to take the time to brush it out because she wanted to be fresh and, yes, as beautiful as she could be for him.

Through the open window drifted the scent of honeysuckle. A tangle of vines grew along the edge of the inn. Honeysuckle. Here was an omen.

After Mrs. Donaldson delivered the water, Mary shut the door and set to work.

Tye did not like waiting. He paced the floor. Mr. Rivaling and Tom were drinking on his tab. When they started to help themselves to a third round, he said, "This one is on you, gentlemen."

Both men set their tankards down. Mrs. Donaldson smiled.

A step sounded in the hallway behind him. "At last," he started, letting his impatience show. But when he turned, all complaints fled his mind.

Mary had changed . . . in every way.

She'd removed her wrinkled traveling dress and put on one of simple light green muslin. Her hair, loose and flowing down her back, had been brushed until it shone. Then, she had pulled the sides of it up and secured them high on her head with honeysuckle vine.

She appeared as beautiful and free-spirited as a wood nymph . . . and as demure and special as a bride.

Mrs. Donaldson clapped her hands and even Rivaling and Tom appeared impressed.

Tye crossed the room. He held out his hand. "Will you be my wife?"

A tinge of pink colored her cheeks. Her lashes swept down and he was entranced. Instead of answering, she placed a shy hand in his.

Tye led her to the others. "Mr. Rivaling, we are ready."

Everyone took their positions. Rivaling set his open prayer book on the bar. Beside the book, he placed the marriage certificate, pen and ink. He cleared his throat. "Miss Gates, what is your Christian name?"

"Mary Somerset Gates." He dutifully wrote it on the certificate.

"Your address?"

"Edmundson, Lyford Meadows." But not for long, Tye told himself. Soon, she would claim Saddlebrook as her home. As *their* home.

"Very well. Are you here of your own free will?" Rivaling asked.

"What sort of question is that?" Tye demanded.

"A question I have to ask," Rivaling replied. " 'Tis the law."

Tye frowned.

"Yes," Mary replied.

"Very well." Rivaling swung his attention over to Tye, who had to answer the same questions.

When he was done, he pushed aside the marriage certificate, picked up the prayer book, and started reading the traditional service of the Church of England.

Tye listened to the words with half an ear. The majority of his attention was focused on the woman standing beside him. He prayed he was worthy of her.

Marriage to Mary would not be easy and yet, at this moment, it was the one thing he desired with all his heart.

A married man. Brewster and Blacky would never believe he'd finally been run to ground without their help.

"Mr. Barlow," Rivaling said, "wilt thou have this woman to be thy wedded wife, to live in God's ordinance in the holy state of matrimony?"

"Aye, I will," Tye answered.

Mary watched him now, the expression in her green eyes serious.

"Wilt thou love her, comfort her, honor, and keep her in sickness and in health; and, forsaking all others, keep thee only unto her, as long as ye both shall live?"

"I will." He added meaning to his words by giving her hand a small squeeze.

Rivaling shifted his attention over to her. A small shiver went through her. Out of fear? Why need she fear him?

"Mary Somerset Gates, wilt thou have this man to be thy wedded husband, to live together after God's ordinance in the holy state of matrimony?"

Her responding, "I will," was so faint Tye had to strain to hear it.

Rivaling continued, "Wilt thou love him, comfort him, and obey him?"

Mary hesitated.

Tye almost groaned aloud. He should have anticipated the word *obey*. Mary would never agree to what she could not promise.

Then, to his surprise, she said, "I will."

He dropped his jaw open. Mary looked at him. She smiled. "There are some things one doesn't haggle over," she reminded him.

In that moment, Tye knew he was in love. But not the transitory love of his youth when he'd been infatuated by the unattainable. Or the love he'd nursed out of his hurt pride.

No, this love shook his whole being to the core . . . and he knew he'd never be the same.

This strong-willed female beside him, this beguiling, frustrating, intelligent, intriguing, and often irritating woman had captured his heart. In truth, the only time she really aggravated him was when she was right and he wrong.

Nor would he have her any other way . . . save one. He'd have her love him. Not just trust him, or need him, or feel affection for him.

He wanted love.

Listening to her repeat the remainder of her vows, he told himself those promises should be enough.

He feared they wouldn't be.

But Tye was a patient man. He'd always gotten what he wanted, and he wanted her more than any one thing in his life. He wasn't marrying for Tanner. He was marrying her for himself.

"Take the ring," Rivaling prompted him, "and place it on her finger with these words—'with this ring, I thee wed.' "

"With this ring, I thee wed," Tye answered dutifully and then added, "Forever and ever, until death we part." He slipped the ring on her finger. "You are mine, Mary. Mine."

"I pray you never regret this day," she whispered.

Rivaling finished the ceremony in a voice that rang through the rafters. "Then, what God joins together let no man put asunder. I pronounce you man and wife."

Mrs. Donaldson clapped her hands. Tom started around the bar, heading toward the ale keg, but Tye had different plans.

For two long days in a coach, he'd had her sitting beside him, twisting, turning, and he could not touch her. Her kiss had branded him and now the time had come to finish what they had started.

He'd waited long enough. "Ms. Donaldson, where is our room?"

"Down the hall."

He swung his wife up into his arms and without a backward glance headed toward the bedroom.

Chapter 18

Mary didn't know whether to laugh with joy or protest in embarrassment. As they left the room she saw Mrs. Donaldson watching with a bemused expression and Tom and Mr. Rivaling grinning from ear to ear.

She started to say something but stopped. His expression was that of a primal animal intent on mating. The moment had come. Barlow had tired of waiting.

He kicked open the door to the bedroom she'd used earlier to change. He pushed it shut with her feet, walked her over to the bed, and dropped her on the mattress next to the valise.

The cotton-stuffed mattress was lumpy and out of shape. The bed ropes sagged in the middle.

The valise tumbled into her lap. She pushed it off onto the ground and braced herself.

She knew what to expect. The marriage act held no mystery. Yes, it had been years ago, but her life was breeding. There would be some pleasant kissing, some groping. Then, if she shut her eyes and let him have his way, it would be all over. All she had to do was keep quiet and lie there.

He stood over the bed, looking down at her. The white curtains in the window lifted and shifted in the spring breeze. She knew he wanted her. His leather breeches and the tightness across the crotch left nothing to the imagination.

With slow, deliberate movements, he removed his brown wool jacket. He folded it neatly over the carved wood footboard. His gaze never wavered from hers.

She waited, her heart hammering against her chest.

Then, he spread his arms and fell face first on the bed beside her, boots and all.

She yelped her surprise, falling back. The bed ropes bounced. His weight rolled her toward him. His arm stayed her, his hand resting on her hip.

Tye turned his head on the pillow. For a long moment, he studied her. Laughter lurked in the depth of his eyes. "Wasn't what you expected, was it?"

She shook her head no . . . and waited, anticipating any moment for him to start hiking up her skirts that were already up to her knees.

"I'm not him, Mary."

"Who?" But she knew.

He traced a circle pattern on her hip with his thumb and didn't answer.

She shifted her gaze to the knot in his neck cloth. "I know you aren't him. Why did you think I was expecting something else?"

"You are tense. Your knees are pressed so tight together I'd need a vise to separate them. The expression on your face is far from loverly. In fact, I imagine you've approached the task of sheath cleaning with more relish." His hand left her hip. He folded the pillow beneath his head and rested the weight of one leg over hers. "The next move is up to you."

"I don't understand."

"Mary." His tone let her know he expected better. "You know what I mean. If I were to jump on top of you and ravage you senseless—even as pleasant as I find the idea—you'd be comparing us. You already are."

"No, I wasn't." But she had been. When he didn't respond, she said, "Then what are we going to do? Just lie here?"

He rubbed his leg against hers, an unthreatening gesture and yet intimate. "I hope not. But it's your choice."

"What if I just go to sleep?" She feigned a yawn.

He laughed softly. A lock of his hair fell over his forehead. "You won't." He leaned closer. "Because you want me as much as I want you."

He was right. She could feel the heat of him and felt an answering response in her own body. Now that she was over her initial anxiety, she almost ached for his touch.

Still . . . "What makes you believe you know everything I'm thinking?"

His eyes softened. "Ah, Mary. Every thought your active, lovely mind possesses crosses your face. I can tell when you are afraid or when you are going to dig in your heels and be stubborn. I almost know your expressions better than my own." He pulled her hair around and over her shoulder. He slid his fingers down the length of it to just below her breast. "But what I'd really like to see is joy. I've yet to see such a thing change the lines of your face."

"I've not known much joy in my life," she said soberly. "I don't know how one even goes about finding it."

"Ah, Mary, it finds you. And one day, when you least expect it, you realize you've had it all along."

She considered his words, then smiled. "I didn't know you were a poet, Barlow."

An arrested look crossed his features as if he'd had a thought from somewhere else. "I suppose

I'm becoming one," he said slowly, a hint of wonder in his voice.

She smiled, then made the first move. She touched the side of his face and traced the line of his whiskers. He turned and gently kissed her fingers.

"Why do you care so much?" she asked. No one had ever worried about her.

"I'm your husband."

His answer went straight to her heart. Before she could stop herself, she threw her arms around him.

Tye was ready for her. He gathered her close, rolling her over so she rested on top of him. She looked down into his rugged, handsome face and her heart surged with gladness. This man was *hers. Her* husband.

She leaned down and kissed him with everything she had.

'Twas all it took. His arms crushed her to him. He kissed her back, greedy, hungry. Mary returned it. She wanted all of him. He was hers.

They started to undress each other, tugging and pulling at clothing, eager to remove all restrictions. His fingers were more skilled than hers. He had laces undone and her dress down around her waist in no time.

She managed to remove his neck cloth and shirt, but the hardest was his boots. When she sat up to pull them off, he followed, causing her to straddle his lap. His arms held her there while he pressed his lips against her chemise, sucking one nipple through the thin material.

Mary couldn't breathe. She couldn't think. She curled her fingers in his hair, lost in sensation. No one had ever touched her in this way before. The blood surged through her veins. Her nipples were hard circles. He cared for each one. His tongued teased and stroked, movements echoed deep within her, at her very core.

Then he slid his hand beneath her petticoats to touch her . . . intimately.

Mary started.

"Shhhhhh," he steadied. "Relax. Let yourself feel." His fingers circled the sensitive nub, round and round until her breathing began to hasten. She pressed herself closer to him and he slipped his fingers inside her just as he covered her breast with his mouth.

She squeezed her knees against his hips, digging her nails into his shoulders. The heat of his mouth, and his touch, his magic, magic touch robbed her of reason.

But her body knew what to do. She tightened around him. Arching against his hand, she begged, "Please, please."

He knew her body better than she did. He knew what she wanted, why she begged. He answered her desires. "Tye," she whispered.

His fingers thrust deeper—and Mary left the

earth. Suddenly everything went bowstring taut. Then, 'twas as if she'd turned into a shooting star. A bright, beautiful, flaring star.

She cried his name, hugging him to her, wanting him deeper. Who had known anything such as this had existed? She hadn't. Ever.

He rolled her down off his lap and onto the bed. Stretching out beside her, he ran his palm up across along her waist to cup her breast. The air from the window chilled her hot skin, but Mary couldn't move as wave after wondrous wave flowed through her.

Staring down at her, Tye watched Mary lost in the throes of pleasure, marveling at how passionately responsive she was. He wanted to shout a thousand hosannas that this incredible, mercurial creature was his. Of course, it had taken all his willpower to give her this.

She opened her eyes, her gaze focusing on him. "What did you do?" she asked weakly.

In answer, he circled the wet material around her tight, jutting nipple with his finger. She sighed, the sound enchanting.

"You called me Tye."

Her lips smiled. "Did I . . . Tye?"

He kicked off one boot, then another. They fell to the floor with a dull thud. She eyed him with lazy suspicion. "You could remove them all the time?"

"Ummm-hmmm. But it was more fun to let you do it."

She rose up on one elbow, her hair hanging loose over her shoulder. Her eyes reflected the aftermath of passion. "Is it always like this?"

"With me," he corrected. The jealousy he'd felt all these years for Jergen evaporated. The other man no longer existed in his mind. He was gone.

And now—it was his turn.

He rolled on his back, placed his hands behind his head and ordered quietly, "Unbutton me."

Her eyes widened at the command, then narrowed with interest. He loved watching the play of emotions across her face. She tossed her hair back and did as he asked, running her fingers down the center line of his chest.

At the first brush of her fingers against his skin, Tye sucked in, her touch sending a delicious wave of anticipation through him.

His reaction intrigued her. She circled his navel—and would have playfully retraced her path, except he'd had enough.

He captured her hand and brought it down to the front of his breeches where he was so damn hard, he must find relief fast or else he didn't know what he'd do.

She freed the top button. Her gaze met his. She unbuttoned the second with more expertise. The tip of her finger grazed the head of his arousal. He jerked, straining toward her.

A slow, knowing smile spread across her face. She slipped the third, fourth and fifth buttons from their holes and slipped her hand beneath the leather of his breeches.

Ty thought he'd shoot straight up through the ceiling. He covered her hand with his. She'd unman him if she kept this up.

Her gaze met his, her expression somber. Then she surprised him. She leaned over and rubbed her smooth cheek against his velvety head.

Tye almost roared with need.

He'd had enough of play.

With swift, practiced movement, he shucked off his breeches and socks. He turned to her, boldly naked.

She sat on her knees, her heart beating so loud he could hear it. Her dress was still around her waist. She shrugged off the straps of her chemise, freeing her taut breasts. The nipples were still dark red and hard as pebbles from his loving. She pushed her skirts down. He helped her pull them off and toss them aside.

He moved closer. The tip of his erection brushed her stomach. He pulled at the ribbons of her garters holding her stockings in place until they were all undone. She rubbed the tips of her breasts against his chest.

Her body had been shaped and honed through hard work. She was nothing like the plump, pleasant lovers of his past. Her breasts were firm, her arms strong. Her sex was still wet and ready—and Tye could wait no more.

He took her by both arms, pushed her back on the bed and slid himself in her with one smooth thrust.

She felt like heaven. Her muscles tightened. For a second she couldn't move. She *was* heaven.

He thrust himself deeper. Her legs came up to cradle him. Buried to the hilt, he whispered, "What is my name?"

With a shuddering sigh, she answered, "Tye, Tye, Tye."

He began moving. She didn't meet him at first, but lay docile. He kissed her neck. "Come with me, love," he urged.

'Twas all he needed to say. Jergen may have had sex with her, but Tye was her first lover.

She started meeting his thrusts, timid at first but with a growing ardor. She was so tight, so hot . . . and had a fierce passion to match his own. She gave as good as she took. She was his mate, his other half, his wife.

He could feel her muscles quiver with the beginnings of release. She cried out his name, her legs wrapping his waist.

Then, and only then, did he seek his own. Three long, strong thrusts and he let himself go within her . . . filling her.

It had never been like this. Never.

* * *

Tye held himself as long as he could and then he collapsed, gathering her up in his arms, as if she was his anchor in a raging tide. She wrapped herself around him just as tightly.

Lost in the aftermath, they were both quiet.

From the open window drifted everyday sounds. An oxen called for his supper. Birds sang. The curtains flapped against the window.

But there on the bed, Tye knew his world had been changed forever.

A shiver went through her as the breeze cooled their flesh. Reluctantly, he moved, leaving her warmth. He flipped the bed covers over them.

Mary relaxed against him with a contented sigh. Cuddling, she closed her eyes and soon fell asleep.

Tye watched over her, awed by what had taken place.

What had David once said? He'd been describing his feelings for Jane. Tye remembered: David had called her his light, his reason for being.

Tye had laughed. Now, he understood.

He lowered his lips close to Mary's cheek. "My light," he whispered. "My reason for being." He settled in next to her. "My love."

Mary woke to find herself buried in the covers, her body spooned against her husband's. Tye was still fast asleep. By the light through the window, she could tell it was late evening.

She ran her hand across his back. Her body still tingled in its secret places from his lovemaking. She wanted more and contemplated what would happen if she woke him.

The gold of her wedding band on her ring finger glowed in the dim light. She touched the warm metal. She was Mrs. Tye Barlow, wife of the Parish Buck.

The sobering thought was that her husband hadn't married her by choice, but out of obligation. Like a legendary knight of old, he had rescued her from her own follies and mistakes. She didn't like the idea ... but she told herself he'd also wanted Tanners Darby Boy.

And even if he hadn't married her for love, she was suddenly fiercely filled with enough love for both of them.

She wrapped her arms around him, and kissed his back, tasting the warm texture of his skin.

His body moved. He rolled over to face her, the covers up around his shoulders. His face was lined with sleep, his hair boyishly mussed.

"Hello," he said, his voice rough and deep.

"Hello."

He grinned. It was heart-stopping, that little grin was. Heart-stopping and full of mischief. "I know another way of saying hello," he said.

"What is that?"

He raised a devilish eyebrow. His hand slid to her waist and, in one smooth movement, she was on her back. He settled against her, hard and ready.

She wiggled. "I'm not certain what you mean?" she teased. "Perhaps you should show me."

He did.

Mary and Tye didn't come out of their room for three days. Mrs. Donaldson delivered hot meals. What she thought of them, Mary didn't want to know or care. She was too lost in her own passions to think beyond the confines of these four walls.

They made love two, three times a day and all night. She couldn't seem to get her fill of him. Tye was an inventive lover, a passionate man who enjoyed all of his senses. They made love in every position possible, including in a tub of warm bath water with their bodies covered with soap. Of course, he was such a large man, he barely fit in Mrs. Donaldson's small hip tub, but they had fun trying to get both of them in it. In the end, they made a terrible mess, but the endeavor had been well worth it.

When they weren't making love, they were entwined in each other's arms, content enough to be together. They didn't talk much. If they did have conversation, she noticed it was mostly about their horses—a safe topic.

He enjoyed making plans for Tanner. But Mary had lost her enthusiasm for the subject. Yes, she

wanted Spender's Stud. But now, she was more
nervous about what would happen between
them when they returned to Lyford Meadows.
There were moments when she wished they
never had to leave Scotland.

There were even moments when she was jealous of the place Tanner held in his imagination.

He never tired of making her say his name.
'Twas a source of great pride to him and she
laughingly obliged. She toyed with the idea of
professing her love—and yet, she wanted a sign
from him before she could be more open.

However, save for making love to her until she
was sated with desire, Tye said nothing. And
she'd been too seasoned by life to believe that the
act of making love was love itself . . . although the
alchemy between them was powerful.

Occasionally, she would catch him watching
her, the expression in his eyes unreadable. She
asked him what he was thinking. He hesitated before answering. She waited, her heart pounding
in her thought.

He smiled. "I was thinking about how much I
want to be in you right now."

They made love then . . . but Mary sensed his
thoughts had been in a different direction.

The night before they had to leave, he spread
their monies out on the bed and they counted it
all. She wore her chemise. He was naked.

"I left a deposit with Lord Spender of four hundred pounds," she told him. Then added, "He is going to be surprised when he learns whom I've married."

Tye stopped counting and sat back. "What *did* you tell him back then? I admit, Mary, your ability to haggle any deal amazes me. I prided myself on being a good bargainer. You're better."

She laughed, pleased with the compliment. "I told him the marriage was one my father had arranged."

Her words did not earn the answering laugh she'd expected. Instead, he looked up sharply. "Your father is probably turning in his grave right now."

"Hmmm, yes," she agreed.

There was a pause. Carefully, he started stacking the coins. "Does it bother you he would have disapproved?"

Mary swung her hair over her shoulder. "What do you mean?"

"You know he didn't like me. Or the thought of us together." He leveled off two stacks, moving the additional coins to start a third.

" 'Twas a long time ago. In the past."

He nodded absently . . . and then pushed over the stacks of coins. "Some people will have his same reaction."

She didn't understand his meaning. "Because my father was the squire?"

"And I a mere groom's grandson?" He did not look at her.

She came up on all fours. "Tye, this can't bother you, can it? I mean, it doesn't bother me, or Jane. Niles won't care. In fact, he has a bit of hero worship of you."

He started picking up the money. She stopped him by placing her hand over his. "Tye?"

He looked up then. "But what of you, Mary? There have been times you've made my place clear. Or that I am no gentleman? When we return to Lyford Meadows, will you regret your decision?"

She sat back on her heels. "So you have wondered the same thing I have worried over."

"Which is?"

"What happens when we return to our homes, to the world we both know?"

His brows came together. "What do you think?"

She reached for three of the coins and rubbed them between her fingers, uncertain how much to reveal. Especially now that she knew the same doubts had crossed his mind. "I think we shall go on like we are now."

He poured a handful of coins into the money purse and said, "You married down, love. Are you going to regret it someday?"

"I'll honor my wedding vows. I'm your wife."

"I know." He paused, a muscle tightening in his jaw. "I know."

"I'm the village eccentric. For years people have accepted me, but they have also laughed. Are *you* going to have any regrets?"

He shook his head. "You are clever, Mary. I've a woman with the mind of a solicitor."

"I've married a man whom I am proud to call husband." She did not confess love. 'Twould be giving too much of herself away.

Her answer clearly pleased him.

However, he did not answer in kind.

Instead, he pushed the money bag off onto the floor and reached for her, pushing down first one shoulder of her chemise, then another, before pushing her back onto the bed.

She opened to him. She was learning she could not resist him, a curse of her passionate nature. But the doubts she harbored had been reinforced.

They made love. He took his time and no matter how impatient she was, he insisted they progress slowly until she was panting with mindless need.

'Twas almost as if he were demonstrating the power he held over her. If she confessed her love, what would he do then?

When they'd finished, she turned on her side, away from him.

He rose up over her. "Mary, is something wrong?"

She pretended to be asleep.

The next morning, they left their haven and returned to the real world. They left for Lyford Meadows.

Chapter 19

Mary and Tye took the mail coach again until they had to change and hire a post chaise to carry them on to Lyford Meadows. The mail coach was crowded and there was little privacy for conversation.

Consequently, whether real or imagined, she sensed them drifting apart. Her growing sense of insecurity was spurred on by her ambivalent feelings about going home.

Home, in her mind, meant Edmundson. And yet, it was no longer her home. She knew without asking Tye would not entertain a suggestion that they live on her family's estate. In all of his talk about the future, Saddlebrook figured prominently.

She twisted the gold band on her finger. She'd

never stepped foot in the hallways of Saddle-brook. She'd spied on the house once because she'd been curious to see what it looked like. That had been years ago. The main house had been built on the ruins of an old abbey. It was a sprawling building, all on one floor. In her mind, his house lacked the stately grace of Edmundson.

'Twas said Tye had made great improvements over the past ten years. She wondered if they would make a difference in her reservations.

As the miles flowed by, Edmundson became the representation of the freedom she had given up through marriage.

She wanted to believe her sacrifice was worth it—and perhaps it would be, if Tye sacrificed too. But in her agitated mind, she feared he had gained all and she nothing. Her doubts created through her active imagination a premonition of impending disaster.

She could not explain her pessimism save to say experience had been a hard teacher.

The first day of their trip, she experimented with compensating for her fears by attempting to be the most docile, pleasant wife a man could ever have.

Tye asked her if she was feeling herself.

She dropped the pretense.

When they hired the private post chaise—a single horse vehicle with a post boy, a lad of eighteen, riding the horse as driver—he waited until they'd pulled out onto the road to say, "You've been very quiet."

She almost sighed her relief. He wanted to talk. Maybe now, they could clear the air between them and settle her mind.

But then, his arm slid around her shoulders, his other arm around her waist. "I've needed to be alone with you." He began to nibble the sensitive line of her neck.

Immediately, Mary felt the quickening inside her his touch inspired—and she panicked.

Was this all that was between them?

"Tye, the driver—"

"Is busy." His hand cupped her breast; his thumb grazed her nipple. His tongue outlined her ear. "Dear God, I missed this." He shifted, bringing her up to sit in his lap. He nuzzled open the pearl buttons of her blue and white muslin dress, opening them with his teeth. His breath heated her skin.

"Tye?" She placed her hands on his shoulders, uncertain whether to struggle or give in to desire.

He began unbuttoning his breeches while still nuzzling her breast.

"We shouldn't," she said, her body opening and ready for him. "I mean, how will it appear when we arrive home?"

"You're beautiful." He tasted the lace on her chemise.

"But shouldn't we t-talk?" she asked, the tip of his tongue on her skin sending a shiver through her.

"Later," he murmured. "We'll talk later. I need you now." He lifted her skirts and shifted her weight over him. His mouth covered her breast . . . and she was lost. He thrust, entering her with one smooth motion.

Mary closed her eyes, letting his powerful legs do the work for both of them. But she felt, oh dear Lord, she felt every movement, especially when coupled with the sway of the coach.

I need you, he'd said. And her woman's heart wept a little. She needed him—but she also wanted his love.

And still, she could not stop from losing herself in the pleasure of their joining. She couldn't resist him. He never took without giving. And when at last her muscles tightened and she reached the pinnacle of fulfillment, when her body and senses were full of him, he claimed her.

For a shining moment as he filled her, she pretended to believe he loved her.

He hugged her tight, his breathing heavy. He kissed each breast and raised his gaze to hers. With a lazy grin, he boasted, "I didn't even muss your hair."

Mary heard him as if from a distance. Her body still hummed with fulfillment but she felt . . .

common. Something she had refused to let herself think when she was dealing with the scandal of John.

And she was sadly coming to the realization that what she wanted was Tye to love her—and nothing less would do.

She slid off his lap.

He knew something was wrong. She could feel him watch her, even if she couldn't meet his gaze as she straightened her skirts. She checked the pins in her hair.

"Mary, what is the matter? You've been distant ever since we left Gretna."

I'm in love with you. "I'm nervous, I suppose, about Tanner and going home."

There was a beat of silence. "You're not"—he hesitated—"sorry, are you?"

Deliberately, she pretended ignorance. "Sorry about what?" She forced herself to look at him, wanting him to say the words.

For a long second their gazes held. Something was going on inside his mind, but she could not divine what. She could tell him how she felt . . . but if she did, and even if he said what she wanted to hear—would his words be true?

"Why do you believe I should be sorry?" she prodded.

"No reason." His mouth twisted into a grim parody of a smile. "Forget I asked."

He righted his clothes then, his movements ef-

ficient, economical. But when he was done, he
slid to the other side of the chaise. He still took up
most of the cramped quarters of the coach, but he
became so distant, he might as well have been in
a separate vehicle.

For a long time, they sat silent, the tension
thick between them.

Then, unexpectedly, he said, "I don't know
what you want, Mary. I don't understand you."

His words were tight, angry.

She had an answer but her pride held it back.

And then, there was no time for any response,
because the pace of the coach changed. Tye lowered the glass window. They had reached the outskirts of Lyford Meadows.

"We're home," he said.

"Yes, home," she echoed.

His hand came across the seat, searching for
hers. Her nerves were stretched too taut. But
when he touched her, she clasped his fingers.

It was enough.

A rain shower had gone before them. The slate
roof tops and stone paths were shiny wet and
smelled of fresh earth.

They drove by the smithy. Blacky was nowhere
to be seen. His brother tended the fire. He
stopped pumping the billows to watch the chaise
drive by. Tye waved but Ned didn't recognize
them.

"I wonder where Blacky is?" He sat forward,

his blue eyes keen with anticipation. "We'll see if Brewster is in. Then we'll call on Spender and claim the horse."

She nodded.

He leaned out the window and called out directions to the post boy. Almost as if they heard his voice, several women stuck their heads out of their doors. In truth, they were testing the weather after the rain. However, when they saw the chaise, they came out. Children poured out behind them, ready to play.

Tye waved. Several people recognized him. A post chaise and the return of a villager was big news in Lyford Meadows. The children started running after their coach, calling Tye's name and asking if it was true he was married.

Brewster was waiting for them outside the pub. He opened the door before the coach rolled to a complete stop. "Come now, both of you, out! What is this we've heard? Is it true you've married?" The children and several village women gathered around, curious to hear the news.

Tye jumped to the ground. He greeted Brewster sounding like the happiest of men. " 'Tis true. I'd like you to meet Mrs. Barlow." He said her formal title with a touch of defiance that was not lost on her.

Mary pasted a smile on her face and leaned out of the coach to wave. She'd known these people all her life, but she was unprepared for their reaction to her.

Brewster's jaw dropped. "Miss Gates, you're a lady."

Several women surged forward. One woman, Mrs. Peters, who was known for her active service to the church, said, "My prayers have been answered. She's in skirts. Ah, Mr. Barlow, you have worked a miracle."

Mary looked down at the blue striped muslin dress she wore. It had been a long time since anyone in Lyford Meadows had seen her without breeches. Tye held out his hand. She picked up her straw bonnet, tied the ribbons around her neck, and climbed out.

Brewster shook his head. "You are a vision, Mrs. Barlow." To Tye, he said, "At first, I suspected you were marrying her to get that horse for yourself, but now . . ."

He indicated with a flourish of his hands her change of dress, but his words went straight to her insecurities. Especially when Tye didn't correct him in any way.

Mrs. Peters started questioning Mary about London and Scotland. She tried to answer as best she could, but gave the woman only half an ear. Her real attention was focused on what Brewster was saying to her husband.

Tye was being teased unmercifully. Two other

of the village lads joined Brewster, and some of their low comments brought heat to Mary's cheeks. Those sorts of things stopped when Vicar Nesmith approached.

"What is this I hear?" he chided Tye. "I was upset to hear you'd run off. As were my daughters. Still, my congratulations. When are you coming in for a proper church ceremony?"

Mary strained to hear Tye's answer but at the same moment, the village seamstress Mrs. Darby asked if she could have a closer look at Mary's London bonnet. As Mary removed it and handed it to her, she heard Brewster interject soberly, " 'Tis bad news about Lord Spender."

"Aye, 'tis," Vicar Nesmith agreed.

Mary took a step toward the men even as Tye asked, "What do you mean?"

"His soul has been commended to God," the vicar said.

"Aye, he popped his cork the day after you left," Brewster clarified in his blunt way.

Mary grabbed Tye's arm, uncertain if she believed her own ears.

"He couldn't be dead," Tye said in disbelief. He looked to Mary. "He appeared healthy last time I saw him only three weeks ago."

"We never know when God will call us home," the vicar responded.

Mary had a more pressing concern. "What of the horse? What of Tanners Darby Boy?"

"Why nothing, I suppose," Brewster said. "Spender's fop of a nephew returned in time for the funeral and has taken over the estate. I imagine the horse is still there."

She turned to Tye. "I left a deposit on him," she reminded him.

"I know." His brow furrowed with concern. "He should honor the terms of the sale."

Vicar Nesmith added helpfully, "I do know a solicitor was up from London to see the nephew yesterday. The approval may have already been given for the title. Spender had no other family so there was really no question in the matter."

"Yes, well," Tye said, "I'll feel more at ease when Tanner is in my stable. Let's go, Mary."

She climbed into the chaise, but his choice words, such as *"my* stable" and *"I"* were not lost on her. He gave directions to the post boy and joined her in the coach. Brewster called out an invitation for them to come by for a pint when they had Tanner settled.

They rode in silence. Mary put on her bonnet, tying and untying the ribbons. She didn't know what she would do if she'd lost Tanner. Not after everything she'd done to buy him. And, of course, Tye would have married her for no reason.

He said, "You don't want to be married to me, do you?"

His words shocked her. She turned in the seat toward him. "Why do you say this?" Was he preparing to tell her he was through? Her heart pounded against her chest.

"Because it's written all over your face," he said bitterly. "And in the village, you ignored the women while they congratulated you. You acted as if you didn't want to hear a word about our marriage."

"No," she said quickly. "I was trying to eavesdrop on what Brewster was saying to you."

He sat back in the far corner. "You were worrying, too. I'm accustomed to plain speaking, Mary. So pardon me if I don't dress up the words, but you've changed your mind, haven't you? Every day since Gretna, you've grown quieter and quieter. Earlier, in the coach, between us . . . something was bothering you, but you don't want to confide in me, do you?"

Mary placed her hand on his leg. "You're wrong. I've never thought such a thing." The moment she said the words, she felt guilty because she hadn't trusted him.

He read the guilt on her face. His fist hit the door with surprising force. "Enough, Mary! You could try a saint. You've got something on your mind. I know. Well, go ahead and say it. If it is the horse that is holding you back, well, here, I don't want him. I'll help you buy him, but he's yours. I'm done with it. I'll not be wasting my time trying to be the gentleman you think you deserve."

He was giving up the horse?

He cared for her more than Tanner.

Stunned, Mary had to collect her scrambled brains. "Tye, I never felt the way you think I do. Not ever. And after London and all you've done for me, I don't believe there is a more noble man in this world than you."

His frown deepened. "Noble? *I'm* noble," he said to the coach in general, sarcasm lacing his words. "I'm bloody, bloody noble."

"And-I-love-you." She said the words fast, running them together before she lost her courage.

For a second they seemed to shimmer in the air between them.

She waited, unable to breathe.

Tye tilted his head as if uncertain he'd heard correctly. "What did you say?"

She placed a hand against her stomach. She didn't know if she could admit love again, not without some sign from him . . .

"Mary?" he prompted.

The coach turned up the drive leading onto Lord Spender's estate.

Tye slid closer. He brought his arm behind the seat behind her. "Go ahead, Mary. Say what you said again."

She drew in a deep breath. Her hands shook and she clasped them in her lap. "I love you." Another deep shuddering breath and with more courage than she'd thought she possessed, she repeated, "I love you, I love you . . ." She paused and added softly, "I love *you*."

Tears burned her eyes. She blinked them back. She didn't know what she would do if he rejected her love.

"You love me," he said simply.

She nodded. "I think I fell in love with you the night of Mrs. Willoughby's soirée, when you talked me into going inside. Or maybe it was the night you bopped John in the nose. Perhaps it was when you had me so angry in the park, I could spit. I do know I liked the kiss—"

His mouth covered hers, swallowing her words. He kissed her, but this kiss was different. Softer than the others, yet more possessive. She put her arms around his neck and kissed him back.

At last, they had to break for air. Mary opened her eyes and what she saw in his face made her soul dance.

Tye touched her lips with the pad of his thumb. "Dear God, I'd never hoped to hear those words from you. I love you, Mary," he said. "I've always loved you."

"Always?"

He nodded. "I may have pretended the horse was the motive, but in truth, I married you because I couldn't let anyone else have you. 'Twas the reason I followed you to London, although I didn't know it myself. I believed I'd gotten over you. In truth, I've been in love with you since we first kissed. But I couldn't imagine *you* would ever love me."

"Tye, how could I not? I've spent my life comparing all others to you."

"Including Jergen?"

"No," she admitted. "I believe my infatuation with him had to do with his being the exact opposite. And for years, when other women would make eyes over you, I realize now that I was jealous. I had to tear you down in order to make the whole situation palatable."

He laughed. "And you were always the one woman who never bored me. Even when we were at cross purposes." He kissed her again, taking his time. The world could have stopped and she'd not have given a care as long as she was in his arms.

They hadn't even realized the chaise had stopped moving.

Someone cleared his throat. Reluctantly, they ended the kiss. The post boy stood by the window. "We're here, sir, where you wanted to go." He lowered his voice. "That's the butler there waiting for you to get out of the coach so he can announce you." He opened the door.

Instead of being embarrassed, Tye and Mary both laughed. "Good advice," Tye answered. He took a moment to straighten Mary's bonnet. "You're beautiful," he said. "Now, let's go buy the finest stud in all England."

"Yes," she agreed.

He helped her down from the chaise, picked up the valise containing their money, and together they walked up the house's front steps. Black mourning crape draped the door beneath a wreath made of the same stuff. William, Lord Spender's butler, wore a black armband.

Somberly, he said in greeting, "Miss Gates, Mr. Barlow."

Tye removed his hat. "We're married, William. We've come to pay our respects. Please announce us as Mr. and Mrs. Barlow."

William had known Mary most of her life. His smile was warm and genuine as he said, "Jolly good, Mr. Barlow. Jolly good. I will tell the new Lord Spender you are here to see him. You may wait in the front sitting room."

"We're fine here," Tye said, placing his hat on a side table in the front hall. Once again the room was filled with bandboxes and trunks.

"I'll announce you, sir," William said, and walked down the center hallway.

Mary shot Tye a glance as she untied her bonnet ribbons. "The old Lord Spender never announced anyone." She patted the top of a stack of hat boxes. "This hall appears almost exactly as it did during my last visit. Apparently, the new

Lord Spender is not going to let grass grow under his feet before leaving for London."

She placed her bonnet beside Tye's hat. "Funny, but I expected to be more nervous at this moment. Instead, after the confession I made to you in the coach, purchasing Tanner is—well, anticlimactic."

He smiled his agreement.

They ended up cooling their heels for a quarter of an hour before William returned. "Lord Spender will see you." He led them down the hall to the same library where Mary had last pleaded her case for Tanner. The mirrors and portraits were all draped with black crape.

Mary would miss the old lord and she was sorry he was not alive to see her make good on her promise. He would have been surprised, and yes, pleased, about her marriage to Tye.

William stepped into the library. "Mr. and Mrs. Barlow." He moved to the side for Tye and Mary to enter.

The nephew hadn't changed much since she had seen him at the horse sale. He still favored loud waistcoats—this one was a brilliant blue and orange stripe—and starched shirt collars that reached his chin. A black ribbon banded the sleeve of his sunny yellow jacket.

He sat behind his uncle's desk and looked very much like a young boy playing at being a man. He didn't offer them a chair, so they stood in front of his desk like chastised children.

Tye spoke. "My lord, we are sorry to hear of your loss."

To his credit, the nephew appeared to wipe a tear from his eye.

"You are planning a trip?" Mary asked, adding "my lord," as an afterthought. She was unimpressed with the nephew.

"To London," he replied tersely. Setting his elbows on his desk, he steepled his fingers, letting them know he did not want to waste time by saying, "What may I do for you?"

His thick-headedness concerning their reason for being here made Mary uncomfortable. Tye must have shared her sentiment because he came directly to the point. "We're here to collect Tanners Darby Boy." He set the valise with their money on the desk.

The nephew frowned as if he'd never heard the name before. Intuition warned Mary he was playing games. She said, "You know the horse. It's the one I bought at your uncle's sale."

"Yes, I do know him," came his irritated response. "Unfortunately, you can't have him."

"And why not?" Tye asked.

The nephew spread his hands to show they were empty. "Because I sold him."

Chapter 20

"Sold him?" Mary said incredulously. "You *couldn't* have sold him."

Tye could hear her temper rising. He didn't blame her. He felt the same. "My wife had an arrangement with your uncle. Money was paid toward the horse. You shouldn't have sold him."

Lord Spender's ruddy complexion turned redder. "Miss Gates—" he started.

"*Mrs.* Barlow," Tye corrected.

Annoyed, Spender corrected himself, "Mrs. Barlow did not have the money she bid. My uncle chose to give her a chance and to honor the bid. However, as his heir, the horse became mine and I chose to sell him to someone else."

"Whom did you sell him to?" Mary demanded.

"The duke of Marlborough. His groom collected the horse this morning."

"And at what price?" Tye asked.

Lord Spender hesitated and then said crisply, "Seven hundred pounds."

"Seven hundred!" Mary rolled her eyes. "We would have paid one thousand."

"Well, you didn't, did you?" Lord Spender shot back testily.

"But you received *less*," Mary said as if the concept were beyond her. "And my sister returned from London several days ago. She's the wife of David Atkinson, the best horse doctor in these parts. If you'd asked, she would have assured you of payment."

He stood with a sniff. "Mrs. Barlow, I don't have the sort of time to traipse through the village asking after your welfare."

"Oh, no, you must go to London," she mocked him. Then added less than respectfully, "My lord."

Tye knew they were in for it now, but he didn't blame Mary. He was just as disappointed.

Lord Spender replied coldly, "The duke's man Harlan made his price worth my time."

"Obviously not with money," Tye observed.

"No, he offered influence." Spender came around the desk. "You see, Mr. and Mrs. Barlow, next Wednesday I am to dine with Marlborough himself in his London home. He's entertaining the Prince Regent, who is horse mad. Who knows what doors will be open to me through His Grace's influence?"

"We had a bargain," Mary insisted. "Your uncle agreed."

"The horse is *gone*, Mrs. Barlow," Lord Spender said. "Besides, an animal like Tanners Darby Boy was destined for greater things than can be found in village stables."

Tye reeled at the insult. "What did you say?"

Lord Spender lifted his plump chin. "I never repeat myself."

Her expression shrewd, Mary answered, "He said, my husband, he doesn't think we are capable of managing a horse of Tanner's quality. Isn't that correct . . . my lord?"

His lordship eyed Tye warily. He took a step back toward the haven of his desk, which was wise. Tye had taken the insult to heart.

No one questioned his horsemanship. No one. He leaned on the desk, his thoughts about how he might avenge such an insult plainly clear on his face.

Lord Spender paled. "I must ask you to leave. I have another appointment."

"Not so quickly, my lord," Tye said. "We are not done with our business."

"You can't have the horse. He's gone," Lord

Spender said, and Tye knew he was right. Marlborough would never give Tanner up, not after paying such a good price.

Instead, Tye said, "You owe my wife money."

"Aye, 'twas the collateral on my bid," Mary chimed in.

Greed crossed Lord Spender's face. "Money?"

Tye counseled the popinjay, "I wouldn't attempt to deny any of this. My wife has witnesses in the form of her sister and myself. You may think us provincial, but to the good people in this village, our word is our bond. For four hundred pounds I'll take you through every court I can."

Lord Spender made an impatient sound. "Oh very well." He took a key from his pocket, opened the middle drawer, and pulled a heavy coin purse. "Here, take it. I wash my hands of the lot of you."

Tye scooped up the purse and tossed it to his wife. "Good day to you, my lord. Enjoy your life in London."

Mary turned on her heel and left the room. Tye followed. Behind him, he heard Lord Spender mutter something about "proud peasants."

The surly little lord hadn't seen anything yet.

She'd barely made it out the front door of the house before she exploded. "He's a robber! Taking my horse away from me. And I have no recourse, do I? No recourse at all!" She tied the ribbons of her bonnet with such force she could have torn them off.

"Not one you would win." Tye put on his hat and led her down the steps to the waiting post-chaise.

"He *stole* Tanner from us and then had the nerve to inform us we weren't worthy of such a horse!" She was dancing, she was so angry.

Taking both of her hands in his, he said, "Listen, Mary, we will show him and Marlborough, too. That arrogant runt will rue the day he cheated us."

Now he had her attention. "I'd like a reckoning of some sort. But what can we do? We *both* needed Tanner for our stables."

"There are other stallions. And we've got a thousand pounds between us to buy one, even two."

"But there is none like Tanner," she said sadly. "A stallion with his stamina and bloodlines is rare."

Tye moved his hands to her shoulders. "Mary, to breed great horses, it takes more than the stallion. Between us is more horse knowledge than in all the horsemen in England combined. Just because we don't have Tanner doesn't mean we can't make our stables into the finest in the land."

She started to refute his words. After all, her mind had been focused on Tanner for so long. But protest died on her lips.

"Think on it," he encouraged her.

Understanding dawned in her eyes . . . along

with hope. "*Our* stables. Yes, our stables," she said softly, then added, "We never really did need Tanner, did we?"

In a flash of blinding irony, Tye realized she was right. They looked at each other—and both burst out laughing.

Lord Spender had apparently been spying on them from a window. He came out on his step, his butler and a footman at his side. His presence made them laugh all the harder. For a moment, they couldn't stand but had to lean on each other.

Mary sobered first. Their faces were inches from each other, her eyes bright. "We never needed to go to London."

He shook his head. "Yes, we did. Because if we hadn't, I'd never have noticed."

"Noticed what?" she asked, the smile on her lips telling him she already knew the answer.

"How much I love you. If we'd stayed in Lyford Meadows, we'd still be feuding. We needed to leave in order to see each other with new eyes. And to get you out of those breeches and back in a skirt."

She feigned displeasure by tapping him on the cheek for his impudence, which she followed with a laughing kiss on the same spot.

Lord Spender interrupted them. "Is there something the matter? I thought you were leaving."

"We are," Tye promised. "After I do this."

He kissed his wife and he took his time about

it, too. What Spender thought, he didn't give a tinker's damn.

"Ummmm," Mary said when he'd finished. She opened her lovely eyes. "We're going to show him."

Tye agreed. He helped her into the coach, giving the post boy directions to Edmundson. The butler, footman, and post boy were all grinning. Spender turned on his heel and walked inside.

Mary removed her bonnet and settled into Tye's arms with a contented sigh. "How dare he call Lyford Meadows provincial," she complained without heat. "I hope they eat him alive in London."

"They probably will. Then he'll come running back here and expect us all to lick his boots."

"I don't believe that will happen," Mary answered.

They drove the distance to Edmundson discussing horses.

As Tye talked of ways they could make their stables legendary, Mary felt a surge of pride. Her husband matched her in ambition.

They could do it without Tanner. Between them they had the mares and when they found a good stud, the possibilities would be endless.

She was so involved in listening to him, that she didn't even notice they'd arrived at Edmundson until they pulled into the drive. Then she sat up, watching the familiar scenery, cautious as to what to expect when she saw her home.

Tye started to direct the driver toward the house but Mary stopped him. "No, let us go to the stables." She wasn't ready to see the house yet, and she missed her horses.

Old Peter and the dogs came out to greet them. The elderly man pulled his forelock with respect when he saw her. She climbed down from the chaise. "I have some news, Peter. I married Tye Barlow."

A grin split the old man's face. "Miss Jane drove over yesterday and told me. That's good news, Miss Mary. He's a good horseman. The two of you will be a fine pair."

"I think so, too," Mary said, linking her arm in Tye's. The three of them walked through her stables. The horses stuck their heads out of their stalls. Portia nickered a greeting and several mares kicked their stall walls to let her know they were displeased she'd been gone.

Whiskers, her troublesome cat, followed them yowling loudly, as if he hadn't had cream since she left. Tye scooped him up and scratched his chin. To Mary and Peter's surprise, the cat let him.

"You have a way with animals, sir," Peter said. "That cat doesn't purr for anyone else but Miss Mary." He added with lusty country humor, "I imagine you make her purr too."

Heat rushed to Mary's cheeks, but both she

and Tye laughed. And Mary was struck by how much she'd changed since before she'd left for London. She no longer felt as defensive . . . or as angry. Anything was possible with Tye at her side.

Proudly, she introduced him to the horses. "Do all these belong to Niles?" he asked.

"Portia and Willow are mine." She knew they were the two finest mares. "But we will handle Niles's horses for him until he returns from school."

"Of course," Tye said. He smiled thoughtfully and said, "I have family now."

"You have no other relatives?" she asked.

He shook his head. "I've been alone since Father died. Our marriage has given me a brother and a sister."

His words and his obvious pleasure touched her. He was so popular in the village she'd not considered him as ever being lonely. They'd had more in common than they'd both thought.

He addressed Peter. "You will stay on?"

The older man shuffled a bit and admitted, "I've only been here to help the mistress. I'm more than past ready for my pipe and chair in front of my hearth."

"Of course, I will pension you off," Mary said. "I feel ashamed. I could have done it sooner."

"No, Miss Mary," he told her. "I'd not have left you high and dry. But you're in good hands now."

Her gaze drifted to her husband's. "Yes, I am."

Tye smiled back at her and for a moment, she could think of nothing else but how much she loved him.

He took her arm and they started back to the waiting post chaise. "Do you want to go to the house?" he asked.

She stopped and looked at the building that had been her home. She thought of the portrait of her parents hanging on the sitting room wall and of her father. He would not approve . . .

"No," she said quietly. She climbed into the coach and they left for Saddlebrook.

As at Edmundson, they also immediately went to the stables. Tye paid off the post boy, dropped the valise inside his front door, and escorted her inside for a personal tour.

Eighteen horses filled his stalls and he had three grooms to help him. Dundee was happy to see them. Mary recognized many of the lads and they knew her. The news of their marriage had traveled fast.

Tye also had almost as many dogs and barn cats as she did.

He'd also been right about an important matter—his more modern stables were impressive. His mares were as good as hers. Mary scratched the nose of Dundee's dam, Gypsy. "Tanner would have thrown magnificent foals off of her."

"We'll find a good stud," Tye guaranteed. "I believe between Portia and Gypsy, we'll breed foals that will give Tanner a run for his money."

"I pray so."

He held out his hand. "Come. I want you to see the house."

They walked arm in arm. As they left, Mary overheard one of the stable lads say to another, "Who would have thought they'd been at each other's throats only a month ago?"

Tye had overheard, too, and they both laughed.

He clearly wanted her to like his home. She noticed the door was tall enough for a man his size to walk through without stooping.

He opened the door, spilling the late afternoon sun over the stone floor. The stone was original to the days when the house had been an abbey.

Mary stepped inside. The air was cool. The walls were whitewashed so that the heavy, dark wood furniture stood out. This was a man's house. No frills. Nothing fussy.

And she felt completely at home.

The rooms flowed one into the other without a hallway. She walked from the vestibule into the front room. A huge stone hearth dominated one end. A fire had been laid but not lit. The bank of windows provided lovely light and a view over the yard and beyond to the stables. Someone had planted a vegetable and herb garden right outside the windows.

"My housekeeper, Mrs. South, comes in every day. She doesn't live here," he said from behind her. "She prepared the hearth and probably has something waiting for us in the kitchen. I'm certain she'd heard word we've returned."

"I know her." Mary walked a few steps around the room. Her long-dormant domestic instincts stirred. " 'Twould be nice to have colorful rugs, cushions, and fresh cut flowers on the table."

"You like the house?" he asked.

"Very much."

He relaxed. "You can do whatever you wish. I'm not choosy. Perhaps there are personal things from Edmundson you would like to bring. Even the portrait of your father."

She looked at the blank wall waiting to be filled, then said, "No . . . I believe I'll save that space to hang portraits of our winning horses . . . and our children."

At the mention of children, Tye came up behind her and put his arms around her waist. "Tell me again," he ordered.

She smiled, placing her hands over his and looking out the window to the stables. "That I love you?"

He nipped her ear.

"I love you," she whispered.

"We'll build a racing dynasty," he promised.

She cuddled in to him. "I like the sound of that."

"Then let me show you the bedroom," he said, and took her hand.

Epilogue

JUNE 1822

David drove the hired landau through Epsom to the field where the Derby would be run. Mary, Jane, and the children filled the vehicle to capacity.

Tye had come the day before with the horse they would be racing, The Highest Bidder. Mary had thought of the name herself and had saved it for a very special horse. They called him Bidder around the stables. She wished she could have accompanied Tye but she was in the next to the last month of her pregnancy by her reckoning, and Tye didn't need to worry about the horses and her both.

David had advised her to stay at home, but she was not about to let their first three-year-old colt run the Stakes and not be there. Especially since

Bidder was running against a colt thrown off Tanners Darby Boy.

White fencing marked off the course. The area by the finishing line was already crowded with vehicles and people. The noise was deafening and the atmosphere was that of a fair. Several spectators were mounted.

"They shouldn't let them have horses around the course," Mary worried. "What if one of them spooks and distracts the racers?"

David nodded agreement, his pipe in his mouth. He steered the landau to a midway point for the race and set the brake. He jumped down.

On the seat across from Mary, Jane was quieting her rambunctious twin six-year-old sons. "Remember, I want the two of you to stay with your father—at all times."

"But we want to be with Uncle Tye," they said practically in unison. They were seconded by Mary's two daughters, Crystal and Livvy, ages seven and five.

"He'll be busy," Mary said. "He has a race to win. You will either listen to your Uncle David or stay here with us." None of the children wanted to do that. They kissed their mothers and scrambled to the ground.

Mary drew her wool shawl around her and wished she could get closer to the track. If she weren't pregnant, she would climb over into the driver's seat, no wider than a bench really, David had just vacated. Unfortunately, she wouldn't fit, and the thought of climbing over anything required a Herculean effort. She hated being so large.

David pulled his pipe from his mouth, tapped the ashes and held out his arms for Jane to pass him their baby, Dorothea, a charming toddler. Dorothea was plainly delighted to be included with the older children. She wrapped her arms around her papa's neck and waved good-bye to her mother.

"Come along, children," David said. "Let's see the sights and maybe take a taste of those pies for sale over there before the race starts."

Excited, they shouted, "The one Bidder is going to win!" They'd been schooled to that response from the moment Tye and Mary had decided to enter their horse.

Mary watched him walk away, children dancing around him. "He'll be able to watch all of them?" she asked Jane. "Don't you think you should help him?"

"I'm staying with you," her sister said firmly.

Mary released an exasperated breath and rested her hands on her belly. "I hate the last month."

"We all do."

Someone called their names. Mary and Jane looked around and then saw Niles making his way through the crowd to them. He was Squire

Gates now, and promised to marry Vicar Nesmith's youngest daughter at the end of August.

He leaned against the landau. "Well, do you think Tye's ready? I'll warn you now, the money is on Tanners's colt."

"He doesn't stand a chance," Mary said with conviction. "Not against Bidder." She felt a special bond with this colt. His dam was her Portia. Tye had tried some new training programs and they both knew he was going to win. They refused to think of any other outcome.

"I'll put money on him," Niles said, "and with those odds, he'll pay me well."

Mary stood, scanning the crowd of horsemen and spectators, hoping for a sign of her husband. A gentleman in a coach close to them frowned at her obviously pregnant state. Mary ignored him. It was so hard to believe there were those who felt a woman should stay home and out of society during her confinement. The idea was so old-fashioned. She did as she pleased.

"I wish I were with Tye," she said to Jane.

Almost as if she'd conjured him, he came walking through the crowd toward them. She sat and reached for his hand. He leaped up on the step close to her and rested a hand on her belly. "How are you feeling?"

"Oh, pregnant," she admitted in a wobbly voice.

He cooed a suitable response. Mary didn't care what he said as long as he commiserated. During the final trimester, she was not a good pregnant woman, a fact understood by not only her family but by everyone in Lyford Meadows. As Blacky liked to say, "You tiptoe around Mary Barlow when she's about to foal."

Tye looked to Jane. "I was expecting you all earlier. What held you up?"

"Nothing," Mary said, even as her sister countermanded her.

"We would have been here but your wife had difficulties."

"Jane, I didn't want you to tell him," Mary said.

"Poo," Jane answered.

"What difficulties?" he asked, his suspicions raised.

"Nothing," Mary reiterated. " 'Twas a small matter. The baby felt heavy. That's all."

Tye frowned. "What do you mean, 'the baby felt heavy'?" He didn't wait for her response but turned to Jane. "What does David think? I should know better than to ask for a straight answer from my wife on race day."

Mary rolled her eyes. "David is a horse doctor. Do I look like a horse?" She quickly amended her statement, "Not size-wise. Person-wise."

"David said she should stay home," Jane answered. "He thinks she is carrying the baby too low."

"He's not a midwife," Mary shot back. "Helly Nelson says I've got another month, perhaps two. And she's always been right about my babies."

Niles excused himself. "This is not my conversation. I'll go help my brother-in-law with the children." He left—quickly.

Tye lowered his head, clearly put out. For her ears alone, he said, "I thought we agreed that if this trip were too much, you would stay home."

Mary covered his hand on her belly with hers. "I couldn't stay home, Tye, not today. This is *our* day."

He was not happy. Still . . . she knew he understood when he said to Jane, "If anything happens, send Niles for me. And watch her carefully."

"I will," she assured him.

The horn blew, a signal for the horses to be readied. Tye pressed a kiss on Mary's forehead. "Be careful," he admonished again and then went to see to the race.

The jockey would be Josh Francis, a Lyford Meadows man with Derby experience. He and Bidder had a good rapport. Mary prayed the fates were in their favor.

The horses started to line up. David and Niles returned with the children. Livvy's face was covered with berry jam, but Mary didn't care. Every fiber of her being was with her horse.

Tanner's colt was a chestnut like his sire. With an experienced eye, Mary had to admit he was a fine animal.

Bidder, on the other hand, appeared too leggy and he was acting up. He pulled at his rider and didn't seem ready to listen to anything.

"Do you think Josh can handle him?" Mary worried to David.

"He's been riding the horse for a year. If he can't, no one can."

Mary tugged nervously at the ribbons of her bonnet. The other jockeys had far more control over their animals at the line. She spied Tye on the other side of the field. He stood beside Alex Harlan, Marlborough's stable manager. She would not have been such a good sport!

She sat down. "I don't think I can watch."

Livvy twisted over the driver's seat to pat her on the hand. "Poor Mama. She has nerves," she informed Jane with such seriousness that the adults all laughed, breaking the tension.

A blast of the horn and the horses were off with a roar from the crowd. Mary sat, her back turned.

David, Jane, and the children were on their feet shouting with everyone else. Mary listened to the cheering and the names people shouted. She didn't hear Bidder's name from anyone besides her family.

What was the matter with people? Didn't they recognize a quality racehorse when they saw one?

Nor could she see sitting down! She stood and her heart almost stopped. Tanner's colt led the pack. Bidder was back almost two lengths. The horses approached the point where they sat in the landau.

Mary leaned over the seat. He couldn't lose. She wouldn't let him. She and Tye had bred that horse to win and win he would. "Go, Bidder. Bring it up, bring it up."

As if he heard, Bidder lengthened his stride and began working his way to the leader.

Mary shouted harder. The children echoed her cries, jumping up and down on the seats and shaking the carriage. Dorothea laughed with delight. Niles took off along the track, waving his hats and shouting Bidder on.

Steadily, Bidder moved forward until at last he was neck and neck with Tanners's colt. For one dramatic moment, they hovered there and then Bidder put his long legs to use and spurted past the leader.

He won by a length.

Across the field, Mary saw Harlan remove his hat and throw it on the ground. Tye went running for the finish line.

David offered to take the children down there and the mothers said yes. Dorothea began fussing and claimed Jane's attention.

Mary rocked back on her heels, exhausted from the exertion. Bidder had done it. All the hard work over the past several years had been repaid tenfold. She and Tye had bred a winner.

Now, all she wanted to do was sit for a moment

and take the weight off her ankles. As she stooped, she felt a trickle down her leg. "Oh. Dear."

Jane looked up from Dorothea. "What is it?"

Mary half-turned, afraid to move. "I think the baby's coming."

"Oh. Dear," Jane echoed. She stood. "David?" He was gone. She leaned out of the landau and begged passersby to fetch her husband.

The man in the coach next to Mary's who had frowned over her obviously pregnant state took one look out his window at what was happening . . . and slowly sank down in his seat out of view.

Mary didn't blame him.

Edward Derby Barlow was born in Epsom on the fifth day of June, 1822, in a private room of the Horse and Horn pub.

The doctor in attendance was David Atkinson, horse doctor, who said he never wanted to birth another human again. Especially one he was related to.

Mother and baby were doing fine—and there never was a father more proud.

Young Edward, with his sisters and The Highest Bidder, were, indeed, the beginning of a dynasty.

Six Tips for Finding Mr. Right
From the Avon Romance Superleaders

Meeting Mr. Right requires planning, persuasion, and a whole lot of psychology! But even the best of us needs help sometimes . . . and where better to find it than between the pages of each and every Avon Romance Superleader?

After all, Julia Quinn, Rachel Gibson, Barbara Freethy, Constance O'Day-Flannery, Cathy Maxwell, and Victoria Alexander are the experts when it comes to love. And the following sneak previews of their latest tantalizing, tempting love stories (plus a special bonus from Samantha James) are sure to help you on the path to romantic success.

So when it's time to find the man of your dreams (or, if you've already got him, to help your friends find equal success) just follow the lead of the heroines of the Avon Romance Superleaders. . . .

Tip #1:
Ballroom dance lessons really can pay off.

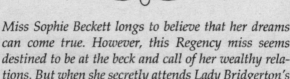

Miss Sophie Beckett longs to believe that her dreams can come true. However, this Regency miss seems destined to be at the beck and call of her wealthy relations. But when she secretly attends Lady Bridgerton's annual masked ball, she's swept into the strong arms of handsome Benedict Bridgerton. Sophie knows that when midnight—and the unmasking—comes she must leave or risk exposure. But she won't do so before she accepts . . .

An Offer From a Gentleman

Coming July 2001
by Julia Quinn

Sophie hadn't seen him when she'd first walked into the room, but she'd felt magic in the air, and when he'd appeared before her, like some charming prince from a children's tale, she somehow knew that *he* was the reason she'd stolen into the ball.

He was tall, and what she could see of his face was very handsome, with lips that hinted of irony and smiles and skin that was just barely touched by the beginnings of a beard.

354

His hair was a dark, rich brown, and the flickering candle-light lent it a faint reddish cast.

He was handsome and he was strong, and for this one night, he was hers.

When the clock struck midnight, she'd be back to her life of drudgery, of mending and washing and attending to Araminta's every wish. Was she so wrong to want this one heady night of magic and love?

She felt like a princess—a reckless princess—and so when he asked her to dance, she put her hand in his. And even though she knew that this entire evening was a lie, that she was a nobleman's bastard and a countess's maid, that her dress was borrowed and her shoes practically stolen—none of that seemed to matter as their fingers twined.

For a few hours, at least, Sophie could pretend that this gentleman could be *her* gentleman, and that from this moment on, her life would be changed forever.

It was nothing but a dream, but it had been so terribly long since she'd let herself dream.

Banishing all caution, she allowed him to lead her out of the ballroom. He walked quickly, even as he wove through the pulsing crowd, and she found herself laughing as she tripped along after him.

"Why is it," he said, halting for a moment when they reached the hall outside the ballroom, "that you always seem to be laughing at me?"

She laughed again; she couldn't help it. "I'm happy," she said with a helpless shrug. "I'm just so happy to be here."

"And why is that? A ball such as this must be routine for one such as yourself."

Sophie grinned. If he thought she was a member of the *ton*, an alumna of dozens of balls and parties, then she must be playing her role to perfection.

He touched the corner of her mouth. "You keep smiling," he murmured.

"I like to smile."

His hand found her waist, and he pulled her toward him. The distance between their bodies remained respectable, but the increasing nearness robbed her of breath.

"I like to watch you smile," he said. His words were low and seductive, but there was something oddly hoarse about his voice, and Sophie could almost let herself believe that he really meant it, that she wasn't merely that evening's conquest. . . .

Tip #2:
Mothers across America proven wrong—
sometimes looks __do__ count!

────────── ◊ ──────────

*The gossips of Gospel, Idaho, all want to know—who
is Hope Spencer and what is she doing in their town?
Little do they suspect that she's a supermarket tab-
loid reporter on the run from a story gone terribly
wrong . . . all they can learn is that she's from Los An-
geles, which is plenty bad. Even worse, she's caught
the eye of Dylan Taber, Gospel's sexy sheriff—the only
good looking man in three counties. He's easy on the
eyes and not above breaking the laws of love to get
what he wants. And before you know it, there's plenty
to talk about in the way of . . .*

True Confessions

Coming August 2001
by Rachel Gibson

'Can you direct me to Number Two Timberline?" she asked.
'I just picked up the key from the realtor and that's the address he gave me."

"You sure you want Number Two Timberline? That's the
old Donnelly place," Lewis Plummer said. Lewis was a true

gentleman, and one of the few people in town who didn't outright lie to flatlanders.

"That's right. I leased it for the next six months."

Sheriff Dylan pulled his hat back down on his forehead. "No one's lived there for a while."

"Really, no one told me that. How long has it been empty?"

"A year or two." Lewis had also been born and raised in Gospel, Idaho, where prevarication was considered an art form.

"Oh, a year isn't too bad if the property's been maintained."

Maintained, hell. The last time Dylan had been in the Donnelly house thick dust covered everything. Even the bloodstain on the living room floor.

"So, do I just follow this road?" She turned and pointed down Main Street.

"That's right," he answered. From behind his mirrored glasses, Dylan slid his gaze to the natural curve of her slim hips and thighs, down her long legs to her feet.

"Well, thanks for your help." She turned to leave but Dylan's next question stopped her.

"You're welcome, Ms.—?"

"Spencer."

"Well now, Ms. Spencer, what are you planning to do out there on the Timberline Road?" Dylan figured everyone had a right to privacy, but he also figured he had a right to ask.

"Nothing."

"You lease a house for six months and you plan to do nothing?"

"That's right. Gospel seemed like a nice place to vacation."

Dylan had doubts about that statement. Women who drove fancy sports cars and wore designer jeans vacationed in nice places with room service and pool boys, not in the wilderness of Idaho. Hell, the closest thing Gospel had to a spa was the Petermans' hot tub.

Her brows scrunched together and she tapped an impatient hand three times on her thigh before she said, "Well, thank you, gentlemen, for your help." Then she turned on her fancy boots and marched back to her sports car.

"Do you believe her?" Lewis wanted to know.

"That she's here on vacation?" Dylan shrugged. He didn't care what she did as long as she stayed out of trouble.

"She doesn't look like a backpacker."

Dylan thought back on the vision of her backside in those tight jeans. "Nope."

"Makes you wonder why a woman like that leased that old house. I haven't seen anything like her in a long time. Maybe never."

Dylan slid behind the wheel of his Blazer. "Well, Lewis, you sure don't get out of Pearl County enough."

Tip #3:
If he's good to kids,
he'll be good to you.

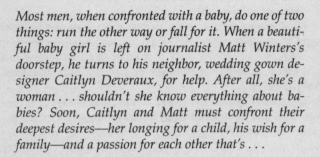

*Most men, when confronted with a baby, do one of two
things: run the other way or fall for it. When a beautiful baby girl is left on journalist Matt Winters's
doorstep, he turns to his neighbor, wedding gown designer Caitlyn Deveraux, for help. After all, she's a
woman . . . shouldn't she know everything about babies? Soon, Caitlyn and Matt must confront their
deepest desires—her longing for a child, his wish for a
family—and a passion for each other that's . . .*

Some Kind of Wonderful

Coming September 2001
by Barbara Freethy

"Oh, isn't that the cutest outfit?" Caitlyn ran down the aisle
and pulled out a bright red dress that was only a little bigger
than Matt's hand. "It has a bonnet to go with it. You have to
get this one."

"This was a big mistake," he said, frowning at her unbri-
dled enthusiasm. With Emily nuzzled against his chest and
Caitlyn by his side, he felt like he was part of a family—a
husband, a wife, a baby. It was the American dream.

"It's one cute little dress," Caitlyn said, putting it in the cart. "Diapers, we need diapers." She walked around the corner and tossed several large bags into the cart, followed by baby wipes, bottles, formula, bibs, socks, a couple of sleepers, a baby blanket, and a pink hair ribbon that she couldn't resist. By the time they headed down the last aisle, the cart was overflowing with items Caitlyn insisted that he needed.

"You know I'm not a rich man," he told her.

"Most of it is on sale."

"And most of it we don't need—I don't need," he corrected. "She doesn't need," he said, finally finding the right pronoun.

Caitlyn simply offered a smile that told him she could see right through him. To distract her he stopped and looked over at the shelves, determined to find something else that they didn't need so she would coo over it and focus her attention anywhere but on him. That's when he saw it: an enormous chocolate brown teddy bear with soft, plush fur and black eyes that reminded him of Sarah.

"Emily would love that," Caitlyn said.

"It's bigger than she is," he replied gruffly.

"She'll grow into it." Caitlyn took the bear off the rack and sat it on top of the growing pile, daring him to take it off.

"Fine," he said with a long-suffering sigh.

"Oh, please, you don't fool me."

"I don't know what you're talking about."

"I'm talking about that sentimental streak that runs down your back."

"You're seeing things with those rose-colored glasses again, princess."

"And you're a terrible liar."

Tip #4:
Sometimes it's good to take charge!

Charles Garrity is a man out of time . . . one moment it was 1926, the next, 2001! But he doesn't have a single minute to figure out what's happened, because he's faced with rescuing his rescuer—a very beautiful, very pregnant woman who says her name's Suzanne McDermott. Charles quickly realizes that all has changed except for one thing: Love is an emotion that can transcend time, and that nothing else matters but what you feel . . .

Here and Now

Coming October 2001
by Constance O'Day-Flannery

"Who are you anyway?"

"Charles Garrity, ma'am. And thank you again . . . for pulling me out of the river." He didn't know what else to say to this confusing female, and he certainly had no idea what to do with a woman about to give birth.

"I'm Suzanne. Suzanne McDermott. Now let's just make it to the car so both of us can get some help."

Charles kept looking at the odd automobile. "You drove this?"

"Of course, I drove it."

Charles shrugged, then reached down behind her legs and, with a grunt, swept her up into his arms.

"No! Wait! You'll drop me!" she yelped.

"Just stay still, ease up, and we'll make it," he gritted out.

As they approached the machine Charles took one last step and set her down as gently as he could next to it.

He pulled on the metal latch on the automobile and stared in wonder as the door opened easily and exposed the luxurious interior.

"You're going to have to drive us to the hospital," she said.

"I am?" he asked.

"Yes, you are. You have driven a car before, haven't you?"

"I've driven an automobile," he insisted, straightening his backbone.

"Good," Suzanne answered. "Let's get out of here. I want a doctor when my baby arrives."

"Let me help you," he said, wrapping his arm around what was left of her waist and assisting her. When they managed to get her onto the back seat, he stood panting.

She felt like she was instructing a child as she patiently began rattling off instructions. A wave of relief swept over her as the engine cranked and the motor began humming.

"This is astounding," he said with a breath of awe.

Suzanne knew now was not the time to ask questions.

The car lurched forward. He must have hit every single rut on the back country path, and he stopped when they finally came to the main road, even though there were several times when he could have safely merged.

"What's wrong?" she asked.

Charles Garrity stared at the unbelievable spectacle before him. Automobiles of every color and size whizzed past him with more speed than he'd ever imagined. Something was wrong—*very* wrong—for this was no place he'd ever been before.

Tip #5:
Sometimes men like it
when you play hard to get.

⟨◇⟩

When pert, pretty Mary Gates gets her chance for a London Season, she sets her cap on someone far more lofty than Tye Barlow, the local rake. The insufferable man thinks he's the world's gift to women! But though he drives her crazy when they're together, she finds herself longing for him when they're apart. Then a daring bet between them ends in matrimony, and Mary must decide whether she's lost—or won . . .

The Wedding Wager

Coming November 2001
by Cathy Maxwell

Tye Barlow's hand came down on top of hers, pressing it flat against the horse's skin. He held it in place. In spite of the beast's impressive height, Barlow glowered down at her from the other side.

Mary wasn't one of his silly admirers. She knew better than to trust a man who could make a woman's brain go a little daffy. But when he was angry like this, she had to concede he was rather good-looking. He boasted sharp, cobalt blue eyes, straight black hair, broad shoulders, and a muscular physique that made other men appear puny.

364

However, Mary knew what sent female hearts fluttering was not his perfections, but his imperfections. His grin was slightly uneven, like that of a fox who had raided the hen-house. A scar over his right eye added to his devil-may-care expression, and there was a bump on his nose from the day years ago when he, Blacky, David, and Brewster had brawled with a neighboring village.

They'd won.

Now her face was inches from Tye's, and she could make out the line of his whiskers and smell a hint of the bay rum shaving soap he used. For a guilty second she was tempted to blurt out the truth . . . then pride took over.

How *dare* he manhandle her. And the state of her affairs was her business, not his.

She gave his black scowl right back at him. "I can afford the horse, Barlow, and I've bought him. He's mine. And you are a sore loser."

Her words hit their mark. His hold on her arms loosened as if she'd struck a physical blow. She jerked away. Two steps and she could breathe easily again.

"Your stubborn arrogance will ruin you, Mary."

His accusation stung. She wasn't arrogant. Proud, yes; arrogant, no. Calmly, forcibly, she said, " 'Twas a business decision, Barlow. Nothing personal."

The daggers in his eyes told her he didn't believe her. "And how do you think you are going to find the funds to pay the horse's price?" His low voice was meant for their ears alone.

"I have plenty of money," she replied stiffly.

"God, Mary, stop this pretense. You're done up. It's not your fault. Your father—"

"Don't you dare mention my father. Not after what your family did to him—"

"I did nothing and if you think so, then you're a fool."

His blunt verdict robbed her of speech. They were back in each other's space again, almost toe-to-toe.

"If I was a man," she said, "I'd call you out and run you through."

"But you're not a man, Mary. Yes, you are good with horses, but damn it all, you are still a woman. . . ."

Tip #6:
Sometimes fainting isn't such a bad idea.

───────◊───────

Lady Jocelyn is no shrinking violet, but even she knows that sometimes a lady has to fall into a swoon—and if you're caught in the arms of sexy Randall, Viscount Beaumont, so much the better. Of course, Jocelyn had always dreamed she'd be marrying a prince . . . or at least a duke. But Randall's strong embrace and tempting kisses are far more enticing than she'd ever imagined. And then a surprising twist of events makes it possible that she just might become . . .

The Prince's Bride

Coming December 2001
by Victoria Alexander

He caught her up in arms strong and hard and carried her to a nearby sofa. For a moment a lovely sense of warmth and safety filled her.

"Put me down," she murmured, but snuggled against him in spite of herself.

"You were about to faint."

"Nonsense. I have never fainted. Shelton women do not faint."

"Apparently, they do when their lives are in danger."

Abruptly, he deposited her on the sofa and pushed her head down to dangle over his knees.

"Whatever are you doing?" She could barely gasp out the words in the awkward position. She tried to lift her head, but he held it firmly.

"Keep your head down," he ordered. "It will help."

"What will help is finding those men. There were two, you know. Or perhaps you don't." It was rather confusing. All of it. She raised her head. "Aren't you going to go after them?"

"No." He pushed her head back down and kept his hand lightly on the back of her neck. It was an oddly comforting feeling. "I have my men searching now, but I suspect they will be unsuccessful. One of the rascals is familiar to me. I was keeping an eye on him tonight. He is no doubt the one who threw the knife."

"Apparently, you weren't keeping a very good eye on him," she muttered.

He ignored her. "I have yet to discover the identity of his accomplice and I doubt that I will tonight. It's far too easy to blend unnoticed into a crowd of this size." He paused, the muscles of his hand tensing slightly on her neck. "Did you recognize him?"

"Not really," she lied. In truth, not at all. They were nothing more than blurry figures to her and dimly remembered voices. "He could be anyone then, couldn't he?"

"Indeed he could."

It was a most disquieting thought. Well matched to her most discomforting position. "I feel ridiculous like this."

"Quiet."

It was no use arguing with the man. Whoever he was, he obviously knew what he was doing. She was already feeling better.

She rose to her feet. "Who are you?"

He stood. "I should be crushed that you do not remember, although we have never been formally introduced." He swept a curt bow. "I am Randall, Viscount Beaumont."

The name struck a familiar chord. "Have we met then?"

"Not really." Beaumont shrugged. "I am a friend of Lord Helmsley."

"Of course." How could she forget? She'd seen him only briefly in a darkened library, but his name was all too familiar. Beaumont had taken part in a farcical, and highly successful plan to dupe her sister, Marianne, into marriage with Thomas, Marquess of Helmsley and son of the Duke of Roxborough. "And an excellent friend too from all I've heard."

"One owes a certain amount to loyalty to one's friends." He paused as if considering his words. "As well as to one's country."

At once the mood between them changed, sobered. She studied him for a long moment. He was tall and devastatingly handsome. She noted the determined set of his jaw, the powerful lines of his lean body like a jungle cat clad in the latest state of fashion. And the hard gleam in his eye. She shivered with the realization that regardless of his charming manner, his easy grin, and the skill of his embrace, *this* was a dangerous man.

And because you can never have enough handy tips
when it comes to meeting a man,
we give you a bonus!
In case you missed it, it comes from
The Truest Heart
by Samantha James
Available now from Avon Books

Bonus Tip #7:
A good man is hard to find . . . and sometimes a bad man is better.

~~~◊~~~

When Lady Gillian of Westerbrook discovers a near-mortally wounded warrior, she takes him in and nurses him back to health. He has no memory of his past, but as Gillian tends to him he begins to remember . . . and she realizes he is none other than Gareth, lord of Sommerfield, the man sworn to betray her to a vengeful king. As Gillian succumbs to his masterful touch, she is forced to choose—between her family honor and her heart's truest desire.

"You are a man who knows little of piety and virtue."

There was a silence, a silence that ever deepened. "I do not know. Perhaps I am a thief. An outlaw."

Gillian looked at him sharply, but this time she detected no trace of bitterness. "I think not. You still have both your hands."

"Then perhaps I'm a lucky one. Now come, Gillian."

Outside lightning lit up the night sky. The ominous roll of thunder that followed made the walls shake. In a heartbeat

Gillian was across the floor—and squarely onto the bed next to him.

He laughed, the wretch!

"Perhaps you are not an outlaw," she flared, "but I begin to suspect you may well be a rogue!"

He made no answer, but once again lifted the coverlet. Her lips tightened indignantly, but she tugged off her slippers and slid into bed. He respected the space she put between them, but she was aware of the weight of his gaze setting on her in the darkness.

"Are you afraid of storms?"

"Nay," she retorted. As if to put the lie to the denial, lightning sizzled and sparked, illuminating the cottage to near daylight.

She tensed, half-expecting some jibe from Gareth. Instead, his fingers stole through hers, as had become their custom. Comforted, lulled by his presence, it wasn't long before she felt her muscles loosen and her eyelids grow heavy. 'Ere she could draw breath, long arms caught her close—so close she could feel every sinewed curve of his chest, the taut line of his thighs molded against her own.

There was no chance for escape. No chance for struggle. No thought of panic. No thought of resistance, for Gillian was too stunned to even move . . .

His mouth closed over hers.

America Loves Lindsey!
The Timeless Romances
of #1 Bestselling Author